PARAMEDIC'S HUNTER

JAMIE DAVIS

MEDICCAST PRODUCTIONS

For my mom who talks about my books to everyone she meets.
Thanks, Mom!

Get the prequel book "*The Vampire and the Paramedic*" Free

Go to JamieDavisBooks.com/send-free-book

—

Extreme Medical Services Books

Book 1 - *Extreme Medical Services*
Book 2 - *The Paramedic's Angel*
Book 3 - *The Paramedic's Choice*
Book 4 - *The Paramedic's Hunter*
Book 5 - *The Paramedic's Witch*
Book 6 - *The Paramedic's Nemesis*

—

Eldara Sister Spinoff Series
The Nightingale's Angel
Blue and Gray Angel

1

THE WOUNDS WERE SEVERE, at least that was the information coming in from the dispatchers over the ambulance's radio. Dean drove quickly through the nighttime streets of Elk City. He made good time but drove with due regard to safety and all traffic laws. It didn't do the patient any good if the ambulance wrecked on the way to the scene.

The call was for an animal bite. The dispatcher said that the caller was having difficulty stopping the bleeding. There were numerous bites to the patient. Dean worked hard to stay focused. He was distracted lately, ever since he found out his girlfriend, Ashley - an actual angel or, as she preferred, Eldara, had been abducted and was still missing. It was important for him to find her. It was also important for him to make sure he cared for his patients. He redoubled his focus on the on the dark nighttime residential streets in front of him.

Dean glanced over at his new partner. Barry Winston had been an experienced paramedic before he applied for the special Station U community paramedic program in Elk City. He had been unaware, just as Dean had been in the beginning, that their patients were not normal people. In fact, their patients were not human at all. The Station U paramedics responded to calls for emergency medical aid from what other people would call the creatures of myths and legends. Some might even say they were the monsters of nightmares.

Dean had come to know different. They were just people who were trying to live their lives alongside their human neighbors, without anyone knowing how different they were. Barry had been shocked at first, but was coming around. He was adjusting better than Dean had in the beginning. Barry was already a pretty good paramedic and that, plus a predisposition for reading fantasy and science-fiction books, had helped him overcome his cultural biases.

Barry operated the siren while Dean drove, changing the tone of it when they entered an intersection. Once they were through it and speeding down the road on the other side, he looked over at Dean. "What do you think caused the bite? It sounds serious. Could it be a shapeshifter like a werewolf or werebear?"

"Not sure, yet, Barry," Dean replied as he drove. "Whatever it is, it does not sound like a casual bite. Also, most shapeshifters are very careful about who they bite and infect with Lycanthropy. The disease is a blood borne illness and they take it seriously when someone is brought into their pack. It doesn't sound like that kind of bite. Whatever it is, we will see soon enough."

Dean turned the ambulance onto another residential street and started looking at the house numbers as the headlights illuminated the mailboxes lining the street. He was looking for number eleven-ninety-four. He knew he was getting close, and started looking on the right for the even-numbered houses. Most of the houses were modest ranch style single-family homes with large front yards. The street was lined with trees and didn't have any streetlights. Both of these things contributed to deep shadows and only a little moonlight filtering down to the ground.

He saw a flicker of movement ahead and turned the ambulance toward the shoulder of the road to shine the headlights onto one of the lawns in front of them. He saw a person crouched over a figure sprawled on the ground. The crouching individual, a middle-aged man, shielded his eyes from the glare of the headlights and then gave them a frantic wave. This had to be their patient, and the nine-one-

one caller. Barry put them on location over the radio and was acknowledged by the dispatcher's voice in return.

"Careful on this one, Barry," Dean cautioned. "Whoever or whatever bit this person might still be in the neighborhood."

"Got it, Dean," his partner responded as he climbed down from the passenger side of the ambulance.

Dean grabbed the large flashlights from the compartment behind the driver's door on the ambulance, then he went around to the rear, climbed inside and got the heart monitor and oxygen bags out of the back. Walking around to the passenger side, he handed one of the lights to Barry. His partner had grabbed the trauma and medication bags from the compartment on his side of the ambulance. They hung off his shoulders by their straps. Switching on their lights, together the two paramedics walked across the lawn to the patient and caller. Dean shined his light around the yard to check for the creature that caused the bite. He had an itch between his shoulder blades and wished he could see better in the dark.

When they got to the side of the patient, the two paramedics saw she was an Asian woman in her fifties. Her entire shoulder on her left side was laid open so that Dean could see bone and tendon underneath. There were also deep slashing wounds to her abdomen. No wonder the caller couldn't stop the bleeding. It was a wonder she had lived long enough for the ambulance to arrive.

Because he was still on probationary status, Barry took the lead, with Dean observing and in support. The newer Station U paramedic held out the back of his right hand so the male caller could see it, and shined his light on it. That would reveal the hidden, ultraviolet ink stamp placed there. It showed the Station U paramedic emblem. It was invisible to humans, but it could be seen by their patients and other Unusual community members. The man nodded as he saw the fresh ink stamped there and he visibly relaxed. Dean showed his right hand as well. His mark was a more permanent UV tattoo of the Star of Life emblem. If Barry worked out in the long term, he would probably get one, too. All the Station U paramedics did eventually.

"Thank the Gods you are here," the man said. "My wife, she was attacked by some sort of demon-made-flesh."

"I'm Barry, and this is my partner Dean," Barry said as he set to work. "We are going to help your wife the best we can, okay?"

"Thank you," the slight Asian man said. "I'm called Yamo, and my wife is Akiko. Please help her. I did what I could but I'm not as powerful as she is."

Barry nodded as he started controlling the bleeding, slapping large, absorbent trauma pads over the wounds. Dean started collecting and assembling the IV supplies so they could get her some fluids. She had to have lost a great deal of blood.

"What sort of Unusual are you?" Dean asked. He had been unable to figure it out just from looking at them, or from anything that was said so far. That was normal. Sometimes you just had to ask.

"We are Hakutaku," the Asian man said. The woman groaned as Barry continued to work on her, packing her significant wounds with gauze and trauma pads. The groan distracted the man from Dean's inquiry. He knew a little of the Japanese and other Asian myths. The Hakutaku were healing spirits, and generally considered helpful and non-threatening. They were rumored to be related to the Chinese Bai-Ze spirits. It was times like this that his study of the extensive library of myths and legends back at Station U came in handy. It also explained why she was still alive. Her husband must have used some healing magic to sustain her.

Dean shined the light around in the darkness to check the area around them again. "Sir, did the attacker run off, or is it still out there nearby? Do you know what it was? Tell me what happened."

"I don't know," the man said. "We go for a walk every night. We love this neighborhood and enjoy the quiet after dark. It is a good time for contemplation and rejuvenation. Tonight, though, the natural world around us, was upset for some reason. We sought to understand why as we walked, but could come to no conclusion. We strive to bring healing and balance to both individuals and the world around us. This time we couldn't figure what was wrong. That was when the demon jumped out and slashed at Akiko. I was able to conjure a burst of light energy that drove it back. It screamed and ran off into the darkness. I turned my attention to my wife. I haven't seen it or heard it since. That was about fifteen minutes ago."

"You keep saying 'demon,'" Dean said. "What kind of Unusual being was it? A lycan? Another variety of animal shapeshifter?"

"No, no. You do not understand," Yamo said. "I think it was an Oni, a type of Japanese demon. I am sure of that much. I don't know how it got past the wards and entered this world. It must have sensed our true nature and set upon my wife right away. She's the stronger of the two of us."

The hairs on Dean's neck stood up. He had never encountered a demon before. He knew they were the evil opposites of the heavenly Unusuals like the Eldara. Those angels fulfilled the roles of messengers and agents of the gods of good and nature. The demons served another group, who sought to tear the world asunder, or so legend said. They were confined to the netherworld and kept there by a series of wards set in place millennia ago. An Oni was an Asian form of demon, though there were many varieties. Some were intelligent, but others were much more dangerous because of their unpredictable animal natures.

Shining the light around the yard, the paramedic saw nothing but the house and the trees and grass. He turned his attention back to the patient and her husband. If there was an Oni on the loose and attacking people, it would need to be dealt with, but that was a matter for someone else. He and Barry were here to care for this patient. They had to get her to the Elk City Medical Center trauma team.

THE ONI DEMON, called Tegu by its lord and master, watched from the roof of the house nearby. It had been easy to climb up there and watch for the arrival of its true target. Tegu had been told that it would know the one it was to kill by his aura, and the stink of an Eldara on him. The Eldara, the messengers of the gods, were the most hated of the adversaries faced by demon-kind. The master was right. As soon as the strange, loud vehicle arrived and the occupants climbed out, the Oni noticed saw the white glow surrounding the driver. He was one of those touched by one of the hated Eldara. That was the demon's target. The man would not be without some sort of magical protections, so the demon watched and waited for the right opportunity to strike. He must kill this man. The master had ordered it.

DEAN FETCHED the stretcher from the ambulance and took it over to where Barry was finishing up his treatments to Akiko. She was semi-conscious, only occasionally groaning in pain when Barry was forced to move her while binding her wounds. He had stretched out the clear plastic from a roll of plastic food wrap and had wrapped her chest to seal the wounds and help prevent what was commonly called a sucking chest wound. The lungs required a closed system to work effectively. When air was able to rush into the chest cavity without having to go through the mouth and nose, the lungs could not inflate properly. This was one of the causes of a collapsed lung. By wrapping her wounds in airtight plastic, Barry helped seal the wounds and prevent air from entering the chest cavity by another route.

Once the stretcher was rolled up next to her, the two paramedics carefully lifted her up onto it and then began loading their other gear up and around her so they could roll the whole package of patient and gear back to the ambulance in one run. Dean pointed to the ambulance and told Yamo to go get in the passenger seat of the ambulance's cab while they loaded his wife into the back. The two paramedics then rolled her over to the back of the vehicle. They took care on the uneven ground to avoid tipping the top-heavy load.

When they arrived at the back of the ambulance, Barry lifted the head end of the stretcher up and Dean helped him retract the wheels and roll it into the back of the ambulance. Considering his route to the hospital, he closed the doors and started to walk around to the driver's side of the ambulance.

TEGU SAW its opportunity as the two paramedics separated. Its target was alone at the rear and turning to walk to the front of the vehicle. The demon leapt down from its perch on the roof of the Hakutakus' home. This would be the chance to finish off the target for its master. It would be satisfying to kill one of the agents of good. Even if this human was just another minion, it would be satisfying to serve its master this way. As Tegu scrambled from the roof to the ground, the demon failed to notice another dark form detach from the other shadows at the corner of the house, following after it. The hunter was also the hunted.

2

JAZ HAD BEEN TRACKING this particular demon since her clan's oracle had detected its manifestation two days before. The small blonde hunter clanswoman shifted in her hiding place as she took in the scene in front of her. She was careful to make no sound. She crouched next to the bushes at the house's corner. Jaz had been too late to stop the attack on the Hakutaku woman and she didn't understand why the Oni had stopped short of killing the Japanese healing spirit, or her husband. Instead, the creature had moved to watch from a distance as the man wailed and cried over his injured wife.

This was very strange behavior for such a demon, and something that should be observed. She was close enough to see it on the roof above her. Maybe she could teach the other hunters in her clan something new about the Oni. Usually this type of demon was a bloodthirsty ravening animal and never stopped short of killing its target. They didn't stop unless they were killed first. That meant one of two things to Jaz - this demon had been driven back by some charm on the couple in the yard. The old man had manifested some sort of light magic in defense. She had seen that. The second option was that these two were not the creature's target.

The hunter thought back to her instructions, given to her by her father when he sent her out, alone. "Track this creature and when you have the opportunity, make the kill, fast and from hiding. The Oni are treacherous and not to be trifled with." She had already known that. Jaz had seen a lot in her twenty-two years.

She had asked why she was being sent out alone. She wondered if the creature was so dangerous, shouldn't a full strike team be used to kill it? All he would say was that the oracle had said it must be her, alone, to undertake this hunt. The whole situation was very strange. The strangeness continued as she started tracking it around Elk City two nights ago. The creature had made no kills on the previous nights' prowling. It was like it was searching for something or someone and hadn't found what it was looking for. The Oni, like many demons, was weakened by the daylight so it holed up some-where in the city during the day. When it went to ground in the daytime, she lost the trail and had to wait until it surfaced again the next night. After it left its lair tonight, she had tracked it here and thought there was finally an opportunity to strike it down. They were away from the crowds of people that were always nearby in a congested city. Hunters must always try to hide their kills from the public they protected. The ignorant humans could not become aware of how close to death and damnation they were, each and every day, with monsters and demons all around them.

Jaz had tracked the creature here, and the strange behavior continued with the non-killing of the Hakutaku couple. What was this Oni demon up to? She double-checked her triple amulet, a three-sided pendant hanging on a chain around her neck to make sure it contacted skin. The amulet performed three simple magics to help her on her hunt. It masked her heat signature, since most of her prey could see into the infrared spectrum. It reduced her scent from those who might be able to sense her presence by smell. The amulet also allowed her to see nearly as well as any Unusual creature or demon in the night's near-total darkness. It was not perfect night vision, but it was better than any other human would be able to see on a moon-less night like this.

Jaz checked her weapons to make sure all were at hand. The

Glock semi-automatic pistol holstered on her left hip was of little use with this particular demon. The bullets loaded in the magazine were infused with silver and arsenic. Those projectiles would slow it down a little bit, until it regenerated. They were more suited to taking down various shape-shifters and vampires. The small Bowie knife sheathed on her right hip was blessed by a priest, and had been tempered in both holy oil and holy water. That would do the job, but she was loath to get in that close. Those talons looked wicked sharp. She had seen the wounds caused by them on the woman on the lawn. That would leave the katana across her back. She preferred it anyway, truth to be told. It gave her a bit of reach beyond the arm's length of the demon's claws. It was also a holy blade, blessed like the Bowie, but more significant because of the additional power it held. It linked to her very soul and drew power from her life force. Every hunter in the Errington clan was gifted with one such blade upon their coming of age at thirteen years old. It gave the Errington hunters stamina and power few other humans could match. Her blade had been with her ever since and she would have felt naked without it.

The peal of an ambulance siren tore her from her consideration of her weapons and Jaz checked her quarry. The ambulance was likely one of those from Elk City's vaunted Station U. Those Unusual-loving paramedics were always out and about in the city, caring for anyone of the underworld's denizens who called for help. Jaz knew that not all Unusuals were evil. Most weren't, if she allowed herself the truth of it. What she hated was that so many of them tolerated those of their number who were evil, those who had done wrongs to humans. She snorted quietly. Those paramedics from Station U were relegated to a group that included the tree-huggers and rabid animal-rights types in her mind.

Jaz watched the demon vigilantly. She expected it to leave the area with all the attention and noise coming to the home with the ambulance. It didn't move back from the roof's peak but leaned forward, as if with anticipation. That was strange. Observing the Oni's behavior as it watched the ambulance arrive, she noticed it tense and heard a small snarl coming from its position on the roof.

Looking back at the ambulance, she saw that one of the paramedics, the driver, had come around the back of the vehicle just then. Could he be the real target of this creature? She settled back into her hiding spot and watched the scene as the paramedics set to work on trying to save the injured Hakutaku woman on the lawn. The demon watched as well.

The huntress was impressed with the efficiency and professionalism of the two paramedics. Even though they were caring for unusual creatures, they treated their patient no differently than she would have seen if the patient were human. Strange that they took so easily to helping the creatures living unseen beside their human neighbors. Jaz had been taught all her life that, while some Unusuals could be tolerated and even worked with, none of them were to be trusted. She watched while they stopped the woman's profuse bleeding and bandaged her wounds. Then the driver went back to the ambulance on the street and retrieved the wheeled stretcher, taking it back to the patient.

Jaz shifted her gaze to check on the Oni on the rooftop. It was definitely tracking the movements of the driver, ignoring the other three potential targets. She had never heard of an Oni demon leaving a kill unfinished, let alone using one attack to lure its actual target into range of a later attack. Whoever had conjured the demon and controlled it must be very strong. Controlling such a demon reliably from any distance was close to impossible by everything Jaz understood about the process. She didn't know of any human conjurer who would possess such power. The demon was clearly waiting for something. Jaz wanted to know what it was waiting for.

The team of paramedics packed up their patient and rolled her to the ambulance. Jaz watched as one of the paramedics directed the woman's husband to climb into the passenger seat while they loaded his wife into the back of the ambulance. When the paramedics loaded up the woman and the one paramedic climbed into the back with her, the driver shut the door. That was when the Oni moved.

Jaz heard the sound of the rushing attack before she saw anything. The sound of the creature's claws, scrabbling down the roof's shingles, was her first warning. Damn, that thing was fast. Jaz reached over her shoulder, drawing her katana. She sprinted from cover to try to catch the demon as it bounded on all fours towards the back of the ambulance. The huntress caught up to the creature in the street, just as the paramedic driver turned the corner towards the front of the ambulance. It was springing forward to sweep at the paramedic's back with its extended claws. Jaz leapt forward in one last, desperate bound, her blade coming down and across beheading the demon in a single silent, slicing blow. The magical blade, which never needed sharpening, blessed by God, banished this demon back to hell with a single stroke.

The demon's head bounced once on the pavement before the head and body turned to a red mist, glowing in the brake lights of the ambulance, leaving Jaz standing in the street watching the emergency vehicle pull away. She wondered who that paramedic was that made him the target of such an attack. She would have to report back to her father on this development. He would want to investigate further. She stood in the street a bit longer as the lights of the ambulance faded, then she moved back into the shadows and headed home.

DEAN SLID the ambulance into gear, checked to make sure his patient's husband was belted in, then pulled away from the scene. He picked up the radio mic and notified headquarters they were on the way to the hospital. He was a little worried that the creature that had caused such a vicious attack was still out there. He made a mental note to notify James Lee, the vampire lord of Elk City about it, as well as the rest of the Station U paramedics. If one such attack happened, it was likely that more would happen soon.

As he drove away with his lights flashing, reflecting off the surrounding trees on this residential street, he shot a glance in the side view mirror. A small blonde woman with a sword stood there looking back at him. She wore all black, sported a pistol on her hip, and held her sword in a two-handed, Asian-style grip. She was illuminated only briefly by the ambulance's taillights and rear emergency strobes while he pulled away from her, then she was hidden in shadow and gone from view.

Dean blinked to clear his vision. Had he seen what he thought he had seen? He had learned in the recent months with Station U to trust his own eyes and instincts. There were many strange things in the world out there. Lord knows, he had seen enough of them. From diabetic werewolves, to watching his former partner turned into a vampire in front of him, Dean Flynn had seen a lot of things never experienced by other humans. This woman with a sword should have been just another one of them, but something inside him told him that she was important. Somehow, someday, he knew he would see that woman again and he tried to remember her face, framed in blonde hair pulled back in a ponytail.

All the way to the hospital, especially every time he stopped the ambulance to check that an intersection was clear before proceeding through, Dean found himself checking his mirrors. By the time he got to the hospital trauma center, he wondered if he had imagined the whole thing. Then he was distracted by the work at hand as they unloaded their seriously injured patient and turned her over to the ECMC trauma team. Dean told Barry to start on the paperwork on the ambulance's tablet computer, while he took the old man inside and showed him to the waiting area.

Yamo, the old Hakutaku man, took Dean's hand as he turned to leave the waiting room after dropping the gentleman off there. Dean stopped and turned. The paramedic was sure the man was distraught about his wife's condition.

"She was real," Yamo said.

"What?" Dean asked. "Who was real?"

"The hunter girl," Yamo said. "I saw her, too - in the mirror as we left. I think you two are tied together in some way. Beware, paramedic Dean Flynn. Hunters live by their own code, and they don't easily associate with those who befriend Unusuals. You are tied, but for good or ill, I do not know."

The Hakutaku man let go of his hand and returned his gaze to the door to the trauma rooms, waiting for word of his wife. Dean walked away, heading back to the ambulance bay at the hospital, thinking about what the man had said. If she was real, then what was she doing here in Elk City - and what was a hunter? Too many questions on top of his other worries. Dean sighed and walked back to meet up with his partner and put the ambulance back in service for the next call.

3

DEAN KEPT his thoughts to himself as he and Barry restocked the ambulance supplies at the hospital. They drove back to their station, tucked into the back of a run-down industrial park outside of the city. There was so much on his mind. Not the least of which was the woman with the sword he had seen in his mirrors at the scene of the earlier ambulance call. There was also the ongoing enigma of his missing girlfriend, Ashley. He felt guilty that he hadn't been thinking about her more often, but work had him busier than normal with the flood of patient calls coming in to the Station U paramedics.

Ashley was an Eldara Sister, an angelic healer. The Eldara were the messengers of the Gods serving many tasks for the divine beings on earth. She and Dean had been together for several months now. At least they had been until about five weeks earlier, when she had left town suddenly on what she would only call an important errand. Then, early last week, Ashley's twin sister, Ingrid, had shown up to announce to Dean that Ashley had been abducted. Ingrid said she needed his help to free her. Ashley's twin was a force to be reckoned with. She was an Eldara too, of course, but not one of the healing sisters. Ingrid was a warrior maiden, a Valkyrie, intent on collecting the heroes from the world's battlefields and escorting them to the afterlife where they would feast together and wait to return for the battle at the end of days.

Ingrid had left as quickly as she had arrived, giving her sister's boyfriend instructions to await her return. Great! Tell a guy he needed to rescue his girlfriend, then tell him to wait for an indeterminate time frame. That had been a little over a week ago. Since then, Dean had gone on autopilot, working extra shifts along with his regular rotations to keep himself busy while he waited. It was agony. He realized that tonight's call with the demon attack was the first time he had not been thinking about Ashley at all. He felt both guilty and relieved. He knew that he couldn't stay in that constant state of worry forever, which explained his relief. The fact that he had been able to forget her at all explained his guilt. Well that, and his distraction by the blonde girl's face in his rearview mirror.

All of this was on his mind as Dean returned to the station with his probationary partner. Barry was an experienced paramedic, but was new to the world of Unusual patients. Dean was his preceptor and was supposed to help break him in and oversee his adjustment to caring for their particular group of patients at Station U. Overall, the new guy was getting acclimated to their patients pretty well. He was doing his research in the station's extensive library of mythology and legend, and he was open-minded. Those were the keys to being a good Station U paramedic.

Paramedics normally had the mantra of Sempre Gumby - meaning always stay flexible. Every paramedic was forced to adapt and overcome challenges with every patient they encountered, even the humans. With Station U and their unique patients, that mantra became multiplied exponentially as they were forced to adapt to both the medical problems faced by their patients, and adapting to the individual mythical nature of each of them.

Dean pulled into the parking lot at Station U and waited while Barry got out to help him safely back up into their garage bay attached to the station. Once inside, he went about his normal post-call tasks of getting everything ready to go for the next 911 call. There was always a next call. Barry went into the station's squad room to complete his patient paperwork on the computer there, and prep it for sending off to the hospital and headquarters after Dean had a final look at it. Dean was heading over to the squad room door to check on Barry's progress when he got the text from Ingrid.

"Back in town. We need to meet up. Where are you?"

"I'm working," Dean replied back.

"Stay there. I'm on my way."

Ingrid was nothing like her sister, though they looked identical, except for a few extra piercings and tattoos. The differences didn't stop with the superficial items. The Valkyrie was much more direct in her approach to everything, Dean had learned. Ashley had once told Dean that she didn't want Ingrid coming to town to help them solve any problems because she usually left a certain amount of carnage in her wake on the way to getting the job done. He didn't want carnage, but action of any type would be preferable to just waiting as he had been doing.

Dean slid his smartphone back in his pants pocket and went into the squad room. Barry was still working on the computer, writing his patient care report for the injured Hakutaku woman. Since most Unusuals had pretty much normal human anatomy and physiology, the write-ups looked surprisingly mundane to the casual eye. The report system had a separate tab on the software's screen where the Station U medics could enter any additional care or details that pertained to their specific inhuman nature. A gravelly voice to Dean's left drew his attention away from his partner.

"I made a midnight snack for you guys when I heard over the radio you were on your way back. I have some cheeseburger sliders with sweet potato fries," Freddy said. Freddy was the station's resident chef. He was also a zombie. The paramedics had sort of adopted him after his run-down house trailer was firebombed by terrorists a few months before. He could never work in a restaurant again after his voodoo priestess girlfriend had turned him into a zombie for cheating on her. He was just about the best chef Dean had ever met, as long as you made sure all his parts were intact after he was done cooking.

"Thank you, Freddie," Dean said. "That will certainly hit the spot." Dean looked over at this partner. "Barry, how's that report coming?"

"I'm finishing up with it right now," the other paramedic replied. "I just need you to look it over and then we can send it in to the system."

Dean walked over to the other computer workstation and logged in to his own account. Because he was the preceptor, Barry's reports automatically came through his system for his approval before being sent in to headquarters and the hospital, to become part of the patient's records. Barry had been a paramedic for a while, longer than Dean, in fact. He was only getting the probationary treatment because of his lack of experience with the particular types of patients the Station U paramedics dealt with. Dean gave the report a quick review, found nothing that needed changing or adjustment, clicked the checkbox that added his electronic signature, and sent it off.

He was just getting up to go grab one of the mini-burgers Freddie had made when the locked parking lot door opened and a tall brown-haired woman dressed in a head-to-toe black leather ensemble stepped into the squad room. Dean didn't know how Ingrid was able to get past the lock. He knew she didn't have a key. Locked doors never seemed to bother her somehow. She just sort of ignored them. Maybe it was a hidden power of all of the Eldara, or maybe it was a Valkyrie thing. Either way, she always made her entrances unannounced.

"Hello, Ingrid," Dean said as he picked up a burger from the plate. "I'm glad you could make the time to come back. Now maybe you can help me find your missing sister. It's not like I was going crazy waiting for you or anything."

"Dean, you have no idea what I've been going through trying to get some assistance to find Ashley, so don't give me any sass. I'm not in the mood." While Ashley sounded as American as the typical girl next door, Ingrid's British accent gave her a certain aloofness that she used to her advantage. She crossed the room to the table where Freddy had laid out the food for them. She picked up a slider, took a bite and chewed with an eye-roll of pleasure, adding a nod and grunt of approval to Freddy before she sat down in one of the station's recliners.

"I'm simply famished," Ingrid said after she swallowed the first bite. She took another bite, finishing the first mini-sandwich off and leaning over from the chair to grab another off the plate. "I've been working hard to get my regular chores done and seek out information on where my sister is being held. It has been non-stop action since I've been away. Do you know how many small wars and battles there are around the world at any given time?"

Dean started to answer that he didn't know, but she waved him off and kept going.

"The problem is, Dean, I've been told, in no uncertain terms, that I can't go looking for my sister anymore. Partly because I haven't been keeping up with my quota of heroic souls for Valhalla." Ingrid paused to finish off another sandwich and looked up at Dean and Barry who just stood there watching. "You guys think you have a bureaucracy to deal with? You know nothing about bureaucracy compared to my superiors. They are the worst micromanagers of the Universe!" The last sentence was shouted at the ceiling.

Dean suspected that it might have more to do with wrangling an angel, who had what amounted to a divine case of ADHD, than pure micromanagement. He tried to get her back on track with what he wanted to know. What was she doing to find her sister?

"All I know is that she is somewhere in or around the Elk City region. That could mean anything within a few hour's drive," Ingrid said, grabbing a handful of sweet potato fries and dumping them on the paper plate she pulled over to her lap. She continued eating as she talked. "I also know that you are going to have to pretty much find her on your own. I've already done too much to meddle in what I've been told is none of my business."

"Is it Artur?" Dean asked. "Are there more members of The Cause that we didn't find when we broke up the group a few months ago?" Artur was an ancient vampire who tried to organize a hostile take-over of the rule of Elk City from the vampire James Lee. He attempted it by starting a terrorist organization of humans focused on getting rid of the Unusuals in their community. Dean and Ashley had helped shut down the conspiracy, and he thought they had rid the city of the problem. Artur fled the area as soon as his plans fell apart. Dean knew Ingrid and Ashley had a history with the meddling vampire. He also knew Ingrid still sought revenge against him.

"No, it's not him," Ingrid said with a snarl. "As much as I'd like to pin this on the little ferret, Artur is hiding out somewhere in East Asia and has nothing to do with this as far as I can tell. This is some sort of struggle between the powers that be. The divine and nefarious Gods are arguing about something, and Ashley got stuck in the middle. Frankly, it is just like her to get her nose into something with which she has no business getting involved. She was always the crusader for lost causes. Maybe that's why she was so attracted to you, Dean."

"Well, I don't know about that..." Dean started to object.

"Don't take it personally, lover boy," Ingrid continued, shoving another sweet potato fry into her mouth. "You're not the first stray pup she took under her wing. All things considered, you are one of the better ones and you might actually be useful since you are the one who is going to have to track her down and free her all on your own."

"What do you mean, 'on my own'? Aren't you going to help your sister escape from whoever has her?" Dean asked.

"Like I said. I've been told that it is not my job," Ingrid repeated. "I was not asked to stop. I was not requested to stop. I was told, in no uncertain terms, 'stay out of it'." She finished the last of her fries and got up to check the refrigerator. "What? No beer?" She grabbed a Mountain Dew, opened it and took a long swig from the bottle. "Look, Dean, I did some checking when no one was looking, and whatever Ashley is mixed up with falls into the realm of humans. That means some human or humans need to work to solve it. She found out that someone on the side of evil was making a direct assault on the area. That's a violation the rules the Gods set up a long time ago. Still, the forces of good are going to play by the rules and rely on humans and other free-willed creatures here to solve the problem on earth. So that means it is up to you to figure out."

"Me?" Dean asked. "But I don't even know where to begin. How am I supposed to find Ashley if I don't know where to start looking?"

"Calm down. I was able to dig up a few items that might be of help to you." She glanced at the watch on her wrist and walked over to one of the windows overlooking the parking lot. She glanced outside and turned back to Dean. "I don't have a lot of time, so listen carefully to what I tell you. You can't find her on your own. You will need the help of two others." She rolled her eyes again. "This is so typical of how my bosses operate, by the way. They love to operate in threes. It has something to do with being a prime number or something. Anyway, back on track. You need three things to work in tandem to find Ashley and free her. You need a magical human, an anti-magical human, and a mundane to find her. You're obviously the mundane. I mean, look at you. You are the perfect average guy, just the kind of person the Gods use in all the stories."

Dean wasn't sure he liked the way she blew him off as average. He was, after all, the one who helped defeat the recent takeover attempt in Elk City. He was an accomplished paramedic, and had become something of a hero to his Unusual community of patients. He didn't think he was average or mundane at all.

Ingrid interpreted the look on his face correctly. "Don't take my words personally, Dean. Heroes don't look like some action guy in a film. They are ordinary men and women who choose to do extraordinary things. Don't forget that. What makes a hero is that they are mundane until they are called to act."

"So, if I'm the mundane in this equation," Dean asked, "How do I determine who I'm supposed to choose to fill the other roles? I mean, knowing I have to find the right person among both magical and anti-magical beings doesn't give me much to go with here."

"Hey, it would not be a quest if there weren't some work involved," Ingrid said with a shrug. She started towards the parking lot door. Grabbing the knob and pulling the door open, she turned and looked at Dean. "I may be able to come and help you, but only once. If you need me - really need me, you have the power to invoke me by saying 'Ingrid, I need you.' Don't use it frivolously. I'm counting on you to free my sister. If you don't, I'll be very cross with you." The Valkyrie turned and walked out the door, letting it slam shut behind her.

Dean just stood where he had been rooted to the floor the whole time she had been in the squad room. Ashley had once called her sister a force of nature. It was a good description of her. He looked at his partner. Barry had been eating a plate of food and watching the whole exchange as if he were watching a movie. He had a slight grin on his face when he caught Dean looking his way.

"Dean, you Station U paramedics certainly have interesting lives," Barry said with a laugh. "Where do I sign up for the supernatural girlfriend? I'm between ladies at the moment."

"I'm beginning to think they're more trouble than they're worth sometimes, Barry," Dean replied absently. His mind was distracted by the cryptic instructions from Ashley's sister. He had to find two others, two individuals who seemed to be polar opposites at first glance. He didn't even know where to begin. He told Barry as much.

"I have read a lot of the stories in our library since I got started with things here at Station U. Heck, I've read of stories like this my whole life. Maybe you're making it too hard," Barry suggested. "In all the stories, the party of heroes just sort of find each other. That is what makes it all so much fun."

"Well, Barry, this isn't a story. This is my real life and the life of my girlfriend." Dean sat down and started eating some food while he thought about Ashley.

4

————

DEAN HAD the next two days off after his string of twelve-hour night shifts. He used that time for some in-depth research into what the instructions Ingrid forwarded to him could mean. He was supposed to assemble a team for a quest to get Ashley back, and that team was supposed to have three specific parts. Despite that information, as well as doing some targeted Google searches and reading, Dean felt no closer to getting Ashley's rescue underway.

He spent much of the two days in the Elk City Library's main branch, looking at every mythological and legendary reference on quests and searches for missing characters in the stories. He re-read and skimmed stories like the section from the Lord of the Rings trilogy where Aragorn, Gimli and Legolas hunted for the lost hobbits. Dean spent time searching online resources for tales of classic trios of heroes, all to try to narrow down what type of people he was looking for.

At the end of the two-day intensive search, Dean was only sure of one thing. In most quests, the heroes ended up together almost by chance. They ended up in a location to do one thing and soon found themselves tied together by common bond that none of them really understood. He supposed it made for a good story, but from the viewpoint of living inside the unfolding tale, it just sucked. It was midnight on the last of his two days off when he finally threw up his hands and gave up. He hated to say it, but he had nothing to go on to lead him to Ashley. He was stumped.

The realization brought him to near tears when it hit him. Part of that was the exhaustion and the lack of sleep that hounded him. The other side of it was his intense connection to Ashley, and from his experiences alongside her during the previous months since he started at Station U. Ashley and Brynne, his former paramedic mentor and partner, had been important parts of his life over those stressful months. Now Brynne was a vampire and could no longer work as a paramedic. Ashley was kidnapped and held for some reason he didn't understand, and he was left alone to pick up the pieces. It was almost too much for him to bear. In light of that, he decided he might have to give up on all of them because he wasn't sure he was up to the task laid before him by Ingrid and the divine forces she and Ashley served.

Sleep eventually rescued him from his thoughts. It was the kind of sleep that took you when you had pushed yourself too long and too hard beyond your physical and mental limits. It was the kind of sleep Dean knew he needed and he surrendered to it, not caring about anything else anymore.

HE WAS AWAKENED by the usual alarm for day shift on his smart phone. It was four-thirty in the morning. Time to get up, get some breakfast and get ready for his first day shift back in the rotation. He swiped to open his phone and saw that he had an urgent text message from work. Checking the message, and then looking at his emails for more detail, he saw that fire headquarters was pulling in all the paramedics by shift to undergo some sort of self-defense training.

An additional text message from Chief Ari, the fire department's deputy chief for emergency medical services, gave more detail on why the sudden need for this training. It was more informative than the department-wide email. Ari informed him that it was a response to the recent demon attack that he and Barry had responded to. There had been similar, but unconfirmed, demon attacks around the city. It was thought that a special set of scene awareness and defense trainings might help the EMS and Fire crews avoid dangerous situations until the culprit or culprits were found and stopped. The Station U crews would benefit from it especially.

He and Barry were to meet with all the city's C-shift paramedic crews for training at the academy that morning from eight-thirty until twelve noon. Then they would all head to work at their stations.

Dean looked at the email again and found some information on the outside contracting organization involved with the training. They were a security firm Dean had heard of, but only barely. Errington Security Outfitters were supposedly a high-end security and body-guard service used by visiting celebrities and other important visitors to the region. They had offices in all the major cities up and down the east coast, but were based here in Elk City, according to their write up in the email. The training for the paramedics would be led by some guy called Jaswinder Errington. He possessed several black belts as well as certifications in martial arts and self-defense techniques.

Dean tried to approach all of their ongoing education classes with an open mind. He had to get over forty-eight hours of training every two years to maintain his Maryland paramedic license. Dean always looked forward to those unusual or different classes over the typical medical ones for which they all had to take refreshers. This self-defense and scene safety class might be one that would come in handy in his specific paramedic practice with the Unusual community. It certainly couldn't hurt.

He jumped in the shower and planned the rest of his morning. Since he didn't have to be at the station at six as usual and the class did not start until eight-thirty, Dean figured he had time to stop in and visit someone he had not had a lot of time to hang with in the last month or so. Plus this friend might have some ideas about where to find his quest partners. After he dried off and changed into his uniform, Dean pulled out his phone and dialed a number, waiting while it rang through to the other side.

"Well, hello Dean," the smooth southern drawl on the other end of the line said. "Long time, no talk. What can I do for you?"

"Hi, Celeste," Dean answered. "I wondered how Brynne was doing and if she was up to having visitors this morning?" Celeste was a vampire, and personal assistant to James Lee, the vampire lord of Elk City. James was the boyfriend of his ex-partner Brynne Garvey, the ex-partner he had decided would live on as a vampire after a fatal gunshot wound. She was still acclimating to the turning and was not always up to meeting with humans in the flesh. Their human heart-beats and freshly pulsing blood could be distracting to her, and that could be problematic for the object of her distraction.

"She has been doing much better, and I think with James and I present to watch over her, she would love to see you," Celeste replied. "When were you thinking of dropping by?"

"I have a training class downtown this morning at eight-thirty, and I thought I might come by there around seven to visit before class."

"That will be perfect," Celeste said. "I'll tell Brynne and James you are stopping by. They will be so excited you are coming over. See you later."

For a while, Dean and Ashley had lived in James' building down-town in an effort to protect him from attacks from The Cause. It had been fun living there like a stay at a posh hotel, but there was no place like home. Dean had moved back to his apartment in the suburbs, where he lived above a detached garage owned by a nice elderly couple. His landlords, Mr. And Mrs. Baxter, were very nice and he caught a break on his rent by doing odd chores around the house and yard for them. It was a good arrangement and he was glad to be back home.

Dean left his place, made sure he locked up, and headed down the exterior stairs to the driveway and the residential street where he had parked his white Ford pickup truck. It was still dark out, although the light of the coming dawn was starting to brighten the eastern sky. Dean unlocked the door and climbed in, starting the truck and heading towards the expressway that would take him downtown. He didn't see the red glowing eyes perched above the roof of his apartment, watching him leave. The eyes blinked twice, then the creature that owned them folded in on itself and disappeared in a red mist.

5

DEAN STILL HAD a keycard pass for the Nightwing building downtown, from when he lived in the building. He pulled up to the underground garage and slid the card in the reader, driving forward as the gate to the ramp rose. Driving down under the building, he parked in one of the open slots near the elevators and rode upstairs, again using the keycard to access the penthouse level. He walked up to the double doors in the entry hall and rang the doorbell there.

Celeste opened the door. Her smile was framed by shoulder length red hair. The vampire and self-described southern belle had been working for James Lee since sometime around the civil war. She wouldn't say how the two of them met but Dean was sure it was an interesting story. While she was his employee, she was also something of a comic foil, confidant, and companion to the vampire lord of Elk City.

"Dean," she said extending her hand in greeting. "It is so good to see you. We miss you since you moved back to the boring 'burbs."

"I like boring, Celeste," Dean replied taking her hand and shaking it. "I am starting to realize that excitement is overrated. And I miss you guys, too. Is Brynne doing alright?"

"She's still in transition," the vampire responded, her voice quieter. Dean knew that Brynne could overhear if they talked in normal tones and was nearby in the penthouse. "It took me almost a year to reach the point where James could trust me around potential meals unattended. Just be patient. She'll be her normal self again soon."

"I know, I'm just second-guessing myself and the choice I made on her behalf, that's all," Dean said.

"She is her normal self when it is just us vampires around. I think she misses all her human friends, but understands the reasons why she can't see everyone whenever she wants." Celeste turned and led him into the spacious penthouse. It had an open floor plan off the entry foyer. There were large plate glass windows around the perimeter that were carefully tinted to block most of the sun's harmful ultraviolet rays during the daytime. As he looked around, the blackout shutters were closed as the sun was already coming up. Brynne was too sensitive to sunlight to tolerate even a little bit of filtered UV light. It was another change her new existence had forced upon her.

Dean followed the red-haired assistant into the large open living room. All the furniture and carpets were white. Seated across the room were Brynne and James, together on the leather love seat. Celeste gestured for Dean to sit in a spot on the end of the sofa opposite them and she seated herself next to him. Dean was used to the precautions from his other visits to his old partner. With James and Celeste to intervene, Brynne could not get to Dean and feed without them stopping her.

Brynne was paler than she used to be, but otherwise looked the same. She was dressed in a pair of faded blue jeans and a vintage black Led Zeppelin concert t-shirt. Dean knew it was probably not a reproduction but one from a time when James had attended the concerts back in the 1970's. Her red-tinged eyes met his when he sat down.

"Hello, Dean," Brynne said. "I'm glad you came up to see me again so soon. I'm sorry for the need for the constant chaperones."

"Not me, Boss," Dean said with a chuckle. "You'd eat me without them. Right?"

She sighed and smiled a bit. "Yes, that is true. Sorry, but you do look delicious." She licked her lips, exposing the elongated canines in her mouth. James laid his hand on hers from where he sat next to her. He was in his characteristic all black outfit, this time black jeans and a black long-sleeve button-down shirt to match his dark eyes and hair.

"Uh, I'll leave that one where it is, Brynne," Dean said.

"It is unusual for you to call and come by on such short notice, Dean," James said. "Is there something you needed? Have you gotten any more word on Ashley's whereabouts? You know if there is anything I can do to help you, you just have to ask. It concerns me that an Eldara Sister has gone missing from my domain."

"I thank you for that, James," Dean replied, "and there is something I need advice about." Dean proceeded to tell them all about his encounter with Ingrid two nights before. He tried to include every detail of the conversation he'd had with the Valkyrie, every item of information he had gleaned from her. If there was something important he was missing, James, with his millennia of experience, or even Brynne or Celeste, might have some inkling of what he was supposed to do next. He talked about his research and all the dead ends he had reached. When he was done dumping everything he knew, he stopped and looked at them each in turn.

James pursed his lips and thought for a moment. Dean heard Celeste utter a quiet "Oh, my," from where she sat next to him. Brynne was the one who broke the silence.

"Dean, just to be clear, she said you need both a magical being and an 'anti-magical' being?" Brynne asked. Dean nodded and she continued. "I agree with Ingrid that you are the mundane in the equation. She sure has you tagged correctly. What do you think, James?"

"I agree with you and Ingrid about Dean, but I'm not sure I can offer much to help you with the other two parts of the team you must assemble to find Ashley. A magical being could be any number of

Unusuals or magical humans from a Djinn, like our friend Kristof Algar, to that crazy half leprechaun who owns The Irish Shop downtown. It's the anti-magical part that is interesting. Usually that is reserved for those opposed to us, the humans who would have us gone from their communities."

"What about one of the Hunter Clans?" Celeste offered. They all looked at the red-headed vampire. "I mean they are human, right? But, they are diametrically opposed to the use of magic to influence and lord power over their fellow humans."

"The problem is that they are unpredictable," James said. "A few of them have some sense of honor and can be dealt with on a limited basis. Others are little better than terrorists like The Cause group we just defeated here in Elk City."

"Hunter Clans?" Dean asked. He had never heard of them and wondered why. Brynne had been very thorough in educating him when she was his supervisor and mentor at Station U.

James sighed and answered. "It dates back to the very beginning of human-kind's dealings with the Unusuals in the world. There were some who took it upon themselves to protect their communities from the more predatory of us. In the beginning they just served as defenders of human-kind, but eventually most of them turned into clans of human predators against any Unusuals. Modern society and social norms have mellowed some of those predatory practices, at least here in the United States, Canada, and Western Europe."

"So they don't hunt you all anymore?"

"Not unless they perceive someone as acting outside of the law and can't get our leadership to act first. Now they mostly focus on the beings of the netherworld who break out into this world," James clarified. "Don't misunderstand me. Even the best of them would just as soon stake me, Brynne, and Celeste as talk to us. They see us as preying on humans, even if we do it in a consensual way."

"How do they feel about the Eldara?" Dean was concerned about the reaction to Ashley if he took one of these hunters on a quest to find her.

"It varies from clan to clan, Dean," Celeste said. "Some see themselves as squarely on the side of good and tolerate the Eldara as connections to the Gods. Others seek to rid humanity of Unusual influence of any kind."

"It's a long shot, though," Brynne said. "My understanding was always that the Hunters avoided places like Elk City, where the two communities, human and Unusual, were more integrated and tolerant."

"That is true, my dear," James said, smiling at Brynne. "But there are Hunters around from time to time including one family that is based here. They travel a lot but I try to keep tabs on them when one of the clansmen comes to my city. There are a few in town right now, but they appear to be just passing through on business. Most of the clans have set up broad networks of business fronts to support their efforts over the years. They are involved with almost everything in some way, from banking, to import/export businesses."

"So, maybe one of these hunters or maybe not one of them. Which is it?" Dean said, shaking his head. "I'm no closer to finding Ashley than I was two days ago."

Brynne laughed aloud and Dean looked up at her, feeling hurt by her callous outburst. She held up a hand as she got control over herself.

"Dean, you always go down the path of feeling defeated before you've even gotten started," his former partner said. "You said you did your research. You've received word from on high, as it were, that you are to go on this quest. If that is the case, then the members of the quest will assemble around you. You may have already met or encountered one or both of the other two you are to join up with. Trust yourself and your instincts. They will carry you through this mystery and help you find Ashley."

James laughed then, too. "She's right, you know, Dean. It is something right out of a storybook. You're the hero, and just like Robin the Hood stumbled on his greatest companion, Little John, in a seemingly random encounter, you are going to stumble upon your sidekicks in this endeavor. Just keep your eyes open, and be ready to ask for help when you think you need it. The right people will come along to help you soon enough, probably when you least expect it."

"I wish I had your confidence, James," Dean said.

"How's the new probie working out for you?" Brynne asked. "Is he driving you nuts?"

Dean was relieved for the moment with the change in subject matter. "Barry is a pretty good paramedic. He had a lot of experience before he came to Station U, so his learning curve is not as steep as mine was, fresh out of the academy. Plus he already had a lot of the lore and legends under his belt from his penchant for reading fantasy and sci-fi novels. Chief Ari says that they are going to focus on getting more experienced team members like him to fill vacancies in the future. He thinks they will adapt better once they are screened for their open-mindedness."

The discussion changed to talks about the Unusual community and their use of the medical resources from the Station U paramedics and the ECMC emergency department. Dean listened and participated a little, but his heart was not in it. He was still thinking about Ashley as he did almost all the time. He wondered who had her, how she was being treated and whether she would survive the captivity. He knew she could not be killed in the human sense. Eldara were eternals. Their corporeal form on earth could be destroyed for a time, but there was very little out there that could destroy the core of her being. All that would happen to the Eldara if they killed her human form was that she would return to her higher plane for a time while her corporeal form regenerated. Dean didn't want that to happen to Ashley. The process could take up to a hundred years. He couldn't wait one hundred years for her to come back to earth. He would be long gone by the time she returned.

Dean checked his watch. It was time to head over to headquarters and go to this defensive scene awareness class. He told Brynne he would come back and see her again soon, and said goodbye to James and Celeste. The assistant walked him back to the elevators.

"Dean, if you do seek out one of the Hunter Clans for your team, be careful," Celeste said. "They have their own agenda, and they are indoctrinated from birth to follow their leadership's orders. If you, or anyone else you care about gets in the way of what they think is their duty, they will not hesitate to sacrifice you to achieve their goals."

Dean nodded and told her that he would be careful as the doors to the elevator closed in front of him. He would be careful but only as far as he had to be in order to rescue Ashley. That was all that mattered to him. All that mattered in the world.

DEAN PARKED his truck in the municipal parking garage next to the headquarters complex and headed into the training academy building. He nodded to a few of the other paramedics from the C-shift crews around the city as he entered the designated training classroom. There was some idle chatter around him regarding what this particular class would be about. There was a tap on his shoulder and he looked behind him to see Ray Burkhardt from station 7 across town.

"Hey Dean," Ray said. "Have you heard anything more about this Jaswinder guy? He's supposed to be some big security expert and bodyguard to the stars. I heard Errington Security is made up of former Special Forces and other military types who served overseas, but I couldn't find anything about this particular person on their website. I wonder if it's he's related to the Errington that owns the business?

"I don't know anything about them other than what was on the flyer attached to the email I got," Dean replied. "Still, if he has some Special Forces training, it might be an interesting class to take. Not the usual boring same-old, same-old medical topics again and again. Am I right?"

"You got that right." Ray said. "Hey, have you heard from your old partner Brynne? I heard she took a sudden leave of absence. You guys at Station U have some serious turnover, don't you? I suppose it's because it's so boring out there in the sticks."

"I hear from her from time to time. She's alright," Dean responded. "And, yeah, it's nothing like you'd expect a paramedic assignment to be, believe me."

Ray snorted a chuckle and started to respond when a clear soprano voice caused them both to turn their attention to the front of the classroom. A woman in her early to mid-twenties stood at the front of the room with two very large men, one white and one black. She was dressed the same as the two men - all in black, from black cargo pants with baggy pockets and a black belt, to a black t-shirt with some sort of family crest on the left breast pocket. She was also wearing a black baseball cap bearing an embroidered "E," and her blonde hair was pulled back into a ponytail through the hole in the back of the cap. Her piercing blue eyes took in the assembled para-medic crews with a glance as she greeted the assembled students.

"Hello," she began. "I'm Jaswinder Errington, Vice President of Personal Protection at Errington Security, Limited. My companions and I were asked by your Chief to come here and relate to you some concepts and techniques in personal safety and awareness. In the class today, we will...."

She trailed off as the door opened and Dean's new probationary partner Barry walked into the room. He had a cup of coffee and a big grin on his face.

"I didn't miss too much, I hope?" he asked.

"You're late, sir," Jaswinder said. "Do you arrive late for all your important meetings, or just your patients and others you intend to show disrespect to?"

"I was just running late today, that's all," Barry replied, some confusion showing on his face. "The line at the Starbucks was pretty long and I got tied up." He raised his cup of coffee to show veri-fication.

"My colleagues and I were asked here to teach you all as a favor to your Chief, an old family friend, sir," she said. "Who should I tell him thought coffee was more important than what we intend to learn here?"

Barry looked around the room for some support and Dean took pity on him. "That's my probie, Ma'am. If anyone is going to humiliate him, it will be me. I'll take care of his tardiness issue."

The woman spun around and fixed Dean with a glare. Apparently she didn't like to be interrupted. He also got the impression that she enjoyed busting balls in her everyday work.

"And you are?"

"I'm paramedic Dean Flynn, Ma'am," he replied. "That's my probationary paramedic and I'll be the one that handles him and any discipline that needs to be handed out. It's my responsibility."

"Flynn, huh?" she said, fishing in one of her large cargo pockets and pulling out a small tablet computer. She tapped it and scrolled through something there, then looked back up at him. "You and your partner are at the City's U Station?"

Dean nodded in response.

"I would think that the two of you would be much more attuned to what we are trying to teach you here. Attacks and violence against EMTs and paramedics is on the rise, and if I understand my briefing for this class, your station has seen more than your share of these types of negative events. Is that true?"

Dean felt uncomfortable as all the eyes in the room focused on him. This woman, who didn't look old enough to have the experience necessary to teach a class like this in the first place, was a very unpleasant person. He didn't want to end up on her bad side, but it appeared it was too late for that. He didn't know how to get out from under her stare or answer her in a way that would get her off his back, so he lashed out.

"I don't think you, a bodyguard to pampered rock stars, would know much about what I, or my partner, do on the streets," he said. Dean regretted the outburst as soon as he said it, but he was tired, emotionally drained, and distracted with worry about Ashley. He didn't have time for some girl to tell him what he needed to know to survive on the streets.

"I see," was all she said in response. She turned her attention to Barry again. "Take a seat. It's time we got started with a little introduction on the work my team and I do." She gestured to one of her assistants and he walked over to dim the lights. The other one lowered the large projector screen on the main wall of the classroom. She picked up a remote and keyed on the projector. As it warmed up, Dean looked at the image on the screen. It was Jaswinder, standing next to a Humvee in what looked like a village in the Middle East. She was dressed in desert camo, had a black and white checkered scarf around her neck, and sported a military assault rifle. There was a pistol strapped on one hip and a knife on the other. She also had what looked like a sword hilt, of all things, jutting up over one shoulder. It looked like her two classroom companions were in the photo with her, dressed and armed in a similar fashion, minus the sword.

"My team and I just got back from guarding a team of journalists traveling behind the lines in Syria. We filmed civilians who'd been bombed by one side or another in that civil war, watched as emergency crews responded through the carnage and destruction, and fended off three separate attempts to kidnap or kill our clients." Jaswinder paused and looked around the darkened room at her assembled students. "I have been trained as a combat and tactical responder, and unfortunately, have had to use those skills in the field on more than one occasion. The point I make is, we were chosen for this assignment in particular because it was thought our experiences gave us some understanding of what you all have faced here in the civilian emergency medical services sector. I know it's not the same as everything you've all seen, but I believe it gives me the right to be able to share my experiences with you about situational awareness, and to help you be prepared to defend yourselves if you get in a tough spot on the streets." She fixed Dean with a blue-eyed stare. "It also gives me the right to command a certain amount of respect."

Dean felt very petty all of the sudden. He had let his temper get the better of him, and instead of showing some respect for an invited guest speaker at the academy. He knew it was not his best moment.

"Mr. Flynn," Jaswinder said. "Will my qualifications, and the qualifications of my team be suitable to continue teaching this class?"

"Yes, Ma'am," Dean said.

"Excellent," she said. "Then in that case, let us all move forward. We have a lot to cover in the ..." she glanced at her watch, "... two and a half hours remaining, so let's get to it." She clicked to the next slide and proceeded on with her lecture. She covered surveys on violence on healthcare professionals, EMS, and fire professionals, talked about specific cases and situations from the news, and then broke the class up into three groups to discuss and talk about individual's own experiences.

After a brief break, they proceeded to talk about scene safety and situational awareness. She spent a good amount of time on this topic, urging them to not operate as if they had blinders on that kept them from noticing what was going on around them. The final hour of class was spent on specific personal self-defense techniques, including how to use their gear - like their medication or trauma bags, or even their heart monitors to fend off an attacker and keep them at bay. She wrapped up the morning by handing out business cards with her contact information and a request to please send her any information or ideas that she could use to improve the class.

By the time Jaswinder and her team were finished, Dean was feeling like a complete idiot for his outburst at the beginning of the training session. He lingered after class as the room emptied out and waited until the Errington team had packed up their computer and other gear. She looked over at him standing by the door and motioned for her team to carry the stuff from the room, then came over to him.

"Did you have something you wanted to say, Mr. Flynn?" she asked as she walked over to him.

Dean felt his insides squirm, but he clamped down on his discomfort and nodded. "Ms. Errington, I would like to say that I made some hasty conclusions and voiced them aloud at the beginning of this class. I was wrong and should have kept my mouth shut. Your class was both relevant and informative, and I think we all learned a lot." He ended with smile and extended his hand. "I hope that you will accept my apology."

"I appreciate that, Mr. Flynn," she said taking his hand. She did not return his smile. The two of them walked out into the hallway and back towards the academy's large entry hall. Grim-faced, she said, "I meant what I said in class. You and your partners at Station U would be the ones who I would expect to want this class the most. Your, shall we say, unique patients, require you to be prepared for extra dangers and risks all the time."

Dean was surprised that she was aware of the nature of his patients, but if he had learned nothing else over the course of the past three hours, it was to not underestimate this woman. "My patients do present some challenges, but for the most part, I believe they are no more dangerous than most of the human patients out there."

She stopped him where they were walking in the hallway with a hand on his arm. "You really believe that?"

He nodded, "Of course I do. I've seen nothing that leads me to think that my patients are any different when you come right down to it. If you know anything about recent events here in the city, you know that it has been humans who have been the most dangerous by far."

"I fear you are a fool, then," Jaswinder said. "There are many more dangers out there lurking in your patients' community than you know. You would do well to watch your back. For all you know, something could be hunting you right now."

Dean laughed aloud. "I doubt that. I'm not that important. No one has any reason to hunt for me." He said it and kept up a brave front, but inside he was wondering if what she said had some flavor of truth. He had already made an enemy of Artur, one of the oldest vampires in the world. Would that qualify as dangerous? He certainly thought so.

"I have to go relieve my previous shift," Dean said, checking his watch. "I'll remember what you taught us about maintaining aware-ness on our scenes. Thank you again for the excellent class." Dean left her standing there in the hallway, where she turned to talk to her team members who were waiting nearby. He did have to head off to the station. Brook and Tammy would be waiting for him and Barry to get there. He pulled his key fob from his pocket as he headed outside and across the street to the garage where his pickup truck was parked. It was time to go to work.

JAZ WATCHED as the naive paramedic walked away from her. She had been expecting some sort of pushback when she was tasked to lead this class for the city. She dealt with it head-on, just like she always handled the doubters and haters out there. She knew she was young, and a woman, and she knew what that meant to some of the people she encountered in her line of work. She was used to being underesti-mated by men meeting her for the first time. She was also used to putting such men in their place when they got out of line, and to be honest with herself, she looked forward to it.

She told Chad and Grant to head down with the gear to their black SUV where it was parked in the underground garage. She needed to head upstairs and meet with the Chief and her father to give her evaluation on the paramedic crews' preparedness level based on her assessment during the class. The two Station U paramedics in particular weren't ready for what was out there right now. Not ready at all.

7

BARRY HAD GOTTEN THERE a few minutes earlier. As usual, Dean and his probie partner went through the shift checks on the gear and the ambulance.

"Hey, Dean, thanks for drawing fire from me in that class earlier," Barry said.

"No problem. She didn't need to do that to you in front of the whole class," Dean replied. "On the other hand, I don't think you'll be late to class again. Am I right?"

"You got that right," Barry laughed. "Still, she didn't have to be such a colossal bitch about it."

"No, probably not," Dean agreed. "Still, you have to admit that she knew her stuff, and she had the qualifications to teach that class, after all. I can't imagine how tough she must be with all she's had to have seen. She's got to be my age, after all."

"The same could be said about us, Dean," Barry reminded him. "There are things we've seen that we just can't un-see."

"True," Dean said as he zipped up the bag he was checking and placed it back in its compartment in the ambulance. "True indeed."

They were interrupted by the alert tones from the overhead speakers in the ambulance bay, followed by the sound of the dispatcher's voice over the radio: "Ambulance U-191, respond for an injured subject, at 4782 Seventh Avenue."

"Time to load up and do our jobs," Barry said. Dean nodded and headed around to the driver's side so that Barry could take the lead. He was doing a great job, and Dean knew that while his probie was an experienced paramedic in the normal sense, he was still learning how to manage their particular patients. But, he was a fast learner and he was getting to the point where he knew as much about Unusuals as Dean did. He was doing his research and making sure that he learned something from every call. Barry was a good example of the quintessential EMS professional.

Dean navigated across town to the area of the 911 call while Barry operated the lights and sirens to help clear the traffic in front of the speeding ambulance. The follow-up information was not very helpful. The dispatcher had very little detailed information on the call, only saying that another responder was reportedly on the scene ahead of them. Dean hoped whoever it was who was on the scene would be able to fill them in on what was going on.

The ambulance turned onto Seventh Avenue, where some rather large homes were situated on broad lawns set back from the road. This was an old and affluent section of town and Dean had never been on a call here before. Most Unusuals either lived in poorer neighborhoods or tended to blend into the urban counter-culture of the downtown scene. Dean started checking the GPS instructions because the house numbers were not well marked and homes were too far back from the street to easily read the numbers on the front. Then he saw something he knew marked the house in question. There, parked under the overhanging porch roof on the side of one house, was a beat-up white van Dean knew very well. The responder reporting from the scene was Gibbie.

Dean pulled the ambulance up into the driveway behind Gibbie's van. Together he and Barry gathered their gear and went up to the front door, which was ajar. The two paramedics heard voices coming from inside the house, shouting or arguing, Dean couldn't tell which.

"Hello. Paramedics here," Barry called as they entered the home.

As Barry pushed open the door with Dean behind him, something large whizzed by in the air at head-height and crashed onto the wall just inside the entry foyer. No, not just onto the wall. Whatever it was went through the wall, leaving a soccer-ball sized hole in the dry wall on both sides of the foyer. Dean saw that there was even a chunk taken out of the wooden two by four stud inside the wall.

He and Barry started to back out towards the door when the door was slammed shut behind them. Something large impacted the interior side of the front door pushing it closed. Dean looked behind him at the now closed door and saw a large frozen bird carcass, maybe a large chicken or a turkey, lying on the floor. It still had its label and packaging on, and Dean could even see the supermarket bar code. As he looked at it, the frozen bird started quivering and then, without warning, launched into the air, flying past his head in a whoosh, bouncing off the walls down the entry hall before turning the corner, and flying into a room on the left. There were screams of alarm and more crashing sounds.

"Dean, is that you?" A familiar high-pitched voice sounded from down the hallway.

"Yeah, Gibbie. It's me and Barry. What's going on?" Dean replied. Gibbie was a middle-aged, somewhat flamboyant vampire who had been trained as a civilian first responder. He and Dean had run black market EMS calls together when Dean had been suspended from the fire department a few months back. Life was never dull when Gibbie was around.

"Dean, Barry, watch out. There's a frozen turkey flying around," Gibbie called.

"We already figured that out. Thanks for the heads'-up before we got here, by the way," Dean quipped. "Where's the patient? Is he or she with you?"

"Yeah, he is in here with me and Kristof," the vampire responded. "If you keep low, you can usually avoid getting hit by the bird."

"Kristof is in there, too?" Dean wondered just what was going on. Kristof was the owner of a very successful restaurant downtown called Sabatani's. He was also a Djinn, more commonly known as a genie. "Is Kristof alright?"

"I'm fine, Dean," Kristof called over the crashing and Gibbie's swearing coming from the other room. "Sorry about this whole mess. I didn't think it would be a problem."

Dean didn't know what he was talking about, but that was not the problem at hand. There was a patient here, and there was a definite scene safety issue, too. Dean looked back at Barry.

"Let's stay on the floor and commando crawl down the hallway until we can see around the corner into the room they are in."

"Sounds like a plan," Barry said. "I'm certainly not standing up while there's a frozen turkey flying around." The statement was punctuated by the whizzing again at standing head height. The bird crashed into the wall and through into the next room where both paramedics could hear it crashing around, breaking everything in its path.

Dean snorted out a chuckle as he heard the words come from his partner's mouth. The things he had seen and heard while on the job at Station U were the types of things that he never would have expected, even from an exciting job as a paramedic. He turned and pushed the heart monitor in front of him on the ornate tile floor, while he started to crawl down the hallway. Barry came up behind him, pushing the medication and trauma bags in front of him.

When Dean got to the open doorway, he saw a high-end residential kitchen with a built-in double refrigerator against one wall. One of the freezer doors was open. There were custom wood-paneled appliances of other sorts around and two granite-topped islands in the center of the room. Crouched next to one of the islands were the two Citizen Emergency Response Team members, Gibbie and Kristof, and they were bent over another man Dean did not know, who lay supine on the floor. Gibbie held a wad of gauze to the man's head. That must be their patient and he seemed to be unconscious.

"Thank God you're here, Dean," Gibbie cried in his high-pitched voice. In other circumstances Dean might find the situation and his friend's flamboyant nature humorous. Now was not the time to laugh, though. There was a patient to attend to.

"What happened, Gibbie?" Dean asked as he crawled over to the patient.

"It is my fault, Dean, not Gibbie's," Kristof said. "I was paid to offer this man a wish. As one of the Djinn, I cannot refuse a wish once payment is made. I always warn my client of the risks of accessing my wild magic. It's unpredictable at the best of times and I warn them, but that almost never changes their minds."

"So what happened to this guy?" Barry asked. He had crawled up next to Dean and was starting a hands-on assessment of the patient. "Hey, he looks familiar. I've seen him on the TV before, haven't I?"

"Yes, Mr. Jones here is Cam Jones from Cam Jones Automotive Mile over on Route 40. He does those ads where he tells everyone how crazy he is to make deals, and smokes those big cigars." Gibbie said.

Kristof ignored the distraction of the man's celebrity and answered Barry's first question. "His new wife hates his cigar smoking, but he was having trouble giving them up. He said he tried everything from e-cigs to hypnosis, but was unable to quit. He knows me and understands my true nature after selling me several cars over the years. He came to me to ask for help. When he called me over here to his house I thought he was calling to book my restaurant to cater an event. When I realized what he was doing, I tried to stop him, telling him that it was a bad idea. He had discovered the formal words to request the granting of a wish from me, however, and I had no choice.

The frozen bird carcass flew by overhead, careening around the kitchen and bouncing off the cabinet doors before zooming out of the room through an open doorway. Everyone ducked and stopped talking while it bashed from wall to wall above them.

Once it left the room again, Dean looked over at Gibbie. "How did you get mixed up with this?"

"I came along because Kristof's car was in the shop and he needed a ride," the frumpy vampire said. "I was just going to stay in the van since it was daytime, and I needed to stay behind the window tinting. But when we got here and I saw that the carport overhang by the front entrance blocked the sun, I just had to come inside. I love Cam's ads on the TV and I wanted to see if I could get a selfie with him for my social feed."

The frozen turkey flew by again and Dean looked up as it went by overhead. Then he looked at the unconscious patient and smelled the acrid odor of cigar smoke still in the air. He shook his head as it hit him what had happened.

"Don't tell me," Dean started. "He handed you your fee for the wish and then actually said it didn't he? He went and wished he could quit 'cold-turkey'?"

Kristof nodded and looked a little ashamed. "I told him, just like I told you the first time you asked me about it. I can't control how my magic acts. I'm just a conduit for the wild magic. It interprets the words and acts upon them. Sometimes it gets it right, but most of the time, not."

Dean looked at his partner. Barry had completed his assessment. "How's Mr. Jones, Barry?"

"He's unconscious and unresponsive. He has one pupil in his eyes that is slower to react than the other to light, and the whole right side of his head is swollen," Barry said. "He's definitely got a closed head injury and needs to get to the trauma center. He probably has a brain bleed. That means his brain is starting to swell inside his skull. If we don't get him out of here, his brain is going to turn to mush."

"Agreed," Dean said. "My guess is that the turkey is going to follow him unless we can find a way to deactivate the magic." He blinked and rubbed at his eyes. That cigar smoke was really irritating him. He was allergic to smoke. "Kristof, there has got to be a way for you to turn this off. Think. There has got to be something we can do."

"I told you, Dean," Kristof said, chastised. "I have no control over the magic. Once it is activated, it has to play out on its own."

Dean sniffed, and wiped his nose. His allergy was really kicking in right now, probably because they were in an enclosed space of the kitchen with the smoke. Dean stopped and looked around, ducking as soon as the bird flew by once again. He sniffed the air, trying to zero in on the source of the smell. He saw it, as soon as he started looking for it. There was a smoldering cigar against the far wall by the kitchen sink. It had rolled under the lip of the cabinets there. He darted over to it, dodging the frozen bird once again, and grabbed the still-lit cigar. He reached up from his crouched position, flipped up the faucet lever to turn on the water, and held the cigar under the faucet.

Gibbie shrieked, "Look out, Dean."

Dean turned and saw the frozen bird turn and zip right towards his head, but just before it got to him, it fell to the floor and skidded into the cabinet by his knees and lay still. Dean let out a sigh of relief, realizing he had been holding his breath.

"Huh," Gibbie said, letting out a long breath. "That was really easy." He looked at his partner. "Why didn't we think of that, Kristof?"

Dean and Barry shared a glance and then the two of them went to work on their patient. Gibbie had done a good job of stopping the external bleeding, so that was already taken care of. They hooked up the heart monitor and blood pressure cuff to start getting vital signs and then Dean looked at the Djinn.

"Come with me, Kristof, and help me get the stretcher."

The genie nodded and followed Dean outside and to the ambulance. On the way, the Unusual CERT team member tried to apologize the whole way to the ambulance.

"I hate using my wish magic, Dean," Kristof said. "I avoid it at all costs, but sometimes there is nothing I can do."

"Nobody is blaming you, Kristof," Dean said as he pulled the stretcher from the back of the ambulance. "I know you can't control it. You told the guy the truth. It's on him. Besides, maybe this will really get him to quit smoking, right?"

The two of them brought the stretcher back into the mansion and then the four of them lifted the portly used car magnate up onto it. He had to weigh over three hundred pounds. As the paramedics took over rolling the stretcher outside with all their gear, Dean looked at the two CERT responders. They looked a little shell-shocked by the whole incident.

"Come by the hospital while we drop Mr. Jones off," Dean suggested. "I'll get you some supplies to refill the gauze and stuff you used up back there to treat him before we arrived, okay?"

They nodded from the shadows of the Mansion's front door, Gibbie was careful to stay back away from the sunlight. Dean waved after he shut the ambulance's rear doors and then he climbed in, flipped on the lights and siren, and drove their patient to the trauma center.

8

WHEN DEAN and Barry came out of the ER's ambulance entrance to get back to their unit, Gibbie's van was pulled up next to it. Dean had a bag of supplies he had retrieved from the restock room at the hospital. Walking over the to the passenger side sliding door of the van, he slid it open and handed the bag to Kristof.

Barry walked up next to him and laughed aloud. Dean looked at him with a raised eyebrow.

"Oh, I was just thinking of what Ms. Jaswinder Errington would say about staying safe and sound with a flying frozen turkey as your enemy," Barry said, continuing to chuckle.

Dean laughed and turned to explain the joke to Kristof and Gibbie. He stopped when he saw their faces. They had both assumed a shocked and maybe even frightened expression.

"What?" Dean asked. "You act as if we just invoked the devil himself."

Gibbie was the first to speak. "Did you say that Jaz Errington is in town? Is her father, old man Earnest Errington here, too?"

"I don't know her by that name, or if her father is here, but I guess that's the same person," Dean said. "She was in headquarters earlier today teaching us a class on scene safety and self-defense. She was a bit of a hard-ass, but seemed to know what she was talking about. Why do you ask, Gibbie?"

"Because the Erringtons are one of the great Hunter Clans," Gibbie replied. "They are known primarily as demon hunters, but they are just as happy to kill off any Unusuals they encounter who are not playing nice with humans."

"Yeah, Dean," Kristof said. "In the home back there, someone like Jaz Errington would have found another, more permanent solution to the problem of uncontrolled Djinn magic. She would have killed me to cut off the magical flow."

"You're kidding," Dean said. "It wasn't your fault. You warned the guy against invoking it and he did it anyway."

"I'm afraid the Erringtons do not see things that way," Kristof replied. "They are not as bad some of the other Hunter Clans out there. I mean, they don't kill indiscriminately, but they have their own code and they live by it in everything they do. If one of the Erringtons think you are an Unusual who is a risk to humans, they'll take action."

Barry asked, "But what are they doing here? She told us all in the class that they had just got back from a bodyguard mission in Syria."

Kristof nodded, "It would make sense that the Erringtons would want to be involved there. The various terrorists are destroying ancient ruins there because they represent Gods that are not their own. A lot of those ancient holy places were built in their locations because of a nexus with the netherworld. If they break the seals on the gateways during the destruction of the temples, they could cause an opening that demons would use to infiltrate the world. It could cause havoc if left unchecked."

"That's true," Gibbie said aloud. "We Unusuals are all scared of the Erringtons, but demons are terrified of them. They have become very proficient demon hunters over the centuries. Rumor has it that Jaz Errington is the best to come along in the last one hundred years. I'd bet that if she is here, she is following a demon of some sort.

Dean took in all they were saying, listening and filing all of it away for future reference. The thing that had him thinking the most was that nagging feeling of deja vu he had since he had first seen Jaswinder Errington in class that morning. It was the feeling he had seen her somewhere before. Until now, it hadn't occurred to him that the two recent events could be related, but in light of what Gibbie and Kristof were saying, he could not ignore it. There had been a series of demon attacks in town recently. He and Barry had responded to one a few days earlier. Dean could still see the image of the woman with the sword standing behind the ambulance as he drove away. Now he was sure he knew who it was. Jaz Errington had been there that night.

Barry clapped him on the shoulder to get his attention and it brought him back to the present discussion. He looked around and saw the three others just staring at him.

"You alright, Dean?" Barry asked.

"Yeah, you look like you've seen a ghost," Gibbie said.

"I don't think it was a ghost, but I might have seen our Ms. Errington before," Dean replied. "Barry, remember the animal or demon attack our last night shift rotation?"

Barry nodded. "Yeah. That Hakutaku couple claimed that they were attacked by some sort of Japanese demon called an ... Oni, wasn't it?"

"Well, I didn't tell anyone, but as we were driving away, I thought I saw a woman, dressed all in black, holding a sword," Dean said. "I saw her when I looked in the rearview mirror as I pulled away from in front of the house. I looked away for a second, and when I looked back, she was gone. I chalked it up to seeing things after a few long night shifts. Now I have to wonder if she is the reason the Oni demon didn't come back and kill the couple. It would make sense if she was there and killed it before it could return."

"If she was there, Dean, then she has been in town for a little while," Kristof said. "There have been rumors of netherworlders, or what you would call demons, floating around the Unusual community for almost a month. Folks have claimed sightings all over the region. That might be what drew the Erringtons here. If they heard rumors of demons roaming around Elk City, they'd come running to find the source and stop it."

"Whatever the reason she and her family are here in Elk City, it spells trouble for those of us who they might like to hunt," Gibbie said. "I'm going to spread the word of their arrival, and then I'm going to ground for a while. I am not getting staked or beheaded by one of those maniacs." The middle-aged vampire started up the van to punctuate his statement. "Kristof, I'll drop you off at your place downtown, then I'm disappearing for a while."

"It's not fair that you feel like you have to run and hide, Gibbie," Dean said. "Let me talk to James. There has to be some way to reach out to them and see what is going on locally that has brought them to town."

"You can try, Dean," Kristof said. "The Erringtons don't always play well with the Unusual leadership in a town. I doubt that James is going to be able to do anything. Remember, they'd just as soon stake him as talk to him. The only type beings they will not kill, according to their code, are humans and the Eldara. At least that is what the legends about them say."

"Well, if that is the case I guess I'll have to deal with them myself," Dean said. He was getting angry about these groups of interlopers coming into his town and threatening his friends. First it was The Cause, now it was these hunters. "I will have to set up a little meeting with her. I need to have a few words with Ms. Jaz Errington about what she is doing here."

"Yeah," Barry said with a snort of laughter. "Because you made such a good impression on her at the training class this morning. She is definitely primed to listen to you now."

"I don't care, Barry," Dean replied. "Let's load up and get back to the station. I need to figure out how to contact her and set up a meeting. We need to find out what she is doing here before we she goes and kills one of our patients in her zeal to follow her family's calling."

Dean and Barry climbed into the ambulance's cab and waved to Gibbie and Kristof as they pulled the ambulance away from the van at the hospital. Dean was thinking about the connection between the hunter woman and his own situation. James and Brynne had both suggested that there might be a hunter clan connection to him in his quest to free Ashley from her abductors. Was Jaz Errington's presence here in Elk City a coincidence? He doubted it. If Ashley had taught him nothing else, she had impressed upon him how the Gods liked to use little connections and coincidences to influence events on earth indirectly. They were forbidden to act directly by some agreement with the forces of darkness long ago, instead relying on the free will decisions of the people and Unusuals populating the earth. They could put situations in front of people to influence a decision, or even force a decision to be made, even if they weren't sure of the outcome of the decision to be made. Dean wondered if that was what was happening here.

He didn't like feeling manipulated, especially if it was going to force him to work with this Hunter. She stood for everything he was against. She was a killer. He was a healer. She believed in one group of the city's occupants being inherently better than the other, while he believed in equal opportunity and treatment for everyone, human and Unusual alike. Dean didn't know how he was supposed to find the common ground to work with her. He was going to meet her and find a way, though. Ashley was depending on him and owed it to her to try.

9

JAZ WANTED to stomp her foot but she forced herself to stand still and tried her best to appear calm. Her father had told her after their meeting with the Fire Chief that she was to come back and meet him here at their corporate offices downtown. Now she was here in front of him, feeling like a little girl all over again, caught sneaking out to the gun range after lights-out.

"... I said, 'are you paying attention to me', young lady?" Earnest Errington asked his daughter.

Her eyes darted up to meet his too late and she knew he had gotten his answer. His lips pressed together, forming a thin line under his salt-and-pepper mustache.

"Father, I have met the man in question. I tell you honestly, I don't believe he will be much help to us in solving our particular dilemma," Jaz said, keeping her voice level and professional. The fact that did not feel professional was hidden under the surface of her demeanor, barely. Ugh! Why did her father always make her feel this way?

"Jaswinder, I do not recall asking your opinion of the man," her father stated. "In fact, I don't believe I asked for your opinion about any of this. This is your assignment and I'll ask you to fulfill it as you would any other task I assign to you. Is that understood?"

"But Daddy, he is so infuriating, and I've only met him one time," she pleaded with her father. "Imagine what a colossal douchebag he'll be after spending a few days or weeks with him." She snapped her mouth shut, knowing she had gone too far.

"Don't 'but Daddy' me," her father said. "I heard about the way you dressed him down for his unprofessional demeanor during the class. You told both me and the Fire Chief in our meeting after the class. You also heard the way he responded. Dean Flynn is what he called 'one of the most valuable members of our Station U paramedic team.' He went on to call him a natural and intuitive medical professional who knows his job and responsibilities. Perhaps your single meeting was more a matter of your impression on him, and not the other way around?"

"I don't see how that could be the case," Jaz said in defense of herself. "I was putting a late arrival in his place for tardiness when Mr. Flynn stepped in and interrupted me, defending him."

"Who was the man in question in relation to Mr. Flynn?"

"It was his probationary medic, apparently," Jaz replied. "He took issue with me berating his guy."

"So he came to the defense of his direct subordinate?" Earnest asked. "And this makes him a 'douchebag' because?"

She hated when he turned things around with logic. She knew where he was headed with this, and it was making her even more angry. "Look, Father. I know you are going to tell me that I would have done the same thing if someone had laid into one of my subordinates. In fact, you've seen me do it. That makes no difference here. I'm sorry, he just rubs me the wrong way."

"Well get over it," Earnest said, standing up from behind the desk to walk around it in the well-appointed office. "This is not just me saying it. This is not just another assignment. This is for the honor of the whole clan. The clan oracle herself decreed that it must be you to fulfill this responsibility."

"I still don't understand why this is our problem anyway," Jaz complained. "Some angel gets herself abducted and we are honor bound to help because ...?"

Jaz's father sighed. "Jaz, you know the legends. A long time ago, this particular Eldara assisted the Clan by keeping us from being duped by one of our adversaries into doing their bidding. Your great-great-great-grandfather made an arrangement with her that we would watch over her when she required our assistance. This happened just before our clan followed that adversary to the United States in the late 1850s. It is a centuries-old obligation and we will not be the generation to sully the honor of the clan because you don't like one of those who must be enlisted to help. Not under my watch."

"Father, the Oracle said that a hunter, a healer, and a hexen must take up the quest for the missing Eldara," Jaz said. "What makes the Oracle so sure this one is the healer we must use?"

Her father's answer was a burst of laughter that continued until he nearly had tears in his eyes. She was not amused by her father's jocularity. Finally, he composed himself. "Daughter, you have always had a stubborn streak, but I never thought even you would question the veracity of something proclaimed by the clan's Oracle herself."

Jaz started to say something but her father held up his hand to stop her.

"She has spoken and names the one called Flynn as the healer, just as she named you as the hunter," he continued as she listened.

The younger Errington hunter felt herself deflate a little. She knew better than to fight this, but she kept pushing anyway. It stemmed from her need to be the one in charge, and years of having to put men in their place. It was something she was unable to do with her father. Must it always come down to some sort of Daddy issue?

"Okay, so the hunter is me and the healer is this Flynn guy," Jaz asked. "Who is the hexen? How do we discover the identity of this witch we need to join up with? Has the Oracle been of any help with that?"

"The only variable left is the witch. The Oracle was unable to pierce the veil of the hexen's identity, only that she, the witch, was involved or connected to this matter in some way. It is as if she does not exist in this world. The Oracle suggested that you and Mr. Flynn would have to work together to figure out who this unknown witch is."

"So I have to work with him, I get it," Jaz said. "I dressed him down in front of his peers while he openly challenged my authority, and now we have to find a way to make nice and get along for the honor of the clan." Jaz sighed. Her temper and need to outdo everything the guys around her could do had gotten her into trouble before. This was one of those things she had learned to deal with. For some reason, though, this time it seemed to bother her more than the others.

"See, I knew you would figure it out," her father said, a broad grin on his face. His phone chirped on the desk and he picked it up to see the message. His grin widened. "It seems that you will have the opportunity to set forth on your task sooner than you think. Mr. Flynn used our company website to request your contact information. He wants to meet up with you."

"Oh, joy," Jaz said, rolling her eyes.

"I will forward you the contact request and you can respond directly to his request. May I suggest you take a different tone with him this time?"

Jaz turned and left the office to the sound of her father's laughter ringing in her ears.

FOUR HOURS LATER, she rolled into the parking lot at the nondescript diner. The neon sign on the top of the classic diner-car restaurant was supposed to read "Hank's Place" but instead read "ank' lace." Jaz was early. She always liked to arrive at meetings early. It gave her a chance to get the lay of the land and establish an advantage over her opponents.

Jaz did a visual sweep of the parking lot and then sat back in the driver's seat as she parked the black Ford Expedition SUV. Old habits died hard and she never let her guard down, at least not all the way.

The fact that she had just been in Syria hunting a particularly nasty group of demons freed by terrorist radicals there, caused her to be a bit more on edge. That, and the fact that she didn't look forward to this meeting with the paramedic.

Her father drove her nuts, not just because he was the clan's leader and she had to obey him. It was also a matter of his being right every time he ordered her to do something she didn't want to. She knew that this paramedic, Dean Flynn, should not be able to get under her skin so easily. That she had allowed him to do so was a problem. She knew that. The fact she had allowed it to surface in an argument with her father was infuriating.

She settled back and did some deep breathing exercises to calm herself. It would do no good to go into this meeting with her dander up. Her temper was legendary in her family. She chalked it up to being the only girl, besides her mother, in a family of men. Her brothers had all teased her as the youngest of the brood. They told her she could never be the top hunter in the clan. They told her it was a man's job. She had eventually proved them all wrong, but not without cost. She was the best hunter in the Errington clan, a fact she had proven with both individual kills and the successful team raids she had led. But the victory was bittersweet. To be honest, Jaz had never wanted it, never wanted to be a hunter in the field, but fate had a way of twisting everyone's desires to its own pattern. Each of her four brothers had died on missions before she had reached the pinnacle of her abilities. Now, as badly as she wanted to show them what she could do, what she had done, that could never be. It was too late.

Her last remaining brother, Anton, had died in a raid on a demon lair in Siberia six years ago. He had been the eldest, the heir apparent; the golden boy. Now he was gone, gutted by a hidden Scara demon before he even knew what hit him. She had become the Errington clan's heir at that moment, and with it came the powers that went with the title. That was the moment she entered into her own realization of her abilities. She had always been looking forward to going to college and having a somewhat normal life, at least as normal as could be for the member of a hunter clan. Once she became the heir; that had all changed.

Her father changed the direction of her education as soon as word came back of her brother's death. Jaz didn't even have time to grieve. Everything she did became more urgent and everyone told her she needed to work harder. She had always trained with weapons and learned the lore, but it all became more intensive and more real then. She started going on trips with other hunters, shadowing them and learning from them. She went to college, but it was through an online program that focused on criminal justice and military history, not the art history major to which she had previously aspired.

None of that changed the here and now, she knew. Jaz had worked hard to embrace her new role and live up to what she saw as the expectations of her father, mother, and her lost brothers. Now she was here, in this small, boring city in Maryland, fulfilling a quest started by some ancestor in exchange for a debt with which she was not involved. To top it off, she was forced to do it without her usual team, the team of hunters with whom she had defeated some of the worst demons to break through the wards and walk the earth. No, Jaz was forced to do it essentially alone, with an obstinate paramedic who was dedicated to saving the monsters living among the human population. Then, the two unlikely allies were supposed to team up with a witch of all people. The combination was an affront to everything she stood for as a member of those sworn to protect the human race from the things that no one even believed in anymore.

Jaz stopped her rumination on the situation as a beat up white pickup truck passed in front of her SUV and pulled into a parking spot down the line. She checked her watch. It was six-fifteen. It was about the time she expected the paramedic to show up, based on travel time from his station. She was correct, as she saw Dean Flynn climb out of his vehicle and walk up to the diner's doors. She watched through the diner's front windows as he greeted one of the waitresses and pointed to a booth at the back. The waitress nodded and Dean walked back to the booth and sat down.

She did another sweep of the lot then looked at her passenger seat. Attached to the back of the seat, facing the front, was a pocket organizer that held her selection of weapons and other assorted odds and ends. She considered her choices. She never went anywhere unarmed, and as a private security agent and bodyguard, she had a license to carry a firearm. She was also considered a licensed deputy with the U.S. Marshal's office. That was a special arrangement the Marshals had with the Erringtons dating back to the 1860s.

Jaz looked over the weapons before her. Her katana was too unwieldy and long to be hidden, so that must be left behind. She settled first for a brace of throwing knives, which she attached to a Velcro panel inside the left side of her leather jacket. Once those were in place, she took the Glock from the holster mounted on the cargo carrier and leaned forward to slide it into the hidden holster clipped to her belt at the small of her back.

Finally, she took the small Bowie, in its sheath, and clipped it to the slot in her shoulder holster. It held the blade under her right armpit, with the hilt hanging downward towards her belt. She snapped the keeper flap from the knife sheath to her belt to keep the hunting knife in place and settled her black leather jacket back over it. Feeling less naked now that she was suitably armed, Jaz exited her SUV, clicking the key fob to lock the doors. The heavily tinted windows hid the contents of the front seat weapons caddy from passersby. Making another scan of the area, Jaz looked to see that her target was still in his location inside the restaurant, and then headed for the front door. Time to get this mess started. The sooner she found this missing Eldara, the sooner she could return to the work she really wanted to do.

10

_____

DEAN LOOKED up from his phone's email app to see Jaswinder Errington crossing the diner to his booth. He pushed down his discomfort with this whole situation and decided to stick to his guns. He had to find out what she was doing here and what danger she represented to his patients and his friends.

She walked up to him and extended a hand. "Mr. Flynn," she said. "Thank you for getting in touch with me. I am glad we have the chance to follow up on our unfortunate encounter in class this morning."

"Please, call me Dean," he replied, rising to take her hand and shaking it. "May I call you Jaswinder? It really is a very interesting name." He sat back down as she slid into the booth across from him.

"I prefer Jaz, actually," the woman said. "Jaswinder is a family name that dates back to antiquity. Only my father and mother call me by it, usually only when they are annoyed with me."

Dean felt himself smile, despite the reason for the meeting. Even Hunters had families that functioned much like most families out there.

"Well, Jaz," Dean began. "I was surprised you responded to my email so quickly. I had expected it to take several days to hear back from you, if I heard back from you at all."

"Errington Security is a respected business with fully integrated technology resources," Jaz said. "Your contact request was forwarded to me as soon as it was received. It seems that we have a lot to talk about, starting with the words we exchanged this morning. I want to assure you that nothing personal was intended. I teach a lot of military teams and I have found that establishing alpha status as quickly as possible is a useful tool, especially for a female. I'm sure you understand."

Dean did understand, and it surprised him to find himself agreeing with this woman. He had expected to disagree with her about nearly everything. It caused him to rethink his approach to this conversation and he took a leap of faith that his instincts on how to deal with this situation were right.

"I can accept that. Until very recently my paramedic mentor was a woman," Dean said. "What I really wanted to ask you, if I may, was what you were doing behind my ambulance three nights ago out in the suburbs?" Dean watched her face as he asked the question to see if he could discern any clues, should she decide to deny she was there.

"I wondered if you saw me," she chuckled. "I got a little sloppy charging after that Oni demon. It was determined to have your heart for dinner. I decided that I couldn't allow that to happen." She met his eyes with an even stare. "You're welcome, by the way."

Dean stared back at her. He knew he had been right about seeing her, even though it had just been a glimpse. There was a glint in those blue eyes, challenging him in a way. It was disconcerting to think about what she had done if that demon was really there and had almost killed him. He met her eyes, the eyes that held his as if challenging him to deny that he owed her something. He declined to offer to fight, instead opting to defuse the situation.

"Thank you, I guess," Dean said. "We knew the Oni must still be around. I'm glad you were around to help stop it. I doubt I would have been able to avoid being attacked otherwise."

He saw what he thought was surprise in her expression when he didn't take the bait to argue with her. He was pleased with himself. Score one victory for him. He picked up the menu and slid hers over to her.

"I can recommend just about everything they serve here, Jaz," Dean said. "I haven't had a bad meal yet. They serve breakfast all day, too, if that is up your alley."

She nodded, took the offered menu and started to look it over. Dean didn't need to look at his. He knew what he was getting. He looked up and caught Daisy's eye. She was the waitress who seemed to always take care of him when he was in. She came right over.

"Hi, Dean," Daisy said. "What can I get you two to drink?"

He deferred to Jaz and she placed her order for ice water. Dean ordered a Sprite. They were both ready to order so they put in their orders for dinner. Jaz ordered steak and eggs, while Dean ordered a burger and fries. They both watched Daisy leave and then their attention turned back to the matter at hand.

"I guess we should get down to why I wanted to make sure we met up," Dean offered as a start to the conversation he suspected they both were waiting for. "It's because I know what you do and who you are, just as I know that you are aware of what I do for a living and the people I treat."

Jaz opened her mouth to speak but Dean held up a hand. "Please. Wait until I am finished with what I have to say."

She nodded and he continued. "I want you to know that I'm very protective of my patients and I won't put them in a position to be injured or killed by someone on some vendetta based on an old, outdated code of honor. I also want to know why you are here, and what can be done to expedite your mission so that those of us living here in Elk City can all live together in peace again."

He finished his prepared challenge and watched her for any sign of a response. The only thing he decided was that he never wanted to play poker against her. She sat there, stone faced and quiet for a full minute before she answered him.

"You know nothing of what it means to be a Hunter, or what my clan sees as our duty to mankind," Jaz began. "Errington's do not kill any being indiscriminately, unless it is a netherworlder here on earth, bent on destruction, as they all are."

"And who do you consider netherworlders, if I may ask?" Dean leaned forward, ready to argue against her reply.

"Demons, daemons, and all their ilk, of course," Jaz answered. "Creatures escaped to earth and spreading evil intent everywhere they go like the Oni demon I killed while it stalked you."

"So you don't see all Unusuals as creatures to be slain in your quest for a pure human world?" Dean asked.

"I will not lie to you, Dean," Jaz said leaning forward in a whisper. "There was a time when the Hunter clans were charged with killing any that weren't human living among us. But we have, uh, evolved I guess you would say. My family and I are more lenient towards Unusuals now. As long as they bear no ill will to the people they live among, we will ignore them. If they are found to be causing harm and local authorities do not or cannot take action on their own, then we may act in the cause of justice. There are also those, human and Unusual, who collaborate with netherworlders in their plans to do evil on this earth. Those who do so forfeit their lives just as they have already forfeited their souls."

She finished the last statement with what Dean would only call a bloodthirsty grin. She seemed to enjoy this stuff. Was she some sort of psychopath to look forward to killing that way? Dean wasn't sure. He had gotten his answer, though, and it was different than what he had learned from Gibbie and the others about hunters. How could he be sure she was telling the truth? Dean decided that he couldn't know in the near term without seeing what she was doing in Elk City.

"So you aren't here to enact some slaughter of my friends and patients? That is good to know," Dean said.

"I know some of what you all recently dealt with here in the city. That kind of carnage is harmful to all and is not what we are about," Jaz said. "In the end, you were fighting against the vampire lord, Artur Torrence. He is an ancient adversary of ours as well. Had I been in town when these events were occurring, I and any other Errington would have been firmly on your side. In fact we are still attempting to track that particular creature. We owe him a very old debt that we would like to collect. Perhaps someday we will end his cruel machinations on earth."

Dean thought on what she said. Could he have been more wrong in his estimation of her and her motives here? Was she even telling the truth?

"So if you are not here on some sort of a hunt, what is your reason for coming to town?" Dean asked. "I can't believe it was just to teach a class to the paramedics in the city about staying safe on the street."

"You are correct, at least in part," Jaz said. "We do consulting and training work like I did with your class this morning. It is not usually me who does it, but we do that at Errington Security."

She paused as Daisy came back with their drinks and set them down along with two sets of silverware, each wrapped up in a paper napkin. When the waitress walked away, Jaz continued.

"Dean, I am here because of an old debt, a debt we owe to someone as a clan. I understand you are a friend of the Eldara Sister Ashley Moore?"

"Yes, you could say that," Dean said. He didn't want to give away too much about his relationship with Ashley. Where was this going?

"We owe the Eldara a debt earned more than one hundred fifty years ago," Jaz continued. "I am here to seek her out where she is held captive and bring her abductors to justice."

Dean started to ask how she knew about Ashley's abduction but the hunter woman kept going.

"There is more, Dean. I am charged to enlist you in that search, along with one other." Jaz finished and sat back, as if to wait for Dean's reaction.

"You're one of the three, just like me," Dean said. He could see his answer caught her by surprise.

"What do you mean, the three?" Jaz asked.

"Ashley's sister, Ingrid, told me that I was charged to find two others to assist me in looking for Ashley. One was to be a person who was magical in nature; the other was to be one who shunned magical things. I'm guessing the latter is you."

"I, too, have a directive from my clan to gather two others to seek out the Eldara and free her," Jaz revealed. "Our oracle prophesied that we must have a hunter, a healer, and a hexen to make the rescue have a chance at success."

"I get the first two," Dean said. "But what's a hexen? Is it some sort of magical creature?"

"A hexen is our word for a witch," Jaz explained. "What you would call a Wiccan, I believe. As for the other two, you have guessed correctly. You are the healer, and I am the hunter mentioned by our Oracle. There was no guidance on who to choose for the third role. I do not associate with witches so perhaps it was to fall to you to choose one you knew. What do you think?"

"I don't have any close Wiccan friends," Dean replied, making sure to use the correct term for the women who channeled magical powers. "I am acquainted with a local coven, but I already owe them a significant debt. I'm not sure they will let me undertake another debt to them." Dean referred to his agreement during the recent troubles with the terrorists of The Cause, to offer his firstborn girl child someday to the coven, so she can be trained in the Wiccan ways. He didn't think he should tell Jaz about that. He was sure her response would be less than positive.

"I think that is wise," Jaz said. "I would not want to owe a debt to them either. I sympathize with your plight. Still, I was charged to find a witch, and find one I will so that the clan may discharge its debt to the Eldara."

She stopped. The lights had gone out in the diner. The sudden darkness caught them both by surprise. Dean looked around, trying to peer through the darkness when screams started at the far end of the diner by the entrance. He couldn't see anything, but heard rumbling snarls amid the screams, snarls that were coming closer.

"Shit," he heard Jaz say from across the table. "That's another Oni demon and someone has sent it here for the two of us, unless I miss my guess. We need to get out of here. I need my sword and I left it in the SUV outside." He saw her reach behind her in the darkness, and then he saw the unmistakable silhouette of a semi-automatic in her left hand.

"Is that a gun?" Dean exclaimed.

"Yes, but it's not going to do much good against an Oni," the huntress said. "The best I can do is slow it down a little. We need to get out to the parking lot. Is that the only door at the far end of the restaurant?"

"I'm afraid so," Dean said. He was still looking at the gun he hadn't known she was carrying. It was a bit of a shock.

"Okay, get behind me, Dean," Jaz said as she stood up and faced the sound of the snarls and screams coming from the other end of the restaurant. "Grab one of those chairs and bust out the window behind us next to the booth. We'll have to go out that way. Hurry up! It is going to figure out where we are any minute."

Dean picked up one of the diner chairs. It was heavy, made of tubular chrome steel with a red vinyl cushion. He looked at Jaz but she had taken a shooter's stance with her pistol aimed downrange towards the far end of the diner. How was she going to use that thing without killing some innocent person? He could not see more than a few feet past his nose.

"Dean, what are you doing?" Jaz said, turning to look back at him. "Break that window out. Now!"

Dean turned and hefted the chair, holding it by its back and swinging it hard at the window, striking the glass with the chair legs. He was surprised when it bounced off. Then Dean heard two gunshots behind him and he picked up the chair and swung harder. The glass broke under the blow this time, shattering and falling around him on the floor and outside. He turned and saw Jaz squeeze off four more shots in rapid succession, the muzzle flashes illuminating her face in the darkness with each shot. He heard a howling roar of pain from the darkness beyond her.

"You go first," Dean said.

"Don't be an idiot, I have the gun," Jaz shouted. "Get out the window. I'll be right behind you."

Dean used the chair to sweep some of the remaining glass from the window frame and swung his legs over to the outside, then jumped the four or five feet to the ground. The streetlights in the parking lot gave him better visibility than he'd had inside. He turned back to look in the open window to see four more muzzle flashes and then Jaz dove out the window, executing a perfect midair flip and landing on her feet next to him. There was a snarl of rage from inside the diner and then Dean saw the Oni demon for the first time as it reached the open window.

The demon was roughly man-shaped but was covered in scales and patches of coarse fur. The head was elongated like a wolf's and the teeth were the largest the paramedic had ever seen. He stood rooted to the spot while the creature looked in his direction and roared as if it recognized him. Jaz jumped in front of him as he saw her slap another magazine into her pistol and then emptied the fresh clip into the demon's face. Dean saw the bullets impact it, and the force of the impacts drove it backward as it screamed in rage and pain.

Jaz grabbed his hand and yelled, "Come on!" as she pulled him away from the diner and across the parking lot. He turned and ran beside her. She held something up in front of her and he saw the lights of a black SUV blink about fifty yards away. It was an awfully long way off with that thing chasing them. He tried to run even faster and make it to the relative safety of Jaz's car. When they reached the side of the SUV, Dean heard the roar of the demon behind them and turned to see it leap out the window, fall to all fours and run across the parking lot towards them. Jaz threw open the driver's door, leaning inside to grab something. Dean couldn't see what it was. He was focused on the demon chasing after them. No, it was looking straight into his eyes. It was chasing after him. Then his view was blocked as Jaz dashed in front of him. In her hands, held in a two-handed grip, was the sword he had seen her holding in the mirror at the Hakutakus' house days before.

She swept the sword down at something and Dean ducked to avoid the impact from the demon as it charged into Jaz to get to him.

He opened his eyes to a reddish mist surrounding both of them. The snarling and roars had stopped. He stood from where he was crouched behind the hunter and looked around.

"Where did it go?" Dean asked. Jaz was just standing there, her sword held out to her side, one-handed. Her heavy breathing was the only sign that she had exerted herself at all. She was still as a statue otherwise.

"Where did it go?" Dean asked again.

"Shhh. I'm trying to listen to see if there are any others around."

Dean looked around, startled at the thought. Could there be more of them?

He watched in silence as she scanned the parking lot, looking and listening. Then she turned and shoved him over to the passenger side of the SUV.

"Get in," she said. "We've got to get you out of here until we figure out why they are targeting you."

Dean started to say something but thought better of it when another snarling roar sounded in the distance. He went around to the passenger side while she climbed into the driver's side. He couldn't get in because of the weapons caddy attached to the seat. Jaz reached over and detached the strap holding it in place to the headrest.

"Just throw that in the back. Get in."

Dean got in and was still buckling his seatbelt as the hunter gunned the engine to life and, with a squeal of tires, drove off into the night, leaving the carnage of the attack behind them at the diner.

11

DEAN'S HEART was pounding in his chest as he thought about what just happened at Hank's Place. The diner had always been a safe haven and in the past had served as a neutral meeting ground with his enemies, real or imagined. He had met with Mike Farver there several times. His former mentor had turned out to be one of the lead terrorists in the attacks on the Unusual community a few months before. Dean had first learned of his betrayal at the very diner booth where he and Jaz sat this evening. Now there were possibly injured people back there who needed his help and he was speeding away, running from demons who seemed to be seeking his blood.

Another thought occurred to him about the carnage at the restaurant. He turned in his seat and looked at Jaz. She had been part of that carnage, firing her pistol blindly into the darkness during the blackout.

She noticed his attention and shot a glance his way while she was driving. "What?" she asked.

"I'm just wondering how many of your bullets missed the Oni and maybe hit other patrons or staff. Was it a good idea to fire off your weapon blind like that?"

"I was not firing blind, and I don't miss what I aim at," she hissed in reply. She kept the SUV's speed up even as she took a sharp left turn at the next intersection.

"Oh sorry," Dean said, rolling his eyes. "I didn't know you could see in the dark. Why didn't I think of that?"

"I can see in the dark," she replied. "I'm a hunter. It would not do much good if I wasn't on some sort of even footing with my adversaries." Jaz shot Dean another glance as she sped down the road away from the attacker.

"Wait, you're not kidding," Dean said, a bit amazed. "But how? I know you are human like me, and it couldn't be magic. You all hate magic."

"We don't hate magic," she clarified. "We hate when it is used against humans for gain by our adversaries. My hunter amulet gives me the ability to see in the dark, as well as in the UV and infrared spectrums, among other things." She touched the ornate three-sided pendant on a chain at her neckline.

Dean was chastened but not any less curious. He always wanted to know more about the hidden world he had known nothing about only a year before. He was hungry for knowledge about his patients and their lives. That included the hunters, he supposed.

"Can you sense the demons? How did you know there would be more coming?" Dean asked.

Jaz glanced his way again as she continued driving. She looked up into the rearview mirror and then pulled the SUV over to the curb, stopping there.

"I can't sense them any better than you, other than the seeing in the dark thing," she said after they stopped. Dean noticed that she kept looking around as she talked. He guessed it was the bodyguard training she must have had; that or paranoia. "Like I said, I can see in the UV and IF spectrums, too, so I can sense when someone is possessed. In those situations the demon sort of leaks out around the edges and shows up in the person's aura. Other than that, I have to use my normal human senses and sensibilities."

"So possession is real?" Dean asked. "Like as real as in movies like Exorcist?"

"I'm surprised you're so naive, Dean," Jaz replied. "You've seen so much and you are smart and well-read. Why wouldn't all of it be real?"

"I don't know," Dean replied. "I guess I'm just still surprised that so many of the legends and myths are actually true. I didn't grow up in this world the way you did."

"All of the legends and myths are true, at least in part," Jaz responded. "And you grew up with the same stories I did, you just never had anyone tell you they were true."

Dean watched as she checked her mirrors and then scanned the area around them. He got a sense that very little missed her attention.

"Someone is sending the Oni demons after you," Jaz said. "Someone or something. We need to get you somewhere safe, but I'm not sure we can trust any of the normal places. Is there somewhere you can think of that no one would think you would go? Somewhere isolated, where we can think and plan?"

Dean pondered the question. He, like most people, was a creature of habit. He had his apartment, his work, and his favorite places to hang out, like Hank's Place. He liked to go places where people knew him and he could feel at home and relax. There was nowhere he could think of that would give him a place to hole up like Jaz described. There was James Lee's Nightwing building downtown. There was plenty of security there, but that wasn't hiding and it would put more of his friends in danger. Dean looked at the huntress and shook his head.

Jaz took out her smartphone and tapped it a few times. He figured she was sending a text message when she started tapping away with her thumbs in rapid succession. Dean waited while she sent her message. He started looking around. It made him itch to think that there was at least one more of those Oni demons around out there, hunting for him. She finished whatever she was doing and slid her phone back into the pocket of her leather jacket.

"I just sent my father a message that we were tracked to the diner. He'll send a team there to make sure any Oni hanging about will be dealt with," Jaz said. "I also told him that we were going operationally dark. That means no messages, in or out, from now on. Turn off your phone so no one can track you. My phone is scrambled so we'll have to rely on that for now."

"I can't just disappear," Dean said. "I've got work in the morning. I'll lose my job."

"Daddy is smart," Jaz said. "He knows you're with me and he will let your Chief know that you are on an assignment with us as a tactical medic or something. That should cover you. He and your fire chief go way back. Now we need to keep moving until we can figure out where we can safely hide."

She continued to look at him as she slid the gear lever out of park and into drive. She gripped the wheel and started to move. Dean looked forward and saw a girl, palms of both hands outstretched, her eyes squeezed shut. She was standing directly in front of the vehicle.

"Look out," Dean shouted.

Jaz looked forward, jamming on the brakes. They had nearly run the girl over. Her outstretched hands were now resting on the hood of the SUV. Jaz drew her pistol. "Dean, get down. If she can't see you, she might not be able to connect the spell she's casting. She's a hexen; a witch. I can see her drawing in magic."

Dean didn't duck. He was looking in the girl's face. She was only about fifteen or sixteen he would guess, dressed in a flowing long print skirt, with a white peasant-style blouse and a brown vest. She looked like someone from a renaissance faire or something. She also looked sort of familiar, like he had seen her somewhere before, like he should know her.

"Don't shoot her," Dean said on impulse. "I think she's with us."

"What do you mean, 'she's with us?'"

"Look," Dean said. "I know you're a shoot first and ask questions later type of person, but we have to work together here. You said that, not me. I'm telling you that for some reason I know her, even though I've never seen her before. Just look at her, she's not threatening us. She is just standing there."

The girl in front of them had opened her eyes and was staring forward at them through the tinted windshield as if she could see into the darkened interior. She had a wild sort of grin on her face, standing there under the streetlights in front of them.

"I am looking at her," Jaz said. "I can see the UV waves of her spell. She's casting something right now. How do you know she isn't calling the Oni on us?"

"How do you know she is?" Dean countered. He watched as the girl lowered her hands and walked around to the driver's side of the Expedition.

Jaz put the window down but kept the gun in her left hand, just below the edge of the window, ready to use. Dean spoke up before the huntress had a chance to speak.

"Hey, good thing I saw you before my companion here ran you over," Dean said with a smile. "What were you doing standing in front of us like that, if you don't mind my asking? It's kind of nuts, you know."

"I was masking your vehicle from scrying spells," the girl said. "The revenants are already trying to track you both after the attack at the diner." She looked at Jaz, a broad smile on her young face. "You can put the gun away, Jaswinder. I mean you no harm. You both were just about to go looking for me anyway, so I decided to come to you."

"Jaz," Dean said looking at the driver. Jaz turned to meet his gaze and nodded. "I think we found our hexen."

"Yeah, I think so, too," the hunter replied. She leaned forward and reached back, sliding the semi-automatic pistol into its holster. Then she reached up and pressed the button to unlock the doors. "Climb in back," Jaz said to the young Wiccan girl. "We need to keep moving. Even if your masking spell worked, there are still mundane ways to track us."

The girl kind of bounced at the invitation to get in the vehicle with them. She jumped into the back seat and slid to the middle, looking around at the gray and black interior. She extended her hand to Dean when he twisted back to look at her as she got situated. Jaz pulled away from the curb and started driving again.

"I'm Jo. That's short for Joanna," the girl said, shaking his hand. "But I prefer just Jo."

"Nice to meet you, Jo," Dean said. "I'm Dean and this is Jaz. But I guess you must know that already." He noticed she was still bouncing slightly as she sat forward on the edge of the bench seat behind them. "Hey, Jo, sit back and buckle up. We can still talk but you need to be belted in. Okay?"

"Okay, Dad," she said rolling her eyes. Then she giggled and sat back to buckle in.

Typical teenager, Dean thought, viewing any adult telling her what to do as a parental figure.

"What were you doing out here in the first place, and how did you find us?" Jaz asked.

"My coven knew that I needed to come here and help you so they sent me directly to this place and time to make sure I was here when you arrived," Jo said. "They spent a great deal of energy to make sure I was here to help you find the missing Eldara."

"So you know about our mission?" Dean asked.

"You are seeking to free Ashley Moore, an Eldara Sister abducted by revenants who seek to use her divine energy to create a large breach in the warding that separates the netherworld from ours." Jo stopped her recitation and looked from Dean to Jaz and back again. "How'd I do?"

"Pretty well," Dean said. She seemed to know more about this than either of them. There was so much he wanted to know more about. Who were these revenants? Where were they holding Ashley and how could they free her?

"Revenants," Jaz said. "That's not good." Dean saw her make eye contact with their back seat passenger in the rearview mirror. "Are you sure they're revenants?"

"Yep," the teen replied. "They are determined to kill one of us. If they do, it will stop us from rescuing the Eldara. They have their own seers and they know of our quest, too. They know it has to be the three of us."

"Well revenants are high order netherworld demons of a sort," Jaz told Dean. "They are the damned souls of the most evil of men, reformed into magical creatures of the netherworld. They can be very powerful."

"How do we beat them?" Dean asked. In the stories the bad guys always have some sort of weakness.

"I don't know," Jaz said. "I've never faced one of them before."

"You can kill them, or at least banish them with a holy blade, like the one you have Jaz," Jo said. "Beheading will do the trick if you catch them unawares. It just destroys their corporeal form and sends them back to the netherworld but it would be enough for our purposes."

"How do you know all of this?" Dean asked.

"Oh, I feel like I've been preparing for this all my life," Jo said.

"How old are you?" Jaz asked.

"I'm fifteen," she responded. She sounded defensive all of a sudden. "I just passed my acceptance ritual into the coven. I'm an adult now, so don't tell me I'm not old enough to be here doing this."

There's that teenager thing again, Dean thought. Naturally pushing back against authority figures.

Jaz laughed. "You're not going to get an argument from me, girly-girl. I killed my first demon on a hunt at fourteen. It wasn't my first hunt, just my first kill."

"Cool," Jo said. "You'll have to tell me about it. I haven't heard that story about you before."

"Time enough for stories later," Jaz said. "Right now we need to get out of here to someplace safe."

"So, where are we headed?" Jo asked.

"We need a place where no one will expect to find us," Jaz said. "Someplace we can regroup and reorganize while we figure out our next steps."

"How about the mountain cabin?" Jo asked.

"What mountain cabin?" Jaz said.

Dean looked back over his shoulder at the Wiccan teen and saw her looking back and forth between the two of them. She seemed puzzled that they didn't understand.

"There's a cabin in the woods on a lake to the west of here near the mountains," Jo explained. "It belongs to the Eldara."

"That might work, but I don't know what you're talking about." Jaz said.

"No, no I guess you wouldn't. Okay, Ashley Moore owns a mountain cabin she bought from a nurse friend of hers," Jo said. "It's remote and it should be safe enough for now, especially with my spell in place over us."

"Wait, I think I know that cabin," Dean said. "I didn't know that Ashley had bought it, but I know the one you're thinking of." It was weird how Joanna knew so much about them, and Ashley, for that matter. She must be from the local coven and had been briefed on them by Asha and the other women there.

Dean turned to Ashley. "Head south to I-95, then we'll swing over and get on I-70 westbound. The cabin is in the mountains of Western Maryland about two hours from here. I think Jo is right. It will be a perfect place to hole up until we get our bearings again."

Jaz nodded and turned the car onto a nearby on-ramp to get up on the interstate. Dean sat back in silence. He had started that day without a clue about how to get started finding Ashley. Now he had his trio to get to work finding her. Despite the recent events with the demon attack, he felt pleased for the first time in a long time. He finally had the jumpstart he needed to find her and get her back.

12

THE TRIP to the cabin was several hours long and after some time trying to plan out what they were going to do, everyone was quiet for a while. Dean looked back at Jo in the back seat. She was settled back, with her earbuds in, watching something on her phone. Jaz had cautioned her about connecting her phone to anything online and the girl had told her that she would access only stored media on the device. Dean thought about who she might be. He was uncomfortable with running around on this mission with a fifteen year-old child. She had said the coven saw her as an adult, but he noticed that she never said anything about what her parents thought. The more he thought about it, the more he started to think she was some sort of runaway. If that was the case, it could make things worse for them. He would have to talk to Jaz about it the first chance they were alone. There had to be a way to verify her story.

He knew that he needed to have three people in their team in order to find Ashley. He was willing to risk just about anything to get her back. It seemed like Jaz was the right person for one of those slots. She had her own prophecy of some sort that matched up with what Ingrid had told him he must do. The wild card was Joanna. She fit the slot in their team they had open, and there was also the fact that she had found them and identified herself as the one they were looking for. Still, with his concerns about her legal status and age, was he willing to endanger her life to get Ashley back?

He knew what Ashley would say. She would never condone putting anyone in danger just to rescue her. She would say she was the one who did the rescuing. He didn't feel the same way about Jaz. She had demonstrated that she could take care of herself. Heck, she could take care of him, too. With demons chasing after him now, he felt safer with the blonde huntress around. He looked over at her as she drove. He wanted to know more about her and her training. It was a new side of the mythical world in which he found himself at Station U. Dean was always curious to learn new things. Maybe he could learn more about caring for his patients by learning more about the hunters and their backgrounds.

When they stopped for gas about an hour outside of Elk City, Dean learned just how paranoid Jaz was about keeping them off the grid. Dean was going to head in and get a soda to help him stay awake and offered to buy something for the others.

"How much cash do you have?" Jaz asked when he turned to leave the pumps to go inside the WaWa convenience store.

"Not much, but I have my debit card," Dean replied.

"No credit or debit cards. It is just like keeping our phones off or in airplane mode," Jaz said shaking her head. "We can't afford to leave a trail behind us. Come around back of the Expedition."

Dean and Joanna got out and followed her to the back where she opened the lift gate. There were three black Pelican cases lying in the cargo area, two large cases and one smaller case. Jaz looked around to make sure that no one else was around and then dialed in a combination on the embedded lock before opening the small case. Jo laughed as she saw the open case and turned away as if she wasn't that surprised. Dean couldn't take his eyes off the contents. The case was full of cash, stacks of it. The bills were all bundled up in bank wrappers and neatly arranged in rows.

"How much money is that?" Dean asked.

"It's one hundred thousand dollars in various sized bills," Jaz said, taking one of the stacks of fifty-dollar bills out of the case before she closed it and rolled the combination dials to lock it gain. She peeled off a few of the fifties, handing them to him, before putting the rest into an inside pocket of her black leather jacket. "Use that to buy anything you want, I'll take a coffee, one sugar and some half and half. Put the other fifty down on the gas here at pump number 2."

"Ooo, I want a smoothie," Jo chimed in. "I love WaWa smoothies."

"Do you always drive around with that much cash in the back of your car? What if someone tries to rob you?" Dean asked.

Jo laughed aloud. "Rob her? That would be like committing suicide. Come on, I'm thirsty." The teen headed towards the convenience store entrance.

Jaz shot a look at the teenager and then said, "It's about being discreet and careful. I'm never as concerned about the cash as I am about the weapons. And, yes, all our Errington vehicles are prepped to go dark at any time. Since we have to be prepared to provide the best security for our clients, we have to be prepared for anything. That includes doing what we are doing right now, heading to a safe house to regroup. Go get my coffee. I'll pump the gas."

Dean shook his head as he wondered what was in the other cases in the back. She had mentioned weapons and he was sure there were other surprises as well. She certainly liked her mysteries. He walked into the convenience store just behind Jo. The teen Wiccan seemed to take everything in stride as if she was used to traveling around a lot. It made him wonder about her legal status again and he wished he could turn his phone on and make at least one call to ask Asha about her. If the coven really sent her to them, she would tell him.

Dean got Jaz her coffee while Jo used one of the touch screens to order herself a smoothie. He strolled up and down the aisles, looking for something to snack on while he waited for the smoothie to be finished. After all, his dinner had been rudely interrupted. He selected a bag of pretzels large enough for all of them and headed to the counter to pay. He handed the clerk one of the fifties and told him to put it on the SUV getting gas at pump 2. He used the other fifty to pay for their food and drinks. He noticed that the clerk was staring at the back of his right hand. It was where his UV ink tattoo was located that identified him as a Station U paramedic. Only Unusuals could see the mark. He let his eyes come up and met the clerk's eyes. They had a slight yellow tint around the corners of the irises. He was some sort of lycan, an animal shapeshifter. The clerk just smiled at him and made an adjustment on the screen.

"Police and public safety don't pay for coffee, sir," the clerk said.

"I'm not on duty," Dean said. "I don't mind paying." He knew that some places gave discounts and freebies to policemen, fire and EMS crews. He took advantage of them all the time while he was on duty. This was the first time someone had noticed who he was off duty.

"Not a problem, sir. Thank you for your service, I'll just ring up the other items," the clerk said.

Dean nodded in thanks and picked up the coffee cup and the bag with the pretzels and bottle of soda. Jo strolled over with the stamped receipt to pick up her smoothie at the deli counter. Once she had the fruity concoction the two of them went back to the SUV. Jaz was just finishing up filling the gas tank. He was surprised it had taken so long to fill up, even with an SUV the size of the Expedition. He mentioned as much to Jaz.

"It's got dual custom gas tanks so we can go twice as far on a tankful," the hunter explained. She took the coffee from Dean and took out her keys while she climbed in.

"I can drive," Dean offered.

"No, I've got it," Jaz said. "I don't like it when other people drive my vehicle."

Jo laughed from the back seat. "Some things never change."

Dean shot her a glance at the strange comment, but didn't argue with Jaz. If she wanted to drive, that was fine by him. He could get some rest. He was tired after working all day and getting up early.

"How's the free coffee?" Jo asked. "Dean got comped a free cup when the clerk spotted his invisible ink."

"He what?" Jaz said, concerned.

"It's no big deal," Dean said. "A lot of convenience stores offer free coffee and fountain soda to public safety officers. He spotted my

Station U tattoo and said the coffee was free. He was some sort of lycan, if I were to guess."

"He was kind of hot, too," Jo said. "But most shifters have that vibe going for them."

"Dean," Jaz said. "I told you we have to stay under the radar and you go and expose us to the first convenience store clerk we run into. Are you crazy?"

"I told you that it is no big deal. I forget about this tattoo when I'm not working," Dean explained.

"Yeah, but you are one of, what, ten or twelve people in the world with that tattoo?" the hunter asked. "So if word gets around that one of you was here on the way out of town, how long do you think it will take our adversaries to put two and two together and figure out it was you?"

"Wow, paranoid much?" Dean asked. "What makes you think that anyone is going to go to those lengths to track me down? It was a chance encounter, that's all."

"I stay alive by being paranoid. If you let me, I'll keep you alive, too," Jaz cautioned him as she started up the SUV and drove back towards the highway ramp. "We know they are tracking you somehow. Until I figure out how they got to us at the diner, I will assume that any compromise is potentially fatal."

"So if we weren't in a hurry, you'd go back and kill that kid to cover our tracks?" Dean asked, only partially joking.

Jaz shot him a glance and then went back to paying attention to the road ahead. The glance turned his blood to ice. If she thought it would work, that is exactly what she would do. Dean had to remember that at the heart of it she was a killer. Maybe she did it for the right reasons, maybe not, but she was his opposite. If the situation called for it, she'd kill without a moment's thought and without remorse. He shivered and wondered again about who he was teamed up with on this mission.

"How about some music?" Jo offered from the back seat. "It's like riding in a hearse in here. Put the radio on and get us some tunes."

Dean reached up to the dashboard and turned on the radio.

When he switched it on, he caught a Baltimore news broadcast in progress.

"... Identified as Jaswinder Errington, a private security specialist. Ms. Errington is being sought in relation to a savage animal attack where shots were fired in Elk City earlier this evening. Her companion, Elk City paramedic Dean Flynn is also sought for questioning in the incident. They were last seen leaving the scene of the incident in a black SUV and should be considered armed and dangerous. Do not approach them yourself. Call 911, Elk City Police, or the Maryland State Police if you have information of their whereabouts. We'll be back in a minute with tomorrow's weather forecast after these messages from our sponsors."

"I thought you called your father and told him what we were doing? He was going to square things away," Dean said.

"I thought so, too," Jaz replied. "It appears our adversaries have more resources than we thought."

Jo chimed in, "At least they didn't mention me."

"Yeah, but you two are on the security cameras at the convenience store and if that lycan back there puts two and two together, he's going to report us to the police. They are going to have descriptions of all three of us on the radio as soon as he does."

"Well we're only another hour from the cabin," Dean said. "It is isolated and no one will look for us there. There is no connection to us."

"I hope so, Dean, I hope so," Jaz said. "Because isolated cabins make great places for a concerted attack, too, where no one can hear the noise and raise an alarm."

The SUV's occupants fell silent as they drove onward, thinking about that final statement. It did not bode well for them.

13

DEAN PACED the floor in the cabin's open great room while he thought about the situation he was in. "I can't believe I'm being chased by the police again," he complained. "I just got murder charges against me dropped. I promised myself I would never be in that situation again."

"You're not charged with anything," Jo said. "You're a person of interest in an ongoing investigation. The police search is just our opponent's way of getting help tracking us down."

"She's right," Jaz said. She was seated on the sofa against the wall. She had her handgun broken down to its component parts, all laid out on the coffee table in front of her. She was wiping the barrel with a cloth coated with some sort of oil. "This is just a ploy to get the police to track us down for them. It keeps us on the run and not getting on with our task of tracking down the missing Eldara."

"That's easy for you to say," Dean quipped. "You're used to living on the run and being tracked by demons."

"This is a kill or be killed game you're mixed up with, Dean," she said. "And, no, I'm not used to being in trouble with the police. We usually try to work with them and not against them. It makes me wonder what my father is doing to get all of this worked out. Something must be keeping him from getting us off the police's radar."

"Maybe he's got other things on his mind," Jo said. She pointed to the TV she was watching. There was a video of a large building fire. The caption read, "Gas Explosion Destroys Elk City Building."

"Turn that up," Jaz and Dean said together.

"... Fire department investigators are making no statements as to the cause of the explosion, but bystanders claim they smelled gas just before the blast that leveled the Errington Security Building and damaged surrounding structures as well. There are no reports of the number of casualties in the blast and subsequent fires, though there are several reports of firefighter injuries while fighting the blaze."

Dean looked at Jaz. She looked pale and lost all of a sudden. It was the first time he'd seen her with her guard down. He heard a sob from his left and looked over to see that Jo was crying. He didn't know what she was crying about. It was Jaz's father that might be missing after all. Maybe she was just shocked by the carnage.

"Jaz," he said. "We don't know that your father was in the building when the explosion happened. We have to hope for the best until we know for sure."

"He was there, Dean," she said. "He was staying in the clan apartments upstairs. We keep them there for when we are in town. My mom was there, too, along with most of my cousins. This mission was important. All hands were on deck to help out. Now we're on our own." Her shoulders sagged and she turned her head away, probably so he couldn't see her crying.

Jo walked over, wiping tears from her eyes and sat down on the sofa next to Jaz. She put one arm around Jaz's shoulders to comfort her. The hunter started to pull away and then she gave in and the two of them shared a tearful embrace. Dean wasn't sure why Jo was so upset, too, but he supposed it was good she was able to give Jaz a shoulder to cry on, given the circumstances. He had never known his own father and had only the vaguest memories of him. His mother had never talked about him, no matter how many times Dean had asked. He moved over and picked up the remote from on top of the TV and turned the TV off. He looked around for something to do.

With all that had happened to Jaz this evening, his troubles didn't seem so important.

He looked at the cabin. Ashley had made a few upgrades to the place since they'd been here. He had come here once when she had borrowed the key from an ER nurse friend of hers. Since she had bought the place, he found that she had put in a small satellite dish and added a generator to power the place if the main power went out. The pantry shelves were stocked with canned goods and it looked like someone came in periodically and cleaned and dusted the place.

He wondered if the caretakers were members of the nearby Unusual community. He and Ashley had helped a family of Dryads living in the forest nearby when they had been here before. They had saved the oldest daughter from a life-threatening infection and he was sure that family would have felt obligated to help the Eldara again if they knew she bought the cabin. He might want to try and contact them. He thought he could find their place through the woods again if he tried. He looked at his watch. It was nearing midnight. Would that be too late, or should he wait for morning?

"I'm going to go for a walk. I've got to connect with someone who might be able to help us out," Dean said.

"No, we can't afford to let anyone know where we are," Jaz cautioned.

"These are friends of Ashley's and they owe her a debt," Dean explained. "You understand how that works. We need some help, at least in the short term. They could be of service to help us stay supplied and informed about what is going on in the outside world. Trust me. These people can help us."

The huntress just looked at him for a moment with her red-rimmed eyes, the pain showing in her expression, even though she tried to appear in control. She nodded, almost imperceptibly, and he grabbed a flashlight from where he had left it on the counter and left to go and find some Dryads in the dark.

DEAN STEPPED outside the cabin and shined the flashlight's beam
into the woods. It had been a while since he had been here, but he
thought he could find the path that led to the Dryads' house in the
woods. If he could connect with Enric, the head of the family and
one of the leaders of the Unusuals in the mountain valley, they could
hide here in the cabin for a while before anyone found them.
Playing the flashlight's illumination on the ground in front of him,
Dean started to look along the edge of the trees for where the path
began.

It didn't take him too long, no more than fifteen minutes to find
where he thought the path began and he walked into the dark woods,
following the trail. It was probably a bad idea, he thought. Dean was
a child of the city. He had grown up in and around Elk City all his life
and had not spent any appreciable time in anything approaching a
wilderness setting. The forest here was alien to him in many ways. In
daylight, the paramedic might have been able to keep his bearings
while walking, but with the darkness, even with the help of a flashlight, he soon became lost.

The first clue was when he stumbled through an opening in the
trees and found himself on the edge of the mountain lake that filled
the center of the valley. He had started on a path that led away from
the lake. The fact that he had gotten turned around and ended up
next to the water meant that he had no idea where he was. He
checked his watch and realized he had been gone for almost an hour.
The walk to the dryad's cabin, when he had taken the trip before with
Ashley, had only taken about twenty minutes.

Dean looked around in the darkness. It was cloudy, so there was
no help from the moon or stars to lend light to the landscape. He
played the light from his flashlight on the dark waters of the lake and
then turned in a circle, shining the light into the woods behind him.
Dean supposed he could just walk along the lake's bank until he got
back to the cabin, but the cabin was not right on the lake and he was
not sure he would see it in the dark. He was still contemplating his
options when there was a sound behind him. It was a ripping snarl,
like that of a large cat. Spinning around, the light's beam showed the

tawny form of a mountain lion, eyes glowing in the light's illumination.

Dean started to panic. His chances of fending off a mountain lion on his own without even as much as a knife were slim. He held out the flashlight in his left hand, keeping the beam on the lion, which stood watching him from the edge of the tree line. He extended his right hand in a calming gesture, palm extended, fingers wide. Dean didn't know what he was doing, or why, but he knew that if he tried to turn and run, the big cat would catch him without any trouble at all.

Then the lion did something he didn't expect. It sat down and extended its right fore paw. If Dean didn't know better, he would think it was copying his movements. The cat's head tilted as if puzzled by something and it let out a low rumble from its throat. It wasn't a growl exactly, but it did send chills up Dean's spine. He had a sudden thought and turned his right hand from palm out to show the mountain lion the back of his hand. He wasn't sure if the hidden tattoo there glowed in the UV spectrum in the dark so he shined the edge of the flashlight's beam on it briefly, just to illuminate it.

The lion looked from meeting his eyes, to his outstretched hand and then nodded. At least that was the way he would describe it. It looked like a nod. He decided to try something else.

"I'm Dean Flynn, I'm a paramedic and a companion of the Eldara, Ashley Moore. Do you understand me?" His voice sounded loud in the darkness amid the chirps and buzzing of the nighttime insects.

The mountain lion nodded again, and Dean felt his shoulders relax a bit. This wasn't a mountain lion. It was a lycan of some sort who had shifted to lion form. He decided to keep talking since that seemed to be working.

"I was looking for Enric's home, the Dryad chieftain in this valley. Do you know him?"

Again, a nod from the large cat.

"Can you take me to him or his family? I need their help." Dean asked.

This time the head tilted again and then swung from side to side. So it was a no. He wondered why the shifter didn't just turn back into

a human form and talk to him normally. All but a very young shapeshifter could change back at will. The ability to shift forms came with
adolescence and the swings in mood and emotion that came with
puberty also made changing back and forth difficult for the younger
shifters. The change could also be brought on by anything that
altered mental status, but that wasn't the case here.

"Why aren't you shifting back to talk to me as a human?" Dean
asked. "Are you too young to shift back until morning?"

Another nod confirmed his suspicions. Okay, so now he had a
connection to the Unusual community, but he'd have to wait until the
morning to talk to them. For now he was stuck communicating with
the shape-changer with yes and no questions only.

Dean settled down on a large fallen tree trunk at the water's edge
and started thinking of ways to keep the conversation going. He wasn't
afraid of the big cat anymore, but he was afraid the kid would lose
interest in this conversation with the lost human and go about his
business, leaving Dean alone in the woods again. He was still contemplating questions to ask when he heard voices from behind him. The
mountain lion stood back up and looked past him into the woods,
then, with a quiet snarl, turned and bounded off into the darkness.

Dean turned the flashlight the other direction, towards where the
voices were coming from. He thought he recognized them. He
watched as Jaz and Joanna exited the tree line at the edge of the lake
about a hundred feet away.

"See, I told you I could find him," Jo said. "You shouldn't doubt
me. I have skills you don't appreciate."

"I didn't doubt you, I just didn't think it was a good idea to have
another one of us wander off into the woods alone to get lost," Jaz
countered. "Anyway, yes, you did find him." In the illumination of his
flashlight, he could see she carried a large tactical shotgun with a
folding stock, and he could see the hilt of her katana jutting up over
her left shoulder. "You alright?"

"I'm fine," Dean lied. "I was just taking a break. I found a lycan
and we were talking when you showed up."

Jaz cursed under her breath and swung the shotgun back and forth along the trees at the edge of the forest, searching for a target. Dean thought this was going to be an ongoing problem for them if Jaz just assumed that every Unusual was a potential target for her hunter skills.

"Jaz, it was a peaceful encounter," Dean said. "Anyway, the kid ran off as soon as you two arrived. What are you doing out here? I was fine," Dean lied again.

"Jo here said you had gotten lost, that she could sense it," the hunter replied. "She was going to come out looking for you on her own and I couldn't let her do that, so here we all are."

"I wasn't lost, exactly," Dean explained. He was curious how the Wiccan girl had figured out that he was lost. He was pretty sure that sort of spell that required a certain level of intimacy or connection unless she was very powerful for her age. "I got turned around in the woods, but when I found the lake, I realized I could follow it back to the cabin. Then I met the lycan youth."

"How do you know it was a young one?" Jaz asked. She was still watching the surrounding woods, scanning the area with her night vision charm for any movement.

"He or she couldn't change back on their own until morning," Dean said. "The ability to shift at will comes with age and practice. The kid was probably out for a normal night of hunting when he came upon me. I showed my tattoo and we started talking. Well I talked and asked simple questions. The lycan's answers were just head bobs or shakes."

"So what did you learn?" Jo asked. "Can we get help from the Unusuals here?"

"I think so. I was about to get to that part when you all showed up and scared the kid away."

"So, are you ready to head back to the cabin, or did you want to stumble around in the dark a little bit more?" Jaz asked.

"Yeah, Dean," Jo added. "At least let me cast a glamor on your eyes so you can see in the dark."

"Uh, no spells, thank you," Dean said. "I'm happy with my normal human abilities."

He joined them as they walked back along the bank of the Lake. They only walked about five hundred feet before Jaz turned and led the group back to the cabin. Dean felt a little silly that they were so close to the cabin the whole time he was thinking he was lost. He decided to keep that thought to himself.

14

DEAN WOKE up the next morning and stretched in the early morning light coming in the cabin's first floor windows. He had taken the couch for the night, while the ladies shared the queen-sized bed upstairs in the single loft bedroom. He was a little stiff since the couch cushions weren't all that soft or comfortable when it came to sleeping on them. He thought he was the only one up, but then the front door opened and Joanna came in from outside. She was carrying her sandals in one hand and a small bouquet of wildflowers in the other. She smiled at Dean when she saw him sitting up on the sofa.

"I didn't want to wake you up. You looked like you could use the extra sleep," the Wiccan girl said.

"You didn't wake me," Dean said. "I needed to get up anyway. I expect we'll have visitors this morning after last night's encounter with the lycan youth. What were you up to outside?"

"It's a little morning ritual I like to do," Jo said. "It helps me to stay grounded and remember who I am within the world."

Dean did not know what to make of that. He hadn't found much for himself in the spiritual realm. He didn't begrudge it to those who believed in something larger than himself, but Dean had never been that guy. It was surprising considering his relationship with an angel and all.

"You should have let someone know you were going out, that's all," Dean said. "We have to stick together and know what each of us are doing if we are going to stay safe.

"I told Jaz when I got up," the girl said. "I thought she might want to join me, considering what happened to her parents last night. It's a great way to center yourself and lose the worries and cares of the world around you."

"I don't need to forget what happened," Jaz said from the stairs as she descended to the first floor. "I need to keep focused to take the revenge called for by my parent's death."

"It was a fire, a gas explosion, Jaz," Dean said. "The fire department told reporters that. It's tragic, but it happens from time to time. I'm sorry for your loss, but not everything is an attack. It could have been an accident."

"It wasn't an accident," Jaz said with firm belief in her words. "I don't believe in coincidences, and this is too closely related to the time we were attacked at the diner and went on the run. There have been many attacks over the years that have reduced our numbers. This was a final step to remove the Errington clan, once and for all."

"She's not wrong, Dean," Jo added. "The revenants want to bring on the end of the world ahead of schedule. They need certain players out of the way in order to do that. It's why they took Ashley."

Jaz looked over at Joanna. "You mentioned the revenants before. How do you know they are behind this?"

"Very powerful revenants control several levels of the netherworld and would love to be able to freely cross the wards that keep the worlds separate," Jo answered. "I was told by my coven leader that revenants sought a breach in the wards between our worlds."

"I still can't believe I didn't know anything about these revenants until now," Dean said.

"You had all those books on Unusuals, myths, and legends at the Station, Dean," Jo said. "Why didn't you learn more about what you could run in to?"

"I paid attention to the living and corporeal creatures I was likely to see on my calls," Dean replied. "I didn't pay much attention to the part about ghosts and creatures from beyond the grave. And how do you know about the library at Station U, anyway?"

"Uh, I mean, doesn't everyone?" the teen replied. "Anyway, we need to find out where the revenants are holding Ashley. The coven's scrying told us they plan to leech her power away and use it to open a permanent hole in the wards between our worlds."

Dean thought for a moment. "So these revenants are the ones sending the Oni demons after me. Why?"

"We have to figure that out," Jaz said, "among other things. The attack on my family, the attacks on you, and Ashley's disappearance are all tied together. Once we find the common threads we'll...."

A knock at the cabin door interrupted her thoughts. Dean turned to answer the door, but Jaz drew her pistol and jumped in front of him, picking up her katana where it was propped by the door. When she was set with sword and pistol in hand, she nodded to Dean to answer.

A glance through the peephole in the door showed two men. Well, actually a man and a teen boy of about fourteen or so. Dean looked at Jaz, shrugged and opened the door.

"Uh, can I help you?" Dean asked.

"My son said you were here and maybe in some kind of trouble," the man said. When Dean looked at the boy and then back to the father, the man continued. "He said you met last night by the lake?"

"Oh, the lion," Dean said. "Please come in." He stepped back and gestured to the pair. The father led the way and the boy followed. The man stopped and Dean heard a growl deep in the man's throat. He shot a glance back at Dean, showing his teeth.

"You invite us in, but have an armed hunter waiting to kill us?" the man said. He crouched and turned to snarl at Jaz. She shifted to a defensive stance and raised her sword up over her head.

Dean jumped between the two of them. He pressed his hands outwards to stop both of them from advancing on each other. "Stop. Stop right now. I mean it," Dean shouted.

He looked back and forth between the two. Jaz looked ready to kill Dean on the way to the pair of shifters. Her eyes were blazing in fury at him. The man was no less angry but they had halted their advance on each other.

"Jaz, put the sword down," Dean said. "These people have done nothing to harm us. The boy was the lion I met last night during his shifted travels." Dean turned his head towards the man, "Sir, we mean you no harm. We have traveled a long way, and have had troubles with those who follow us. That is why she answers the door armed."

Jaz started to lower her blade, but didn't really relax. The man took a step backwards, though Dean noticed that the fingernails on his hands were slightly elongated and ended in points. He had partially shifted. Still, he had not attacked, and they were ready to talk, not fight, and that was a step in the right direction.

"I'm Dean, Dean Flynn. I'm a paramedic from Elk City." He held up his right hand to show the tattoo to the father.

"I'm Albion Nutt and this is my son Arlo," the man said. "Arlo says you talked to him and he said you needed assistance. He said you mentioned the Eldara who visits this place?"

"Yes, Ashley Moore. She is a good friend of mine." Dean said. "She is missing and in our quest to find her, her abductors attacked us. We were forced to flee here to plan our next actions."

"Way to go, telling everyone our whole plan, Dean," he heard Jaz mutter.

Jo came over and introduced herself.

The man looked at the three of them and gave Dean a crooked grin. "You three are an odd group of companions to quest for a missing Eldara."

Jaz said, "Don't get me started. It wasn't my idea."

That comment made Albion laugh out loud. He kept laughing until he noticed the others staring at him. "I'm sorry. I know this is no laughing matter to the three of you. The whole valley is honored by the visits of the Eldara to this region. It makes us proud that she would choose our quiet lake and forest to make a place of rest and solitude in-between her travels. Of course we will help you.

Albion looked to Dean, "Have you tried to reach out to the Dryads? Their patriarch is the leader of the vale, Enric. He would know best how to help you."

Dean smiled. "That was where I was headed last night when I got turned around in the woods and ended up by the lake with your son."

"Well, we can take you there now, if you'd like?" Albion offered.

"I would like that," Dean replied.

"We would like that," Jaz said after clearing her throat. She looked at Dean. "I'm not letting you get lost traipsing around the woods again. We'll all go together."

"If that is your wish," Albion said. Dean thought he seemed uncertain about taking the hunter along on the trip to Enric's house but decided not to argue about it.

"Albion, my interest in this quest are no less important than Dean's. My family owes the Eldara a debt of honor and I would repay that for my family." She stopped for a moment and stared off past Dean for a moment, gathering herself before continuing on. He knew she must still be reeling from the apparent loss of her parents last night. The fact that she refused to break their radio silence to check on them was a surprise to Dean, but she said that it would only serve to pinpoint them to the enemy.

"A debt of honor I understand," Albion said with a nod. "May I have your assurances that you mean no one in the valley harm?"

"I mean harm to none who don't wish to harm us," she replied. She met the werelion's eyes. The two considered each other for a time and then the elder shapeshifter nodded, as did Jaz. That was settled.

"So, when can we get started?" Dean asked. "I'd like to see Enric, Anya and their family again."

"You know them?" Albion asked, then he snapped his fingers on one hand. "Of course. You are the paramedic who was here and helped heal Enric's daughter, Zora."

"That's me."

"I'm sure they will want to see you as well, then," Albion said.

"They talk about how you helped the Eldara and were her chosen companion. A great honor. Let us go, then."

Dean agreed and he, Jaz, and Jo gathered their limited things for a walk in the woods. For Dean, that meant his duty jacket. He was still wearing his uniform from the previous night. He had no additional clothes. Jo had a few things in her shoulder bag, but not much. Jaz was the most prepared for their sudden departure from Elk City. She had a full evacuation kit in the back of her SUV that didn't just include bundles of cash. She had several changes of clothes and the two large cases that Dean had helped her carry into the cabin the night before. She would not tell him what the contents of the cases were and he was not sure he wanted to know.

Jaz slipped her sword belt over her shoulders so that it settled across her back with the hilt jutting up diagonally over her left shoulder. She already had her pistol holstered on her left side and what she called her small Bowie knife on her belt on the right side. Albion waited while she gathered her leather jacket, which showed a brace of throwing knives still attached by Velcro to the interior of it.

"Are you expecting trouble, huntress?" the shifter asked. "I assure you that none in this valley mean you harm if you come in peace."

"If those who seek us come for us, you will be glad I have come prepared," Jaz said. "Let's go."

Albion and Arlo led the way out of the cabin and Dean brought up the rear, locking the door behind him and pocketing the key instead of replacing it under the fake plastic rock by the front porch where he had retrieved it the night before. He had wondered when they arrived how they would break in to the cabin but Jo got out and went right to the rock even in the darkness and giggled with glee when she came up with the key. He figured she had used some spell to find it.

The five of them headed off into the woods, this time in daylight, seeking the Dryad cabin.

15

THE JOURNEY to the Dryad community did not take that long. The tree fairies lived deep inside the forest and occupied a cabin built into a wooded hillside. Dean knew the rooms extended deeper into the hill than most would expect. Albion, Dean and Jaz were silent on the twenty-minute walk through the trees. Jo and Arlo, however, chattered the whole way there. She asked him about where he went to school and when he said he was taught at home by his mother, she laughed and said that she was home schooled, too, after a fashion.

Dean listened to the conversation with some amusement at how easily teens connected with each other. It was also the most he had heard about Joanna's family life or where she came from since they had met the night before. When Dean and Jaz had questioned her about it, she was evasive and did not give any direct answers to their queries. He wished they were walking longer because of what he might learn from the teens' conversation.

As they entered the clearing where the front of the cabin showed from the hillside, Dean recognized it right away. There was no one outside so Albion went up and knocked on the door. "Enric, Anya, come out. It is Albion and some guests."

There was no answer, and Dean and the others looked around the clearing for some sign of the Dryads. Albion knocked again. As he stood waiting, the door burst outward, knocking Albion backwards from the covered wooden porch. Then the Oni demon was on top of him. Dean watched as the shifter transitioned immediately to his mountain lion form and then the scaled demon and the enormous lion were rolling on the ground, in a snarling and roaring battle for their lives.

Dean didn't have much time to watch. Two more demons burst from the cabin's doorway and ran out at them. He saw Arlo shift form and join his father against the demon he was fighting. The sudden violence caused the shift to happen spontaneously. He heard shots to his left and saw Jaz, pistol in a two-handed grip, drop one of the charging demons with a full clip worth of bullets into its head. He knew it wouldn't stay down for long from the experience at the diner the night before.

The final demon made it past Jaz and was headed straight for him when he saw it intercepted by a bolt of white light from his right. The demon seemed to stop in midair as it was leaping towards him. Then it fell to the ground as the light turned to white-hot fire that consumed it and left the netherworld creature a charred carcass on the ground in front of him. He looked to his right and saw Jo standing there, her right hand outstretched, palm forward, fingers spread wide as if she were trying to signal someone to stop. There was a glowing ball of white the size of a baseball rotating in front of her palm.

Dean turned back to the scene in front of him. Jaz had drawn her sword and held it in one hand as she ran over to the Oni she had shot. It was struggling to rise after taking a flurry of bullets to its head. With a sweeping motion, she hacked through its neck from above and removed its head. As soon as she did so, the demon's body turned into a red mist that dissipated into the air. He turned to see that Arlo, in his lion form, smaller than his father but no less powerful looking, had now latched his jaws on the neck of the Oni demon atop his father. He twisted his head from side to side as his jaws clamped down tighter. That must have done the trick because, with a snap of the younger lion's head on the demon's neck the Oni stopped struggling and went limp. Then, it too turned to mist and the two lions were left there on the ground, glancing around with puzzled looks.

Jaz walked over the still smoking corpse of the third demon and poked at it with her sword. She looked over at Jo. The young Wiccan still stood wide-eyed with the ball of energy or magic or whatever it was swirling in front of her outstretched palm. She looked around at her companions and then back at the demon, a look of disgust and horror on her face, then she raised her hand upward and the ball of white light burst upward into the sky out of sight. The girl then collapsed in a heap, crying, after releasing the pent-up energy. Jaz ran to her side.

Dean looked around and tried to decide what he could do to help. He had been of little value during the attack itself, but perhaps he could do something now. Looking towards the shifters, he saw that Albion had returned to human form. He had a few scratches and scrapes on him from the demon's claws but Dean knew he would heal. Shifters regenerated after a time. Arlo was still in lion form and his father was talking to him in a soothing voice while the lion paced back and forth, letting out occasional growls and snarls. The younger shifter had less control over his transformation and would shift back once he had calmed down.

Dean decided that Jo needed help the most right now and went over to her. She was holding her right wrist in her left hand as she sat on the ground and sobbed. Jaz had an arm about her shoulders but was scanning the tree line and shooting glances towards the cabin door. He knew she was expecting another attack. Looking at Joanna's right hand, Dean saw what looked like a nasty, circular second-degree burn on her right palm. It was already blistering and the area around it looked red and painful. He didn't have a first aid kit with him but he did have a pack of four by four gauze in his uniform pants pocket. He wanted to keep that burn wound clean until he could dress it properly. The gauze would have to do until he had more supplies.

"Jo, I don't know what it was you did back there," Dean said, "but I want to thank you." He opened the pack of gauze and laid it gently on the wound in the girl's palm.

She looked up at him, blinking tears from her eyes. "I couldn't let the demon kill you, Dean."

"What was that?" Jaz asked. "I have never seen a demon outright killed like that. That one will never return. It is dead, dead, dead."

"I've seen you kill a demon before, Jaz, like back at the diner," Dean said. "They just kind of go 'poof' don't they?"

"That is what happens when you destroy their corporeal forms here on earth," Jaz explained. "Their spirit forms return to the netherworld, from whence they came. There they must regenerate for a hundred years before they can manifest again. But what Jo did was something different. She killed it, spirit and all. That demon will never return to kill again."

Jo looked up at Jaz. "It is called sun-fire. I have never done it before and it takes a great deal of power to do it just once. I basically open a small portal to the center of the sun and release a ball of fusion plasma from there in the direction of my choosing. It will consume, body and soul, anything it strikes."

"Plasma from the sun, huh," Dean said. "No wonder you burned your hand. I'm surprised the wound is not worse."

"I was stupid. I summoned another ball before I checked to see if I needed it," Joanna said. "I shouldn't have held it so long. The spell comes with wards against fire and heat, but it's the sun, you know, so it's not normal heat or fire. I also used up my power. I have a splitting headache and there's two of everything I look at right now."

"I have never heard of this magic before, but it seems dangerous," Jaz said. "If it strikes an innocent or one of us, we'll be consumed as completely. You must be careful."

"Of course I'll be careful," Jo said, rolling her eyes at the hunter. She sighed and held a hand to her head. "To be honest, I didn't know I could do it. I'd read about it and learned the theory of it, but no one has been able to cast it for centuries. Then again, no one has needed to try since the demon wars in the dark ages I think."

"That's probably why you didn't know what it was, Jaz," Dean said. "I'm sure she'll be careful using it in the future. If she hadn't used it here and now, though, I would be demon chow." He turned and looked around the clearing again. The last time he was here, there were children playing in this clearing and several families lived here. Where were the dryads? A horrible thought occurred to him.

He stood up and ran to the cabin set back in the hill and went inside. He looked around the outer room and then started to head back the hallway, into the hill's tunnels to the other rooms there. A hand on his shoulder startled him and he turned to see Jaz and Albion standing there.

"Let us go first. We can see better in the dark back here," Jaz said, handing him a penlight. "Here take this flashlight for yourself while we go in."

Dean stepped back as he turned on the flashlight to let the others take the lead. Albion went first and Dean could see he was partially shifted again, his talons extending past his fingertips. Jaz followed with her sword in hand. They hadn't gone far when Dean detected the characteristic scent of death and heard the moans and cries of the wounded. Albion must have been able to smell the stench and hear the cries from the first room. It was why he looked so grim. He kept up with them as they went down the long hallway, checking each room to the right and left. These were the bedrooms belonging to the extended dryad family that lived here. They had shown Dean and Ashley such hospitality in the past when they had traveled to the valley on a weekend holiday.

They got to a room at the end of the hall. There were bodies piled in front of the door. The men in the family must have defended the door to the last against the demons. Albion looked back at them. "This is not going to be good," he said. "Prepare yourselves."

Dean had seen death and dying before but this carnage was beyond his experience. The men and parts of men were strewn about the floor. The smell was overpowering in the enclosed space. Dean heard retching behind him and he turned to see the werelion teen behind him turn and vomit on the floor. Jo had tears streaming down her face and she looked a bit pale, but when she caught him looking at her with concern she stood up straighter and nodded that she was all right. Arlo wiped his mouth with the back of his hand and tried to give Dean a weak grin.

"Arlo," Dean said. "Why don't you go back out and watch our backs. We don't want to be caught from behind by more demons. We've got this covered here."

The shifter boy nodded and looked grateful for the excuse. He turned and headed out to the front of the cabin. Dean turned back to face the door, standing amidst the bodies.

"Thanks for that, Dean," Albion said. Dean nodded in reply.

Dean looked around at the bodies and then saw movement. My God he thought. Some of them were still alive. He kicked himself for not doing his job right away and started gently pulling the grisly pile apart, checking each of the ten or so men and boys for a pulse. Four of them were still alive. When he found the first live survivor, he had to clear a gobbet of clotted blood from the teen's mouth and tilted the head back to open the airway. He wished he had a portable suction machine, but he didn't. Once he had succeeded in doing this much the boy's breathing eased some.

He felt a presence next to him and saw Jo at his side. He looked over at her and, despite the pale and startled look on her face, she nodded and took over holding the boy's airway open while he went on to find the next survivor.

"I need medical supplies, or these four survivors are not going to survive," Dean said.

"I have some things from the SUV back at the cabin," Jaz said. "I'll go with Arlo and bring back one of our medical kits."

"What's in it?" Dean asked.

"It's a standard combat medic's kit. There are two of them, plus a few personal kits," Jaz replied.

"Bring both of the larger kits. Hurry." Dean urged.

While Jaz ran off toward the front of the cabin, Dean took a SOF-T tourniquet out of the cargo pocket of his duty pants. He always carried one and this was another instance he was glad he did. The next survivor was bleeding from a gash in his upper arm and had already lost a lot of blood. The arm below the elbow had been ripped or bitten away. Applying the device and tightening the strap by twisting on the attached windlass he was able to stem the blood flow from the mangled limb.

Two down, two to go. Dean heard Jo ask Albion to hold the tilt on the first victim's head so his airway would stay open. He glanced over at her as he continued his work. She had started tearing strips from her long skirt and pressed the improvised cloth bandages into the worst of the first victim's wounds. There were several areas that appeared to be bite marks on the torso and she was trying to manage that patient's bleeding with her application of direct pressure and wound packing.

"You're doing a good job, Jo," Dean said. "Someone taught you well."

"My father was training me to be an EMT before I left to join the coven. He hadn't finished but we had gotten to the module on traumatic injuries. I can help," the Wiccan teen said.

Dean nodded and went back to sorting the living from the dead. He had pulled the final two survivors out and was continuing to manage their serious wounds with what little he had when Jaz and Arlo returned with two black tactical backpacks. Jaz unzipped the first one so that it opened up with all its medical supplies exposed and laid out for him. Dean started grabbing supplies, including a needle decompression kit that he was going to need for victim number four to manage what he suspected was a tension pneumothorax or collapsed lung.

"Jo, do you know how to set up an IV bag for infusion?" Dean asked.

"Sure," Jo replied. "Doesn't everyone?"

Dean smiled. "I saw two IV bags in the first pack. There are probably two in the other as well. Get two set ups to run fluids for these patients when I get the IV's started on the worst two. Be ready to spike the other two and get them ready if I need them. Okay?"

"Got it," the teen replied and she set to work.

He thought he could get these four survivors stabilized for the time being now that he had the supplies he needed but they were going to have to get to a trauma center in order to survive. He looked around and saw Jaz and Albion pulling the dead from in front of a single door that ended the hallway.

Jaz reached out and tried the door handle but it did not open. Albion stepped forward and set his shoulder against it to shove. It did not move.

"It's barred or blocked from the other side," the shapeshifter whispered.

Dean looked at the men on the floor and then looked at the barred door. "What if there are more survivors on the other side? There are only males here. No women or children," Dean observed.

Albion nodded. "That makes sense. Let me try something." He stepped up close to the door again and called out. "Hello, is there anyone on the other side of the door? It is Albion and some other friends here. The demons are gone. It is safe to come out."

There was nothing so Albion knocked on the door and repeated his message. Finally a muted voice came from the other side. It was a woman's voice.

"Albion, it is Anya," the voice said. "How do we know you are not some trick of the demons? They tried to get past the door with force. Perhaps you are trying to trick us?"

Dean called out from where he was working on getting another IV started, "Anya. It's paramedic Dean Flynn. Do you remember me? I helped to heal your daughter Zora last year. I am Ashley Moore's companion."

"Paramedic Dean," Anya's voice called. "I remember you. Tell me, what were my daughter's injuries?"

"She had two broken legs and a serious infection, Anya," Dean said. "A tree had fallen on her when she tried to stop human loggers from cutting in the forest."

There were murmurs and scraping sounds from the room on the other side of the door and then the door opened a crack with some light from the other side spilling out into the hallway. Albion stepped into the opening. Dean thought he was trying to block the view of the carnage in the hall from those in the room. A face appeared in the partially opened doorway. It was Anya. She looked both worried and relieved at the same time.

"What of Enric and the other men?" she asked. "We heard the fighting and screams and feared the worst."

"There are some survivors, but I'm sorry Anya," Albion said, "most of them gave their lives protecting you. Dean is working to save the few survivors now. We want to get you others out of there, but let us clean up the hallway a bit first. Don't come out until we call you."

The dryad woman choked back a sob, but she nodded at him and stepped back from the door, closing it. Again, Dean heard frantic voices from the other side and then cries and sobbing. He could only imagine what it must have been like to be on the other side of that door, listening to what was happening out here in the hallway.

Jaz said, "I'll get some sheets from the other bedrooms. We can cover the bodies out here and clear a pathway to get them outside. It will shield them from the worst of it."

Albion and Jaz set to work shifting the dead bodies, and parts of bodies, from in front of the door so they lay against the sides of the hallway. Jaz used a pile of sheets to cover the remains. There was now a path through the hallway to the outside.

Dean was finishing up his work on the final survivor when Jaz rapped on the door again. "Anya, it is all right to come out now. Carry the children, and stay to the middle of the hallway."

The door opened again, this time wider, and revealed a small bedroom packed with the women and children of the dryad clan. Anya and Zora were the first Dean saw and the older dryad woman rushed over and pulled Dean close in a hug. He felt Zora join in. He held them while they expressed their relief.

"Come on," he said, breaking the hugs. "Let's get everyone out. I've got more work to do on the survivors, then we can talk and share what happened here together."

Anya nodded and started gathering the women and children. Albion led the way while Dean and Jo continued their life-saving work. Jaz stood by in another doorway. As they passed the women saw the shrouded shapes on the floor and blood on the walls and the crying began. Dean knew he would hear that keening sound in his nightmares for a long time to come. He redoubled his efforts to save the living and went back to work packing wounds and assessing his remaining patients.

16
___

I⊤ ⊤ook Dean and Jo another ten minutes to finish stabilizing the four patients as best they could. Then he used some more sheets to fashion litters to move them all outside. He'd have more light there and could do a better re-assessment than in the darkened hallway with his single flashlight. He didn't know how Jo managed as well as she did and chalked it up to better eyesight.

Anya, Jaz and Albion came back in and helped him move his patients out into the clearing in front of the cabin while Jo stayed inside until the last had been brought out. When they got into the sunlight, he noticed that all the injured appeared somewhat improved. Then Anya and some of the other women began to bring small pots of something over to injured dryad men. The women pushed Dean aside and started peeling off the clothing that Dean and Jo hadn't already removed from the patients. When the men were nearly naked, the women started smearing a green paste on the exposed skin. He watched as the paste was instantly absorbed adding a greenish tinge to the skin of his patients.

"What is that, Anya?" Dean asked.

"It is tree paste," she said. "You would call it chlorophyll. It comes from the trees that sustain us and we use it whenever one of us is injured. It helps the body sustain itself while it heals."

Dean looked down at his four patients. Their bleeding had slowed or stopped soaking through his bandages and their faces had more color. Far be it for him to doubt the healing abilities of his patients. They would still need some sort of advanced medical attention but he could see that it was much more likely now that they would survive.

"Anya, that is a good thing, but they all still need to go to a hospital. They have internal injuries and need stitches," Dean explained.

"Some of the women will take them by car to the city. It will be faster than waiting for an ambulance to get all the way out here," Anya said. "Zora and I will remain here with the others and tend to the children."

Dean nodded. It wasn't a perfect solution but she was right in that it was probably thirty minutes before an ambulance could get here in the remote valley. They could be halfway to the nearby county hospital by then.

"I know you don't like to use human facilities, Anya. Do you want me to come along?" Dean asked.

"No," she replied. "There is a doctor there who knows us and knows of our differences. He trained in Elk City with one of your doctors. He will watch out for us."

She motioned to one of the other dryad women who went and started a beat up old Chevy Suburban parked under the trees nearby. Dean and Jo helped the women package their patients and arrange them in the back of the SUV as best they could. Two other women climbed in with the driver and then the vehicle left.

"At least the demons didn't get all of them," Dean said as the makeshift ambulance pulled away down the long dirt lane. "That has to be one small blessing in all of this."

"But what were those creatures doing here in the first place," Albion said. "I haven't heard any reports of other attacks nearby and our valley is sheltered and off the normal travel routes around the state."

Jaz, Dean, and Jo all shared a look and the elder werelion picked up on it.

"That is what has been chasing you?" he asked, pointing to the burnt carcass nearby. "Why didn't you warn us?" He sounded angry.

Dean spluttered in an attempt to come up with an answer. The fact was he was blaming himself a bit for this, too. Jaz stepped in and spoke.

"I'm not sure they came here for us," the hunter said. "If that were the case, why come here and attack the dryads when we were just a few minutes away? It doesn't make sense. No one knew we were coming here. It couldn't have been us that brought them."

"Well, if you didn't bring them here, what did?" Albion asked. He was frustrated and it showed in the way he flicked his still-manifested talons against each other, making a clicking sound.

"I think it may be this," another voice said, entering the conversation. It was Anya. She approached them carrying a bundle she had retrieved from the cabin. Dean wondered what it was. What could have drawn the demons to attack the dryads here?

"About two months past, the Eldara Ashley Moore came and visited us. She told Enric and me that she had bought the cabin in the woods and would be staying there for a time. She also gave us this bundle and asked us to keep it safe and hidden, telling no one we had received it. We were honored to receive the gift of trust from an Eldara and we owed her a life-debt anyway." Anya glanced down at the long, thin bundle she carried. It was about three feet long and a few inches across. It was wrapped in white cloth and tied up with rough twine.

"Eldara Ashley told us that if she disappeared and did not return to claim it in one moon's passage, that we were to take precautions to protect the cabin. Also, we were only to give this to one known to us as Ashley's friend, relative or companion." Anya held the bundle out to Dean and bowed her head slightly. "Paramedic Dean Flynn, we know that you are companion of the Eldara Sister. I believe she meant this for you if she did not return in the allotted time."

Dean took the bundle. It felt lighter than he expected based on how Anya was carrying it. As his hands touched the cloth, and he ran his fingers along the length of the bundle he thought he knew what it was. At least, he knew what if felt like. He pulled at the knots holding the fabric wrapping on the object and pulled the covering away, revealing a shining silver sword blade. It felt unusually lightweight, considering how big it was and that it was made of metal.

There was a gasp from everyone around him when he held it up so all could see it. Even Jaz seemed surprised by what she was seeing. Albion looked like he was about to bow down before it and Dean both. Only Jo seemed unsurprised by the arrival of the shining sword in their midst. Why had Ashley left some sword behind in the care of the dryads and told them to give it to him when the time came? He filed that away in the list of questions he had for his girlfriend when they reunited.

Dean didn't believe it was a real sword. While it was shiny, it had very little heft to it. He thought it might be plastic painted to look like metal with some sort of glossy covering. He went to wave it and take a few practice strokes in the air, but Jaz came forward and laid a hand on his arm.

"Don't do that, Dean. You act like you have no idea what you're holding," she cautioned.

"It feels like a really well made plastic replica of a sword," Dean responded. "You hold it, but it has no weight at all." Jaz stepped back from him and she had a look of, something, fear or horror in her eyes. "What? I thought you liked swords."

"That is a heavenly blade, Dean," Jaz said. "Every Eldara has one, even the Eldara Sisters. It is the manifestation of their divine power and mission here on earth. No mortal should even be able to touch it. Yet here you are swinging it around like a fool." She tilted her head to one side, giving him a quizzical look. "What are you?"

"I'm human, just like you, Jaz," Dean said. He looked at the blade again, trying to decide what to do with it. He touched the blade end with his thumb and, before he knew it, had cut himself rather badly across three of the fingers on his left hand. The blade was so sharp that it didn't hurt immediately, which was why he had managed to cut himself so deeply before he noticed. Drawing the hand away as if touching a hot pan on the stovetop, he clenched his fingers into a fist to stop the bleeding. As he watched, the little bit of blood on the blade, smoked to ash and fell away, leaving no evidence of it behind.

"See, I'm bleeding. I told you, I'm human," Dean snapped, a bit of anger at his stupidity coloring his voice. "Anyway, you're also partly right. It's a real sword of some sort. That blade is razor sharp." His hand was starting to throb and he held his clenched fist close to his chest while holding the sword away at arms-length. Someone needed to wrap that blade up again before someone else got hurt messing with it.

Anya came in and picked up the cloth in which the sword had been wrapped. Without touching any part of it directly, the dryad took the sword from him and wrapped it back up again. Her daughter Zora came over and helped tie the bundle of cloth-covered sword closed.

Dean watched the blade get put away and when his fingers separated from it, he felt like he was losing part of himself. It was strange, but it was like the blade had connected to something deep inside of him and now that it was taken away, he noticed a hole inside that he had never noticed before. This was not a new void, but one that had always been there, unknown, until his contact with the sword had filled it. It was strange and it made him feel a little queasy.

"Dean?" Jaz asked. She was looking at him with growing concern. "Are you all right? You just turned pale as a ghost."

"I think it's just the pain in my hand," Dean lied. "It will be better soon. I just need to dress the wound and wrap it up." He looked down at his hand where he clutched it to his chest. There was no longer any blood dripping from his clenched fist so he had gotten the bleeding to stop. It would probably start up again as soon as he opened up his hand. He still had a few of the gauze dressings in his pockets. He pulled them out and opened his hand. They'd do the job for now. He was probably going to need stitches. The cuts had been deep.

He looked down at his hand and searched for the wounds amidst the crusted and dried blood on the inside of his hand. He remembered cutting his fingers and still felt the pain, sort of. Come to think of it, he realized he was feeling the memory of the pain. As soon as he thought about it, he realized that the pain was gone. His hand ached from clenching it so tightly for so long to stop the bleeding, but that was it.

He examined the inside of his fingers between the two joints, looking for the cuts from the blade. They weren't there. Instead there were lines of thin, white scar tissue there where the cuts had been. It was like he had cut himself weeks ago and the wound had healed perfectly. The dried blood was there to prove he had done it, but not just minutes before. He didn't want the others to see, so after wiggling his fingers a little, he pressed the small stack of gauze squares against his fingers and closed his hand again.

"It'll be all right," Dean announced to the others watching him. "I got the bleeding to stop and I'll finish bandaging it up when we get back to the cabin." He held out his free hand and took the sword bundle back from Anya, taking care to grip the package by the hilt end of the sword and not the blade.

He looked around and his gaze stopped on Joanna. She was looking at him with a grin on her face. She held a finger to her lips and pursed them in a shushing gesture. She knew he had healed, he was sure of it, but how did she know? He wanted to go over and ask the teen Wiccan, but could not right that moment, here in front of everyone.

"Dean we need to get these women and children situated somewhere," Jaz said. "They can't stay in there and we cannot bring them back to the cabin, either. There's not a lot of room and that is where the next attack will likely take place if there is one."

Dean looked at her, not knowing what to do. She was right about them not staying there until the interior of the dryad's cabin had been cleaned up. He looked to Albion with an arched eyebrow, forwarding the question to him. The elder shapeshifter glanced about the clearing and nodded to his son.

"Arlo, go home and tell your mother what has happened here, then go to the rest of the valley council and tell them the same," he said. "Tell them we need to provide shelter for the dryads and also need the strongest of the area to begin patrolling the valley. If there are more of these demons around, we must find them and stop them before they attack anyone else."

The boy nodded and ran off at a trot for the forest's edge. He was gone from sight in seconds. Dean wondered aloud about what the other Unusuals of the valley could do if the demons returned again.

"Between Arlo, his mother, and I, we can handle a large portion of this side of the valley," Albion began. "There is a small pack of were-wolves that live at the far end of the valley. They don't mix with us often but this is an emergency. They'll do what needs to be done. Then there's Old Barney. He's a werebear. He's more than a match for one, or even two of these things. We'll keep this valley safe. It's our home, after all."

"We need to go back to our cabin and regroup, too," Jaz announced. "Dean and Jo, come on. We've got some planning to do. That sword's presence here gives me an idea of how we can find our missing Eldara, or at least find out what happened while she was here."

Dean didn't want to leave the dryads alone in the woods after their ordeal, but when he looked around, Anya had already organized them into small groups and they were salvaging things from their cabin. They had assembled a few sacks of clothing and were spreading a cloth on the ground to prepare some food. It appeared they didn't need his help right now after all.

Jo and Jaz were already waiting for him at the edge of the clearing. He nodded to Albion. "Come get us if you need anything from us, or if you learn anything new."

The other man nodded and Dean joined the two women at the other side of the clearing. Together they headed back down the trail. He had questions for his two companions about this heavenly blade and what they knew about it. Then they had to plan. It was time to do more than just react to everything that was happening. It was time for them to intervene on their own behalf.

17

THE WALK back to the cabin was a quiet one. Jaz led them with Jo following her. Dean brought up the rear. He held the bundled up sword in one hand while he clutched the unneeded gauze in his left hand. He was looking forward to getting back to the cabin. He knew he needed to clean up that hand and look at it carefully, but still did not know how it healed so quickly. The amount of blood was proof of the severity of the wound. So what had happened back there?

Everyone seemed shocked he could touch the sword. It was a bit like King Arthur removing the sword from the stone. Was he the chosen one in some fashion? Dean was still marveling at the sword, too. He could still picture the silvery, reflective surface, the light weight, and the razor's edge. He also could picture the blood burning off the blade, turning to ash and flaking away, leaving the blade unblemished. If nothing else, seeing that with his own eyes had assured him that the sword was magical in some way.

Jaz had said she had a plan to find Ashley by utilizing the sword. He wondered what it could be. He was still pretty new to the world of Unusuals and knew there were many things that he didn't know. Jaz had been raised in and around the lore of that world, even if it was as an adversary to those he considered friends. She must know a lot more about what can be done with an artifact like the heavenly blade.

He was still contemplating the true nature of the sword when they arrived back at their cabin. There seemed to be no signs of intrusion but Jaz didn't take any chances. She stopped them at the edge of the woods and observed the cabin for a few minutes from a hidden location. Then she had them stay behind her while they approached the front door. The hunter had her sword out in one hand and a pistol in the other. They stepped up on the porch and checked the door. Still locked. Dean retrieved the key, unlocked it, and they went inside. Jaz did a quick sweep of the small building and when she was finished with the upstairs loft bedroom, she nodded.

"It's clear," she announced. She holstered her pistol and sheathed her sword, and then removed the sheathed blade from across her back, propping it against a chair before she sat down.

"I've been meaning to ask you, Jaz," Dean said. "Why do you use a pistol when your sword is needed to kill the demons?"

"Two reasons, really," she said. "The pistol can't stop the demons permanently but it still injures them for a time. A series of well-placed headshots on any demon will scramble their brains. Sure, they'll regenerate enough to keep coming in a minute or so, but that gives you options to do other things like run away, or run in close and finish the job with an enchanted or blessed blade like mine. The other side of it is if you are close enough to a demon to use your sword, they are close enough to reach you, too. All things being even, I'd rather slow them down with a few, well-placed bullets, then banish them back to hell with a sweep of my blade. That's the better option every time."

She got up and crossed to the two large pelican cases they had carried in from the SUV the night before. Dialing in the combination lock on one, she opened it and pulled out a small zippered pouch. She closed the lid before Dean could see the other contents. Walking back to her seat, she unzipped the pouch and pulled out a rag, a can of some sort and some assorted tools, laying them on the side table next to her. He realized she was cleaning her pistol after firing it that morning.

Dean walked over to the kitchen area and turned on the water in the sink, letting it run while he unclenched his left hand. He half expected to see the wound had returned, that he had imagined it healing. When he opened his hand though, aside from the dried blood and a thin silvery scar, there was no evidence it had ever happened. He started washing the blood off in the sink and wondered what he should do.

"Here, Dean, let me help with that," Jaz said. "You can't bandage that hand on your own."

"It's okay," Jo said from across the room. "It's already healed."

"What?" Jaz hurried over to Dean and looked into the sink where he was washing his bloody hand. "That's impossible. I saw you cut it. I saw the blood. It was a deep wound." She looked at him again as she took a step backwards. "Dean, you have not been honest with me. With either of us," she said gesturing to Jo. "Are you some sort of shifter? That would explain the regeneration, though not the fact that you can touch a heavenly blade."

"I'm as human as you, Jaz. I assure you," Dean said. He was pretty sure he was telling the truth, though he was beginning to think he didn't know the truth.

"Well, no human heals that fast, Dean. So come clean. What are you? If you aren't going to tell us your powers and abilities, how can we be a team on this quest? I need to know so we can maximize our chances for success."

"I'm not lying to you," Dean said. He was starting to get angry with her. Why wouldn't she believe him? "Look Jaz, not everyone in the world is out to get you or is your enemy. I'm the same guy I was when you met up with me yesterday. I eat regular food. I sleep in a bed. I walk in the sunshine. I'm as human as you are. Why won't you believe me?"

"Because you are hiding something. You are jeopardizing this mission, and this mission is all I've got left," she said. Dean could tell that she was getting angry with him, which just angered him more.

"Oh, you think you've got a monopoly on this mission's importance? You, the big hunter girl." Dean was shouting at this point. "I've got every bit as much tied up in this mission as you do. Don't try and take this whole thing over for your own agenda."

The hunter stepped towards him poking him in the chest. "If you insist on lying to me, I can't trust you. If I can't trust you then this partnership is over, period. Tell me the truth about what you are so we can get on with things."

He brushed her hand away. "Don't touch me. I didn't give you permission to touch me. And I'm not sure you're the right person for this mission in the first place. You are all 'kill first, ask questions later' and that is not the way I run things."

"Run things?" Jaz shouted at him. "You are not running things here. This is a mission of honor to the whole clan, or what's left of it. I'll not have some half-breed monster of some sort messing that up."

"Half-breed monster!" Dean shouted. He stepped up until he was inches from her face, staring down into her blazing blue eyes. "You trigger-happy whack-job, I told you I'm human. You don't get to label me like that...."

"Mom. Dad. Stop it. You can't fight right now. Not when Aunt Ashley is still in danger. Stop it, stop it, stop it!"

They stopped as Jo's voice reached them. She was standing up, fists clenched, tears rolling down her cheeks. Dean wasn't sure why she was crying and why did she call them that. Was she mocking them?

"What did you say," Jaz asked the Wiccan girl. "Why would you call us that?"

"Because you two fight all the time. I want you to be the parents I remember, not these people, ready to kill each other. I miss you both so much. Please stop fighting." Jo pleaded.

"Wait, we remind you of your parents?" Jaz said. "I mean that's nice and all, but honestly, I'm a bit young to be your mother."

Dean looked from Jaz to Jo and back again. The blonde hair was the same, as was their build. Could it be true? But how? Jaz would never let her daughter become a witch, he was sure of that. Then he froze. She wouldn't do it unless the child was already spoken for - unless someone had already traded the life of her first-born daughter for a spell. Dean's heart sank. This was not going to be good. If the last fight was a bad one, this one was going to be a doozy.

"She doesn't mean we remind her of her parents," Dean said. He looked to Jo. "Isn't that right?"

"You know me?" Jo said taking a step towards him.

"I do, I just don't know how it could be, not yet at least," Dean responded.

"Oh, Daddy, I've missed you so much." The teen ran up to him, throwing her arms around him. He felt awkward as he patted her on the back.

"Will someone tell me what is going on here?" Jaz asked. "I feel like I'm missing something important."

Jo turned to her as Dean let go of the embrace. The girl wiped away her tears as she laughed. "You always hated this part of having me. You never accepted that I had to become a Wiccan, Mom."

"Look, stop calling me that," Jaz said. "It is impossible for me to be your mother. I'm only twenty-two. I can't have a fifteen year-old."

"Asha warned me that you'd resist the truth if I revealed it to you," Jo said, laughing through her tears. "She said I'd have to show you something to convince you."

"Who is Asha? What are you talking about?" Jaz asked. "This is crazy. No Errington would become a witch. It would not be allowed."

"Asha is my coven leader," Jo explained. "Take off your jacket and show me your birthmark."

"What are you talking about? How do you know about my birthmark?" Jaz looked a little frightened. It was the first time Dean had seen something resembling fear in her eyes.

"Your family birthmark," Jo said. "The same one I have. Show it to me."

Jaz slipped out of her leather jacket. She was wearing a black tank top underneath. He saw what Jo was referring to right away. There was a light brown birthmark in the shape of a shield on her left shoulder. She reached a hand up to cover it absent-mindedly.

Jo took off her brown vest and then pulled her white blouse over her head. Dean started to turn away then saw that she was wearing a camisole underneath. There, on her left shoulder was a matching birthmark.

Jaz looked at it, amazement in her eyes. She reached out a hand to touch Jo's exposed shoulder. She touched it, tracing the borders of the birthmark. She shook her head.

"There has to be another explanation," Jaz said, stepping back. "Maybe you're a long lost cousin none of us knew about. I told you, you are just too old to possibly be my daughter."

"Well I'm not from now, Mom," Jo said, laughing. "You don't have me until you're, like, twenty-eight or something like that. I came back from your future to help you find Aunt Ashley. Asha told me I was needed. That's the purpose for which I was born and training had begun. The coven cast the spell to send me back in time to you both. The spell worked better than I thought it would, though I had to run out in the street to stop you before you sped away."

Jaz looked at Dean. "Why aren't you arguing with her? This story is crazy. It's ridiculous." She stared into his eyes. "Isn't it? No Errington would become a witch. It would never happen."

Dean just shook his head. He had no idea how to explain this to her. He thought he had years to go before he would have to address the price he paid a few months ago for a particularly dangerous spell from the Elk City coven. They had demanded his firstborn girl as a price, saying they would take her in as she reached school age and train her as one of their own.

"I didn't have a choice, Jaz," Dean floundered for a way to say this. "The coven demanded a price and when they asked for a child I didn't even have as payment, I just went with it. It didn't seem to matter at the time."

"Wait, you're not kidding," Jaz said, staring at him, the fire returning to her eyes. "You gave away your daughter, my daughter, OUR daughter, to become a witch and you say it didn't matter at the time."

"Look at her," Dean said, pointing to Joanna. "She turned out fine."

"She's a witch!" Jaz shouted. "How is that fine?"

"Here we go again," Jo muttered under her breath nearby.

Dean flinched as he saw Jaz's reaction start to build after their daughter's offhand comment. He steeled himself to take the brunt of it and to take his time explaining himself. This was going to be an epic argument. One for the ages.

18

DEAN PUTTERED around the cabin straightening up and trying to stay busy. To say the level of stress was high in the small enclosed space was an understatement. It had been nearly eight hours since the heated argument between he and Jaz had died down. The sun was getting low in the western sky. It had been a long day. Since the argument, she had not said a word to either him or Joanna. Joanna had drifted off to a corner of the room and had put her earbuds in to listen to music. She was not talking to either of them either. Dean wondered what he was supposed to do.

When he had agreed to the coven's terms for casting their scrying spell a few months back, he had thought he would have years to face the consequences of the decision. Now he had been literally slapped in the face by them. That had been the point where Jaz had walked away from the argument and ceased talking, when she slapped him. Dean's hand drifted up to his face to touch the place where she had hit him. He wondered if this was considered domestic abuse.

He went over and sat down where the heavenly sword bundle still lay on the dining table. Having run out of things to do to keep busy, Dean decided to look more closely at the blade. He would be more careful this time, though he apparently healed from the blade's wounds quickly.

The argument about his 'powers' was still unsettled. It had been deflected by the fight about who Jo was, but it would have to come up again. Jaz insisted that the fact he could even handle the blade made him an Unusual of some sort, and that he had been hiding his true nature from her. How could he get her to understand that if he were different in some way, it was hidden from him too?

Dean reached over and untied the twine that held the bundled sword's cloth wrapping closed. He carefully pulled the cloth aside and looked down at the blade as it was exposed. The sword's brightness and gleam was not diminished in any way by the darkness that had filled the room as night started to fall. It didn't glow exactly, but the reflective surface of the blade seemed to capture any available light nearby and reflect and magnify it. The sword was beautiful, with delicate etching on the blade that seemed to be both decoration and words or runes of some sort. Dean didn't recognize the language or even the letters that made up its alphabet, but he was sure the blade's decoration meant something to the right person. Ashley, Ingrid, or another Eldara might be able to decipher it for him.

Moving his gaze up the blade to the hilt, he saw more intricate work there. The cross guard was of the same silvery metal of the blade and seemed to meet the blade without a seam of any kind, as if it were forged in one piece. The grip of the hilt was covered with a glossy white leather of some sort. When Dean leaned forward to examine it more closely he noticed the leather didn't have grain but tiny scales that made up its surface. Continuing his examination, he looked at the pommel where gripping silver talons, those one might see on an eagle or other raptor, clutched a multi-faceted white crystal.

He reached out to touch the sword and gripped the hilt in his right hand. And then he wasn't in the cabin any longer. It was disorienting and it took the paramedic a moment to realize he was seeing the new location through another person's eyes. They were walking through a cave or a cavern of some sort. No, it wasn't a cave. The walls appeared to be finished in some way. There were squared-off timbers supporting the walls and roof periodically along the passage. Here and there, he saw an old-fashioned oil lantern hanging from one of the supports, providing pools of yellow light along the way.

Dean tried to turn his head and look backwards but was unable to do so. He was locked inside the viewpoint of whoever this individual was. Dean and whoever's head he was in continued on their shared journey down the passage until they reached a junction in the corridor. Turning left down a different, narrower passage, they walked a bit further to a stout wooden door set in the rock wall ahead of them. There was a hinged panel in the door and a white, cadaverous hand reached up and opened the panel, leaning forward to peer through it into the room on the other side.

There was a figure, dressed in a dirty white gown, seated in a chair in the center of the room. No, the figure was tied in the chair, her hands bound to the chair's arms, and her ankles tied to the chair's legs. He couldn't see who it was. The long, dark and filthy, matted hair hung over the face as the person's head sagged down with her chin resting on her chest. He peered closer to see who it was, and as he did, the individual lifted her head and her familiar green eyes looked back into his.

"Dean, you must leave me," Ashley rasped, her voice rough as if she had been yelling or maybe screaming for an extended time. "It is too dangerous."

He tried to answer back as the cadaverous white hand slammed the panel in the door shut. As the latch clicked something rocked his body to the side and jarred his vision. He blinked and then he was back in the cabin. Someone was shaking him by the shoulder.

"Dean, can you hear me? Wake up, snap out of it. Are you all right?" He heard Jaz's voice, but it sounded far away, as if he were in both places at once even though he could see the cabin and the table and sword in front of him. He pulled his hand back from where he had been gripping the hilt and the rest of the vision vanished leaving him firmly in the cabin with Jaz and Jo.

"I said, are you all right?" Jaz repeated. Her annoyance was evident in her tone.

"I saw her," Dean said. "I saw Ashley."

Jo rushed over then. "You saw her? How? Where was she? Is she alright?"

"She's bound and looks like she's been mistreated. She sensed me looking in at her somehow," Dean said, relaying what he had just seen. "She told me to stay away."

"Are you sure it was her?" Jaz asked. "I could have been a delusion of some sort, or a spell cast on you."

"I wasn't a spell, Mom. I would know," Joanna said.

"Don't call me that," Jaz snapped.

Jo spun around and walked back to where she had been sitting. Dean could see she was hurt by Jaz's response.

"You don't have to take it out on her. She's not responsible for this. I am," Dean whispered.

"I know who is responsible and it is not, I assure you, Dean Flynn," Jaz replied. She shot him an angry glare. "You will not get off that hook anytime soon. We will have more than one long discussion on this issue, but now is not the time. I am honor-bound to help find the Eldara, and I plan on reuniting you with your true girlfriend as soon as possible. Then I will put as much distance as possible between us. Now go over what you saw again. Take it step by step."

Dean went over the vision from the first moment he found himself inside the other's head to the moment when he was wrenched back to the cabin and his own body. Jaz asked him several times to describe the hand he saw opening the panel in the Eldara's door. She seemed intrigued by it and Dean asked her why.

"I think you were occupying or sharing the vision of a revenant," Jaz said. "We know they are involved with this, and the dead-looking skin on the hand would match up with what I know about them and how they look."

"I could grab the hilt again and try to reconnect," Dean offered, reaching out to the sword on the table in front of him.

"No," Jaz said. "The revenant might have noticed your presence from either your own bumbling around in its head or from Ashley's direct communication with you. We have to be careful using that link moving forward. Do you know how you activated that ability?"

"I was thinking of her while looking over the sword up close," Dean said. "I jumped into the vision when I gripped the hilt."

"Okay, let's try not to do that until you learn to control what you can do better," Jaz said.

"How come you think it's me and not something the sword is doing?" Dean asked. "I want to understand more of what this blade can do. If it can help us find Ashley sooner, we should be using it."

"There's plenty that blade can do, Dean," Jaz said. "In the hands of a being from one of the higher planes, it is said to be able to heal that which cannot be healed. It also has a negative effect on those from the netherworld, the lower planes. If you strike a fatal blow to a netheworlder, you kill it, not just banish it back to regenerate in a hundred years, as my sword does. That blade severs not just skin and bone and sinew, it severs the soul's connection to the body of the creature it strikes. It's why I, and other normal mortal types cannot touch it. The divine power vested in it would consume us. The fact that you can handle it is proof that you are more than you say you are."

Dean started to object and Jaz raised a hand to stop him.

"I know you don't understand it any more than I do. I accept that. But, just the same, we need to understand it. It could be important to how we act later on in this quest. It could change what we do."

"So what do we do?" Dean asked.

"I could attempt a scrying spell," Jo offered from across the room. "We know that Dad-uh-I-mean-Dean connected with Aunt Ashley somewhere. Perhaps if I center the spell on him it will tell us where she is."

"No, it's too dangerous, Joanna," Jaz said. "That kind of spell puts you at risk if there are any sort of defensive wards in place. You would be opened up to the backlash."

"Aw, Momma, you do care," Jo said.

Dean saw Jaz tense up. He spoke up and tried to defuse the situation before another argument started.

"You can't have it both ways, Jaz," Dean said. "You can't treat her like your daughter one moment and turn around and tell her not to call you Mom the next. I say we treat her as a full member of the team, just as we have since the beginning. It's a calculated risk but one that would get us on the path to completing this quest."

Jaz looked at him and back to Joanna before she nodded. "All right, you can do the spell, but I want you to take precautions. If you detect any sort of wards in place, back off."

"I'm not stupid," Jo said. "Anyway, Asha says I'm more powerful than any of the other sisters in the coven. I can do this, especially now that we have the new connection between Dad and Aunt Ashley."

Dean looked at Jaz. She nodded and he nodded in return. "Okay, kiddo, let's do this. What do you need me to do?" Dean asked.

"I'm going to need to spend a few minutes meditating," Jo replied. She was bouncing a little in her seat in her excitement. "I need to settle myself down a little. This is going to be awesome. Okay, in the meantime, you can try to clear your mind. I don't want you to think about anything. When the time comes, I'll ask you to reach out and touch the sword hilt again but don't try to reconnect with Aunt Ashley. Just think about the blade. I'll make the connection through you."

"All right," Dean said. "You will be careful with this, right?"

"Absolutely," Jo responded. "You get set." I'll be ready in a sec."

Dean and Jaz watched their newly revealed Wiccan daughter settle onto the floor, sitting on a throw rug in front of the cabin's rustic couch. She crossed her legs as she sat down and rested her hands on her knees, then she closed her eyes and was still for a minute or so. The other two in the room sat at the table and waited until she was ready.

Jo opened her eyes and Dean almost thought he could see a white glow surrounding her. It was as if her image was shimmering, like she was a video of a person superimposed on the image of the room. He reached out and laid his hand on the hilt of the blade, working to keep his mind clear as he did it by thinking about random EMS drug protocols. As his hand contacted the sword, the room again vanished from in front of him, swirling away into darkness. It had begun.

19

JAZ SAT AT THE TABLE, watching Dean and Jo as the spell took effect. Dean sat up straight and started staring straight ahead, but his eyes glazed over and were unfocused. Jo sat on the floor nearby, like a statue, immobile and almost humming with magical energy. Jaz' amulet's night vision function let her see into the non-visible light spectrum that humans could not ordinarily see. That let the hunter catch a hint of, well, some sort of waves emanating from the witch girl.

She still couldn't quite wrap her head around the upheaval in her life that had struck her in the last two days. Her mother, father and the rest of her clan had likely been wiped out in the explosion and fire at their offices in Elk City two days ago. She couldn't even come forward to ask for information about them because of the nature of their quest, and the authorities probably counted her among the dead anyway. Then she had discovered, against everything she had been raised to believe, she had a daughter, who had come back from the future in some manner. A daughter who was a witch. Hunter children didn't grow up to be witches and use witchcraft, they grew up to guard against them. But, then, that particular wrinkle was Dean's fault.

Jaz thought about Dean. She knew they had not started off on the right foot with their clash in the self-defense and safety class she taught at the fire academy. To his credit, he sought her out to try and make things right. That didn't make him any less infuriating, however. He was good at what he did, and he knew it. He also had learned to accept the Unusuals in a way she thought she never could. She knew that her upbringing carried a certain prejudice with it. That was necessary to maintain the skepticism and vigilance to catch the creatures that were out to harm mankind. Now it appeared he had some sort of supernatural background himself, not that he was likely to admit it to himself. Jaz accepted that it was something he honestly didn't know and she did not have a clue as to who or what he could be. Touching that heavenly blade uninvited should kill any human or normal Unusual on contact. At the very least, Dean should have received some sort of shock or burn from it.

But he was sitting here in front of her, his hand laid across the hilt of that divinely wrought sword as if it were made of plain steel. It was as if he did not understand the rules, so he just chose not to follow them. There was that sort of obstinacy to admire in the man. He didn't give up easily on a concept or on people he knew. That type of loyalty was hard to come by. Once he joined a team, he was with that team one hundred percent. She had seen it happen with their small team. Or should she call it a family? It was a dysfunctional one, if it was a family at all. She shook her head in disbelief. Somehow, someway, the two of them were supposed to get together and then stay together long enough to raise a daughter who knew them as her mother and father.

As she watched his face, she wondered what he was seeing in that intense stare. She was not aware of any way to join their magical conference call with whatever connection Dean had with the Eldara to whom her family owed a life debt. Jaz chuckled to herself. The man who was to be the father of her future daughter, was the very committed boyfriend of that same Eldara. How was that going to work out for any of them? Jo called her Aunt Ashley, so she knew the woman. It was just that Jaz could not see how she would let any man she was with associate with a former lover after they started seeing each other. Not that there was a whole lot of men in her life. She had dabbled with some random encounters when the mood struck her, but none of them had meant anything to her, and they were certainly not the type who she would count as a long-term love interest.

She had always envisioned that her mate would be someone who would remain behind while she went out on hunter missions and encounters. He would be someone who would understand her non-traditional background and lifestyle. It would almost have to be someone from outside the hunter clans. Men in the hunter clans would never take a backseat to a female hunter. In their patriarchal world, she would be expected to hang up her sword and turn out hunter babies to replenish the clan's ranks. That would be their version of an honorable role for her. The very thought of it disgusted her. No, she would find new blood to bring into the clan. It was not unheard of, and she would have set her own expectations for the newcomer about what a woman in the clan was expected to do.

Her eyes were drawn back to Dean again. He might have been a perfect person to fit that role in her life if she didn't already despise him so much. As she watched him, his back stiffened and his eyes widened as if he were seeing something startling. Again she wondered what might be there wherever his mind was, and what he was seeing. She shifted her gaze to Joanna, but nothing had changed there. The witch girl still held her position on the floor and looked to be silently meditating if it weren't for the barely visible waves of energy coursing from her.

Jaz settled back, taking a whetstone from her baggy utility pants pocket. She drew her Bowie knife. She had been taught an idle hunter was a dead hunter, so she began the long careful strokes of the blade on the stone that honed it to a razor's edge. She was a hunter. She knew how to wait for things, be it her quarry or the answers she sought.

As soon as his hand made contact with the sword's hilt again, Dean found his point of view changed. He was staring out of another' eyes at a forested hillside. His angle of view was from above and looking down the side of a large hill, or small mountain. The dark green of the treetops below blanketed a broad valley with a lake in the center. The sun was just setting beyond the ridge to the west casting the mountain's shadow across the valley floor. The image shifted as whomever it was turned and walked back into a cave set in a mountainside. From the finished look of the cave corridor, Dean was confident this was the same cave system that he had seen before. He was close to Ashley again and he tried to remember and note every detail that might help him and his friends pinpoint its exact location.

He walked back down the long, rough-hewn rock corridor leading back into the mountain, proceeding straight until a side passage to the right opened up. Turning down that branch of the cave system, Dean watched as the individual whose point of view he shared took him down a sloping path until it opened into a cavernous chamber deep in the mountain. There was the sound of running water nearby in the darkness, and though he could see well in the dark given his host's abilities, he could not penetrate to the depths of the large room's far walls.

There was a strange purple glow to one side and that was their destination. On one wall of the cavern there was a large oval of glowing purple energy swirling on the wall. It was easily ten feet tall and six feet wide and looked like a sickly purple and yellow bruise projected on the wall. Whoever his host was, they stopped together in front of the shimmering surface of the energized oval. It filled his field of vision. He heard a raspy voice and it took him a moment to realize that it was his host's voice.

"The hunting party sent to secure the blade has not returned," the voice said. "I fear it has been intercepted."

A second voice answered from the other side of the magical field. "This is both fortunate and not," the second voice said.

It would have sent chills down his spine, if he was in his own body right now, Dean thought. It had the same quality as the scratching of a thousand cockroaches all at once in his head. It continued.

"We have lost more of our Oni brethren and they are a finite resource in this endeavor. That is unfortunate. But our seers warned us that the Hunter, the Healer, and the Hexen were on their way to us. Who else but they would have the power to stop a hunting party of three Oni?" Dean watched as the swirling purple oval pulsed with each of the other voice's words.

"So they are here?" Dean's host said. "How is that fortunate?"

"Because they have not realized their full power yet as questers," the voice from beyond the purple portal said. "They must accept their shared bond in order to become as powerful as they could become. Before they will be able to accomplish that, we will reach our goal and drain the soul of the Eldara in order to hold open this portal indefinitely. Then there will be nothing they can do to stop us from taking this entire area for our own."

"We must still pay our benefactor for helping to secure the Eldara for us in the beginning," Dean's host said.

"He demanded the healer be taken alive and the hunter clan eliminated," the portal's voice pulsed. "We will fulfill our end of the bargain. The clan has been removed from the picture, yes?"

"All indications are that the rest of the clan was consumed in the fire," the host's body said with sickening glee. "There will be no descendants other than the one who has come to us. There will be no one to continue to hound our benefactor's long-term plans, I assure you."

"He will be pleased with that news. Now we must finish the task assigned to us so we will gain the knowledge from him to use the Eldara's soul to maintain this portal indefinitely." The portal's colors shifted and began to coalesce into distinct shapes. "I will send through a larger party of Oni to complete the final part of our bargain. Use them wisely. They are among the last available to us."

"As you wish, Master." Dean's host stepped back from the portal as the shapes continued to solidify. He knew what to expect based on the conversation, so he was not surprised when the first Oni demon stepped from the purple borders of the magical oval on the rock wall. What did surprise him was that the procession of demons continued for some time. Dean lost count at fifteen and was pulled out, back to his seat at the table in the cabin. It took a moment to refocus his eyes and he blinked while his vision returned to normal.

The paramedic looked around the room and saw Jo leaning forward where she sat on the floor, her fingertips rubbing at her temples. A glance to his left showed Jaz sitting in the chair next to his at the table. She had that frighteningly large knife out and appeared to be testing the blade's edge with her thumb. She looked up at him and quirked up an eyebrow in question while returning his gaze.

"Jaz," Dean said. "We've got trouble. They know we are here."

20

"BUT HOW MUCH DO THEY know about where we are?" Jaz asked again. She was pacing from window to window, looking out at the cabin's surroundings for trouble.

"All I know is that they know we are in the valley here," Dean said. "They figured it out when the three demons we killed at the cabin didn't return. Oh, and they have some sort of prophesy or something like it of their own. The voice on the other side of the portal mentioned seers and the three of us."

"Okay, tell me the whole thing again from the beginning," Jaz said. "Don't leave anything out. Every detail could be important."

Dean closed his eyes and, for the third time, recounted what he could see and hear from inside his host's head in the vision. When he was done, Jo jumped up and pointed outside.

"That's it," she said. "I missed it before, but it's obvious now. They are somewhere in the mountains around this valley. That is why the demons came through the portal all at once like that. They are close enough to travel here on their own power. There must be old caves or something in these hills they are using."

"It makes sense, but that is bad news for us," Jaz said.

"Why?" Jo asked.

"Because that means the demons are closer than we think," the hunter said as she resumed her pacing to check the windows as the late afternoon sun streamed in from the southwest.

The knock on the cabin's door made them all jump. They relaxed when they heard Albion's voice from outside.

Dean opened the door as Jaz and Jo walked over to join him in the cabin's entryway. They saw Albion and three others standing outside on the porch. There were two men and a woman who Dean did not know.

"Hi, uh I thought I'd bring the other shifters from the area down to meet you guys while we were on patrol," Albion said. "Dean, Jaz, Joanna, this is Mark, Dawson, and Hannah from the pack at the north end of the valley."

Dean nodded and the three of them nodded in return. He looked at Jaz who stood still just staring at the three newcomers with a suspicious gaze. He nudged her with an elbow and she shot him a glance and then nodded to them herself. Jo stepped out onto the porch and shook all their hands, greeting them enthusiastically.

"Man, we can sure use you guys right now," Jo said. "After what we just found out, we can use all the muscle we can get."

Albion looked from the teen to Dean and Jaz with an alarmed look. "What is she talking about?"

"We just cast a little spell using the Eldara's blade to try and locate her," Dean said. "We think she is being held inside this valley somewhere. I was able to see caves or passages in the mountain rock shored up with wooden crossbeams. It all looked very old and broken down in parts. Does any of that ring a bell?"

Mark scratched his beard for a minute in thought, but it was Dawson who spoke up first. "It might be the old silver mines at the south end of the valley. They have been boarded up and closed for over 150 years now. It would be a good place to hide out."

"It's not just a hideout," Jaz added. "They have opened a nether-world portal there and are bringing demons through to attack the valley. The last count was fifteen demons before we lost our connection."

Albion looked worried and Mark let out a low growl. Hannah was silent, but Dean noticed her fingernails had suddenly elongated into claws. The four shifters shot each other glances and then looked back at Dean and the others in the cabin's doorway.

"Do we know where they are going or what their intentions are?" Hannah asked.

"It seems that they kidnapped the Eldara in order to drain her life force to create a long-term portal to the netherworld. I think they need her sword to complete the process," Joanna said. "The newly transferred demons are here looking for us, since we have the ability to throw a monkey wrench into their plans and rescue her."

Jaz jumped in, "I do not think they knew specifically where we are in the valley, though they will surely check here, and at the dryad's cabin, too."

"We cannot allow them to open a permanent portal here in our valley," Dawson said. "We would all become subservient to them and that is unacceptable."

"I don't know what we can do, Dawson," Mark said. "If they are already in the valley and heading this way, we won't have time to contact other packs to help, and we aren't strong enough to take them on by ourselves. There are only six adults in the pack, plus Albion and Arlo, and there's Old Barney the werebear, if we can find him. Even with the hunter, the witch and this human, it will never be enough to stop more than fifteen demons."

Jaz shook her head. "We need to take advantage of the demons being out in the valley looking for us and not in their hideout. Now is the perfect time to go there and try to get Ashley out." She looked at Dean and Jo.

Dean nodded and when he looked at Jo, the Wiccan teen nodded, too. It made sense, even though it abandoned the rest of the valley's inhabitants to fend for themselves. He wished he could come up with a solution for them. Then he got an idea.

"I might have a way to get you all some help while the three of us head off on our rescue mission," Dean said. "We have to try and shut this portal down and get Ashley out of there before they get too strong. Jaz is right. This is the perfect opportunity to do that. But, there is another person who has a vested interest in this, someone who might be the best solution of all, if what I've heard about her is true."

Jaz looked at him with a curious glance, but Joanna seemed to see where he was going and nodded enthusiastically.

"Ashley, the Eldara, has a twin sister," Dean explained. "For reasons she can't tell me, she is unable to participate directly in the rescue of her sister, but she is a Valkyrie. I suspect she might enjoy coming to the valley to help you all deal with the demons. Does that sound like a good idea? I don't know her very well, and I've heard she makes a bit of a mess wherever she goes, but I think she's a ferocious fighter."

Albion smiled for the first time since he had heard about the demons on the loose in the valley. "A Valkyrie or two would be a welcome addition to our little militia," the werelion said. "I agree. They are strong warriors, and I think they would be interested in ridding the world of a few demons, seeing as how they are destined to face them in the final battle at the end of the world."

"Good, I'll contact her." Dean said. He looked up at the sky outside the cabin. "I don't know exactly how long this takes, but here goes." He took in a deep breath and shouted, "Ingrid, I need you."

"There's no need to raise your voice, you know," the smooth tones of Ingrid's British accent sounded behind him in the cabin.

Dean and Jaz both spun around in surprise. There stood Ingrid, dressed in her black leather pants and jacket outfit, just as Dean had last seen her. Joanna ran forward and wrapped the new arrival in a hug.

"Aunt Ingrid, I'm so glad to see you," Jo said. "Things are a little tense here and I could use a friend right now."

"Hey, Kiddo," Ingrid said with surprise. "What are you doing here and now? Aren't you a little out of place?" Ingrid looked at Dean and Jaz and then back at Jo. "Do they...?"

"Yes, they know who I am," Jo said. "That's why it's been a little tense."

Ingrid let out a long laugh at that statement. "Oh, I'll bet it has been, and more than just a little tense." She looked back at Dean and Jaz, "Don't worry you two. I know it's a bit of a shock, but you will both get over it eventually."

She walked forward and took in the four shifters standing outside. Turning to Dean, she said, "I assume you are using your one chance to call for help? Remember I cannot participate directly in Ashley's rescue. That option has been forbidden to me."

"I told them," Dean said. "But I think we have found a way you can help without directly fighting to rescue Ashley. How would you feel about helping this valley's residents fend off a few dozen Oni demons?"

"Ooo, you've got my attention," Ingrid cooed. "Go on, I'm interested."

Dean and Jaz explained the situation in the valley. Albion and Mark jumped in occasionally to lend their input about what the valley's residents could do. Dean pointed out that if they could tie up the demons in the valley, it would allow him, Jaz and Jo to slip around them and get to the abandoned mines at the caves.

Ingrid listened, asking questions when she didn't understand something about what Dean had learned through the sword's strange connected visions. When they were done explaining what they had in mind, Ingrid gave them a large, feral smile, showing her white teeth.

"This is going to be great fun," the Valkyrie said. "Plus, I think I can persuade one or two of my Valkyrie sisters to join the party, too. We haven't had a good demon hunt in years. I've got to go and make a few inquiries. I'll be back just after dark. We'll stage here at the cabin and lure them in. That should give you, Dean, along with your lady friends, a chance to move around them in the dark and make your way to where they are holding Ashley."

Dean nodded, cringing inwardly at the way Ingrid called his companions his lady friends. Albion nodded too, and he along with the three werewolf pack members trotted off into the woods north of the cabin. They had to gather their forces and get back here before dark.

Ingrid watched them leave and turned back to Dean. "This is going to be our one chance to get Ashley, Dean. You understand that, right?" He just looked at her. "If they can't have her for their portal, they will likely destroy her corporeal form, and her soul will be banished to the heavens until she can regenerate. She will be gone for the next one hundred years. We can't have that. There's a lot she has to do here on earth, so don't screw this up." She held his gaze for a moment longer and then looked up. "I've got to get going if I'm going to bring anyone back with me to help. See you in a bit."

Dean watched in amazement as a set of white-feathered wings spread from behind Ingrid. She launched herself off the porch and into the air, shimmering a little and then she winked out of sight as she flew away through the trees. He watched for a minute then came back to the present when he heard someone clear their throat behind him.

"Are you done ogling your girlfriend's sister, Dean?" Jaz said. "Because we've got some work to do here. If we are going to move quietly and without being seen in the dark by the Oni demons when they approach this house, we need to put some things in place. I have my amulet, but that just works for me. Joanna, can you create a spell of some sort to mask yourself and Dean from demon senses?"

"I have my hunter's amulet, too, I just didn't wear it because I didn't want to give away who I was. You gave me the amulet on my thirteenth birthday, just before I left to join the coven," Jo replied. The teen thought for a bit and said. "I could try something else for Dad, but I have to think about how I can pull it off."

"Good," Jaz said. She looked at her watch and then the surrounding skyline. "You've got two hours to figure it out and get it in place. Get started. Dean and I will pull together the gear we are going to need from the cases we brought in from the SUV."

Dean watched the hunter take charge as they finally had a plan of sorts to act on. This was her element and he was impressed as she opened up the larger pelican cases and set to work. He knew she was right. They didn't have much time.

21

THE THREE OF them set to work. Jo sat down on the couch and began going through her large satchel purse. She had components of her spells and other items in there, including a few items of spare clothing. Jaz called Dean over to where she was opening up the two large cases. He had suspected at the time that the cases carried weapons a hunter might need on their operations. He was half right.

When Jaz unlocked the rolling tumbler locks and lifted the lids, Dean did see a startling variety of weapons. But there were also the two medical bags with two tactical medical kits. She pulled the medical bags out and handed them to him. He took them over to the table and slid Ashley's sword to the side so he could open them up and inventory their contents.

These medical kits weren't the same. He had the two tactical kits they had used with the dryad attack. There was also a standard individual first aid kit also called an IFAK. It was meant to be carried by an individual and had basic trauma supplies to treat and manage immediate life-threatening emergencies. It held a pair of black medical exam gloves, a SOF-T tourniquet, a few various combat gauze dressings, plus trauma shears, a needle decompression kit and basic airway management tools. It was all packed in a black bag with elastic loops to hold everything in place when it was unzipped and fully opened. The bag could be clipped to a belt or pack and was small and compact.

The other small kit was a little bit larger and was contained in a small black backpack carrier. It had everything included in the first kit, plus additional supplies he was glad to see. There was a 500 milliliter bag of lactated ringers IV fluid and a full IV kit. He also found several quick clotting solution impregnated gauze dressings and various bandages. There was a surgical airway kit and some basic field surgery supplies including a small suture kit to do stitches. He was also happy to see a medication pack attached to the inside by Velcro. It carried small containers of ibuprofen and acetaminophen for aches and pains in the field, plus there were also small vials of morphine, and naloxone to counteract an overdose and syringes to administer them. There was even an epinephrine auto-injector for severe allergic reactions.

Dean wasn't sure what he would need and opted to carry both since he wasn't going to be armed. At least he'd be prepared to provide care for Jaz, Jo, and eventually Ashley when he got to her. He attached the IFAK bag to straps on the bottom backpack so that it would sit below the small tactical backpack when it was worn. He was adjusting the straps and making sure it fit comfortably when Jaz came over and dropped something on top of the pile of medical gear on the table. It took him a moment to realize what it was. It was an empty sword scabbard and belt. He looked up at her where she stood next to the table.

"What's that for?"

"It's for your blade, stupid," Jaz said. "I took out the sword that was in there. It should fit your blade pretty well. You can't just carry it in your hand the whole time."

"I wasn't going to carry it at all," Dean told her.

"You can't go on this thing unarmed, Dean," the hunter said. "I need to know you can take care of yourself if everything goes to crap. Try it out and see if it fits, otherwise I'll come up with something else."

Dean thought about arguing further, but opted out. She was probably right. He needed to be ready to defend himself and if he took the sword along, he could return it to Ashley. She might have some magical use for its powers. He picked up the blade and the scabbard. The blade slide home and seemed to fit pretty well for being a replacement. Jaz nodded in approval and walked back to her cases where she was organizing her kit.

Dean took a moment arranging the sword and scabbard on the belt. He was trying to figure out if he should carry the blade like Jaz did across his back or wear it on his hip. He decided that he could attach the scabbard to loops on the side of the medical backpack. He removed the sword belt from it and set to work using some spare Velcro straps to secure the scabbard to the medical bag so the hilt would stand just over his right shoulder. It was a bit thrilling to envision himself in the rig and he put the assembled medical pack on and stood to check out the look in the mirror on the wall.

"Looking good, Dad," Jo said.

"I really don't think you should be calling me that, Jo," Dean said. "I know it is true for you, but it just doesn't make sense in my brain. You are from twenty years or so in my future, right?"

Jo nodded and looked disappointed. It must have been hard for her to hide her true feelings for the two of them when she first arrived. He started wondering what he would do in her situation and started feeling sorry for the teen. He remembered how much he had needed his mom at that age. His dad had never been in the picture and he had only vague memories of him.

"Okay, look," Dean said. "You can call me Dean, or Dad, or whatever you want if that makes you feel better, but understand that I'm not there yet. I'm still wrapping my head around all of this. I know that it's possible you are my daughter come back from the future to help with saving a kidnapped angel. It is going to take me some time to adjust to this, okay?"

He suddenly found himself wrapped in a hug, and then the teen bounced away with a big grin on her face. He smiled back at her and went back to admiring his getup in the mirror. He reached up and tried drawing the heavenly blade free. It slid out of the scabbard easily with a soft rasping sound of metal on metal. He couldn't get the angle right to return it to the scabbard, though and figured that it took practice to do so. He shrugged out of the pack and then replaced the blade in the scabbard. He looked at his assembled pack on the table when he was finished. He was pretty much set to go. He turned when he heard the two women arguing behind him.

"No, absolutely not," Jaz said. She shook her head for emphasis, her ponytail whipping behind her head.

"But why not?" Jo pleaded.

"I'm not giving you a gun, Jo, and that is that."

"Look Mom, you need to get over this," Jo said. "You raised me. Do you think you, the last Errington hunter, didn't teach me how to handle weapons?" The Wiccan teen pointed to something in the case in front of Jaz. "Unload that Glock and I'll show you I know what I'm doing."

Jaz hesitated for a moment, then reached into the case and extracted a pistol that looked like the twin of the one she now wore on her hip. She removed the magazine and racked the slide to check and make sure the chamber was empty. When she was sure the gun was not loaded, Jaz handed it to Joanna.

Jo sat down with the weapon and, in a series of fluid motions that only came from long-practiced muscle memory, proceeded to take the pistol apart. When she was finished she had the component parts laid out on the cushion next to her. She looked up at her mother with a grin. Then she reversed the process in another series of well-practiced moves, handing back the reassembled weapon. Dean had never had weapons around his home growing up, so he wondered again about whether Jo really grew up in a house with him as the father. He did not think he would allow guns in his house.

Jaz took the reassembled gun from Jo without a sound, inspected it. She slid in the magazine and racked a round in the chamber, then removed the magazine. She pulled back the slide to eject the shell in the chamber and expertly caught the bullet as it was ejected into the air. She thumbed it back into the magazine before replacing the magazine into the pistol's grip. The hunter stood staring at the girl on the couch before her for a moment, then reached into the case and pulled out the pistol belt with holster and three pouches full of spare magazines. She handed the pistol and rig to Joanna, who squealed with delight as she took them from her outstretched hands.

"So much for my mother-of-the-year award," Dean heard Jaz mutter and then she went back to work organizing her own kit.

He saw she had pulled out a small backpack as well and was stuffing it full of blocks of something he couldn't make out. The paramedic walked over and watched as she filled the pack.

"I don't suppose I get a gun, too?" he asked.

"Have you ever even fired a gun before, outside of a video game?" Jaz asked him without looking up from her work.

"No," Dean said.

"Then, no, you don't get a sidearm," Jaz said.

"What are those blocks you put into your bag?" Dean asked.

"C-4, detonators, and some preconfigured door breaching charges in case we need them," Jaz said. "And don't tell me it's overkill. We have no idea what we are going to encounter when we get to the mines."

"I wasn't arguing, just curious," Dean said.

Jaz glanced at him and snorted at his pack and sword arrangement.

"What?" Dean asked.

"It's fine, but we need to get you out of that light blue uniform shirt," Jaz replied. She dug in the second case and turned to toss him a black, long sleeve turtleneck. "Put that on. Your navy blue duty pants are fine, but you need a different shirt so you draw less attention, especially at night."

"Thanks," Dean said. He took off the pack, then swapped out the light blue uniform shirt for the new black turtleneck. He caught Jaz watching him change and wondered if she liked what she saw. She wasn't hard on the eyes either, he admitted. If he wasn't so committed to Ashley, he could see himself with a woman like her. Dean looked around, trying to find Jo. He asked Jaz.

"Where did our future daughter go?"

Jaz shot him a glance that wasn't quite angry. "She went upstairs after I gave her the Glock. She's your daughter, why don't you see what she's up to."

"Jaz, I didn't come to that decision lightly, you know. When I was asked to give up my firstborn daughter to the coven, I was thinking of all the people who were hurt or killed by The Cause in their terrorist vendetta."

"Dean, I know that you think you meant well," Jaz said. "But hunter children do not become witches. They are raised to be hunters." She looked to the stairs and then back to Dean. "If she is my daughter, she's the last heir to the Errington Clan after me. There is a lot that goes along with that responsibility. I can't see a way I would give her up to be trained as a witch."

"She's good at what she does, Jaz," Dean said. "And you must have trained her in some hunter stuff, too. I saw her field strip that pistol. It looked like she knew what she was doing. You thought so yourself, or you wouldn't have given her the gun."

They were interrupted by the sound of the teen coming back down the stairs. Dean glanced in her direction and was surprised at what he saw. She had changed out of her long skirt and baggy blouse and vest outfit. She was wearing a skintight black body suit. She had her long hair pulled up in a ponytail like Jaz's and had a holstered pistol on her left hip and a Bowie knife just like Jaz's on her right. Both the pistol holster and the knife scabbard had straps that secured them to her thighs on either side. She looked like something out of a spy movie.

"I don't think you need to worry about her forgetting her hunter roots, Jaz," Dean said. "Damn, in that getup she looks just like you. You could be sisters."

"Where's your sword?" Jaz asked Jo. "If you were raised by me, I'd have made sure you were given your blade when you turned thirteen."

"I couldn't bring it back with me," Jo said, disappointed. "The coven said its magic wouldn't penetrate the time travel spell's field with me when I went through. Besides, you would have recognized it. It was Grandmother's sword."

"I suppose that would make sense," Jaz said. "I would have given you my mother's blade if I had been able to recover it from the explosion."

"I don't need it really," Jo said. "I'm supposed to focus on my magic, Asha says. She says my attachment to weapons of war keeps me from reaching my potential."

Another voice behind them from the cabin's doorway interrupted them. They all turned to see who it was.

"Well, well, well. Don't you all look like one big happy family," Ingrid said, walking through the cabin's doorway.

Dean just stood and looked at her. Two companions followed her into the room. The three Valkyries stood there, looking like they just stepped out of a Wagnerian Opera. They all wore gleaming armor, polished to a mirror finish. Each was holding a winged helmet under one arm.

"These are my battle-sisters, Elsa and Antonia," Ingrid said. Elsa had a large two-handed sword she had propped point-down on the floor. Antonia carried a spear with an eighteen inch long gleaming double-edged blade at the business end. They both nodded in response to the hellos from Dean and his companions.

Antonia looked around and thumped the butt of her spear on the floorboards, giving a wicked smile. "So, when does the fun start?"

22

IT WAS JUST after sunset when the shifters returned to the cabin. Mark, Dawson and Hannah came first with three other members of their pack. Albion and Arlo showed up next and were accompanied by a gray-haired, bearded man who was wearing furs and buckskins like something out of a mountain man movie. Dean guessed that was Old Barney, the werebear. Trailing behind Albion and Arlo were the dryads Anya and Zora. When Dean asked what they were doing there, they told him they were there to defend their valley. They said they could help with any wounded injured during the coming battle.

Dean, Jaz, and Joanna stood on the front porch facing the assembled shape-shifters and the dryads as night fell. The Valkyries stood off to one side, inspecting their weapons, as if they didn't have a care in the world. He supposed they didn't. This was the kind of thing they lived for. Jaz cleared her throat and went over the plan one more time.

"Okay, Albion, you and the rest of the shifters will wait inside the cabin with the lights on to draw the attention of the Oni demons to you." She waited as the group of shifters nodded.

"Anya and Zora," Jaz continued, "You will be upstairs and stay out of the way until you are needed or called for." The dryads both said yes, they understood. The hunter turned to look at the battle maidens.

"Yes, yes. We understand," Ingrid said. "We stay unseen above the forest canopy until the demons are engaged at the cabin's doors and windows. Then we swoop in and pin them against the cabin between us and the shifters inside."

"Zis is going to be zo much fun," Elsa said in her thick French accent.

"Right," Jaz said. She continued, looking right and left at Dean and Joanna. "Dean, Jo, and I will be out to the side, in the woods, watching. Once the Demons are engaged by the Valkyries, that will be our signal to move from our hiding place and start heading south to the old mines."

"Have you figured out how you are going to mask Dean from the demons' senses?" Albion asked. "I can see and smell him clearly. The two of you are nearly invisible to me according to my Unusual senses."

"Jo says she has a solution to that," Jaz said. She hoped it worked. The witch girl had not been very forthcoming about what the solution was, just that she had worked something out. Jo had her own amulet, similar to Jaz's, that masked her scent and cooled the heat pattern to hide it from Unusual senses beyond the normal visible light spectrum.

"Well, you three better get to your hiding places then," Old Barney rumbled. "The forest is telling me that there's trouble coming fast. The demons must almost be here."

"See you on the other side," Ingrid said. She and the other Valkyries spread their wings and launched themselves skyward, winking out of sight as soon as they left the ground. Dean knew that they could mask their presence from anyone if they chose to do so. The shifters started into the cabin with the two dryads, leaving the three of them on the porch. Jaz stepped down to the ground and headed to the northwest side of the cabin followed by Dean and Joanna.

They walked about a hundred feet from the house into and

among the trees until they arrived at a large fallen tree lying on the ground amidst the brush and undergrowth. They climbed over it to the other side and found a sheltered area where the three of them could spread out and lay down on the ground. There was enough open space under parts of the tree so that they could still see the cabin through the brush. They were mostly hidden from view, especially in the dark.

Dean looked around. Now it was time to see if Joanna had been able to come up with a solution to mask his presence from the Demons as they approached the cabin. Once they were engaged, it would not matter as much and they could slip away to the south.

"Okay," Joanna said to Jaz. "I came up with something that will extend your amulet's effects to cover a larger area than just an individual. That should mask Dean as well. The challenge is that the area of expanded coverage is dependent on contact."

"What do you mean by contact?" Jaz asked. She shot Dean a look.

Jo sighed and gave them a sheepish grin. "You two have to be touching, as close as possible, in order for it to work."

"Wait a minute, how close?" Dean asked.

"Really close," Jo replied. "Look, the amulets are our best protection. I can expand their area of effect but it has to be through contact. I decided that if it was with me it would just be weird, so it has to be you and mom."

"When this is all done," Jaz hissed between her teeth, "you and I are going to have a long talk, young lady."

"Oh joy," Jo said, rolling her eyes. "Look, we don't have much time and I have still have to cast the expansion spell, so lie down."

Dean watched as Jaz lay on her stomach behind the log, then he lay down beside her so that their adjacent arms and legs touched. He craned his neck around to look at Jo. She was shaking her head.

"No, you two have to be really close, closer than that," the Wiccan teen said.

Dean looked over to his left and looked at Jaz where she had turned her head to look at him. This was going to get very uncomfortable.

"Fine," Jaz said. She rolled onto her side. "Spoon up behind me, but don't you dare enjoy this."

"I wouldn't dream of it," Dean said. He waited until she was still and then he moved up behind her, pressing his body against hers. He could smell the shampoo in her hair as he got closer.

"And don't breathe on me," Jaz said. "I hate that."

"Don't breathe, got it," he replied.

He heard Jo giggle a little and then she said, "Perfect." He heard her mutter a few words under her breath from behind and above them.

"Okay, the spell's in place," Jo said. "Don't move and it should be fine. I'm going to go over here a little ways and get settled."

As she moved away, Dean whispered in Jaz's ear. "You know this is straight from the child of divorce's handbook. You know, come up with a way to force your parents back together, or in our case, to get together."

"Well, if I detect any evidence that it's working on your part, you're going to be sorry," Jaz hissed in reply.

"Noted," Dean said. He still had to admit it would be funny if the whole situation weren't so deadly serious. He settled in to wait and distracted himself by peering into the darkness towards the cabin. He found he could see much better than usual. It must be part of the amulet's effects. He could make out details in the dark that he would never be able to see under normal circumstances. He looked at the woods to the south of the cabin and tried to see if he could detect movement there that would signal the coming of the demons sent to kill them.

Dean didn't have to wait very long. They were hidden only about ten minutes when he saw something coming through the woods, then another form moved up with the first. He thought they could be deer or something at first. That changed when two changed to five and more of the forms moved up, then more of the creatures were present. The demons were bunched in a group and he couldn't get a good count. They spread out in a line and moved towards the cabin. As they moved into a line, he was able to refine his count. There were eighteen of the demons here. He wondered if there were more kept back at the mine, waiting for them to arrive. That was important to keep in mind.

The closest demon in the line was going to pass within about twenty-five feet of their hidden location. Dean held his breath as the creature passed by. He could make out the scaled hide of the beast as it reached its closest point to them. It paused to sniff the air and Dean wondered if it had picked up on something. Whatever it was, the demon soon continued forward, finding nothing worth investigating.

The approaching line of demons curved around the southern edge of the clearing in which the cabin stood and stopped just inside the tree line. Dean watched them as they took up positions behind trees as if they expected an attack from the house. He wondered what they were waiting for, but then with a unified snarl, the demons all rushed forward towards the cabin. They split into groups. The bulk of them went for the front porch with its front door and single window for access. The others split into groups of two or three and headed for the other ground floor windows visible on the south side of the building.

As the demons reached the cabin, there erupted a chorus of wolf howls, lion roars, and a loud growling snarl that must have been from Old Barney in bear form. Then the melee began. The demons struggled to get in their chosen entry points and the defenders inside, slashing and biting with claws and teeth to keep them out.

"Almost time," Jaz whispered. "Be ready to move."

"Got it," Dean replied.

As if on cue, three shining forms materialized just above the ground. The light they emitted in the UV spectrum, as Dean could now see, aided by the amulet, was blinding. The Valkyries shouted battle cries together and charged into the rear of the mass of demons clustered on the porch. The surprise attack was successful and the cries of the demons were cut short as the battle maidens' blades slashed through their tough hides without effort. As each of the Eldara warrior's holy blades swept home, the demons cried out and then fell to the side in a burning heap of smoldering flesh. Their blades, like Dean's, would actually kill the demons, not just banish their corporeal earthly forms back to hell.

"Okay, now," Jaz said shifting her position behind the log to rise. It was awkward because of how Dean was pressed up behind her. He rolled backward away from her to give her room to rise. He got to his feet and turned to see that Jo had joined them as well.

"Dean," Jaz said. "I know you are not going to be able to see as well where we are going in the woods. We will keep you between us and try to warn you of any obstacles. Try to keep up with our pace. We won't have much time to reach the southern end of the valley before the cabin attack's results are known to the Revenant at the mines."

Dean nodded, checked his gear to make sure was all set and attached where it would not get in his way as he followed the women through the woods in the darkness. Jaz took the lead, with Dean following and Joanna taking up the rear. She set a pretty rapid pace, jogging off between the trees. He already missed his enhanced vision as he stumbled over a root, but he wouldn't let that be the reason they failed this mission. He steeled himself to keep up and watch as best he could for hindrances in the darkness. He would keep up.

The three would-be rescuers set off together into the deep woods of the southern end of the valley. Hopefully they would reach their destination before anything happened to their objective. Dean thought of Ashley. He thought about her and how she counted on him with each step and that kept him going. Soon they were out of sight of the cabin and the sounds that came from the battle there. They could focus on the task that waited ahead.

23

IT TOOK the trio nearly an hour to make it to the foothills that made up the southern base of the valley. Dean considered it a good pace, given that he could barely see the whole time. Jaz didn't seem to agree with the paramedic based on the way she kept pushing him to go faster. As the upward slope announced their arrival at the southern-most point of the valley, the hunter finally called for a halt to rest and start the second part of the journey: finding the location of the mine's entrance.

Old Barney had told them the entrance was likely hidden by a lot of undergrowth that would make it difficult to locate even in daylight. Jo said she had a plan to help with that and both Dean and Jaz looked to her.

"The demons are netherworlders who do not belong here," Joanna explained. "That means they should leave a trace of their passing in a forest this thick. The plants themselves will react to their touch, which will start to destroy the leaves and branches as they pass. I think I can recognize it. Once we find the point where they came down the mountain, we can follow it back to their lair, in theory."

"Are you sure?" Dean asked. "When you first mentioned this to us, you acted like you had cast this spell and seen it work before."

"I mean, it should work," the teen said. "It's just a simple contrasting nature spell."

Dean shared a look with Jaz, but they both chose to keep their thoughts to themselves. Dean figured they had already committed to this plan. They would just have to stick with it until something proved them wrong and they had to adjust.

"What do you need to do the spell?" Jaz asked.

"I need you two to stay behind me while I cast it," Jo replied. "I have to keep it up until we cross their path down the mountain. Once we have that, it should be little trouble for either of us, Mom, to back-track their trail to where they exited the mines."

Dean stood up, adjusting his pack where it dug into his shoulders, and got in line behind Jo. Jaz got behind him.

"I'll stay back here and watch our backs," Jaz said. "Dean, you keep your ears open. Listen for anything that changes in the sounds around you. Things like the insects quieting down or other changes to the usual forest sounds. They could signal the return of the Oni demons from the cabin."

He nodded and started listening, wondering if he, the city boy, would notice anything at all since he didn't know what normal forest sounds were like at night. He paid attention to the sounds anyway as Jo started on a track perpendicular to their first path of travel. She was paralleling the base of the mountain, trying to find the track used by the demons.

They walked for about a half hour before Jo stopped them. She had taken them on a very slow walk. It was so slow, in fact, that Dean had little trouble picking his way along in the darkness. Now he peered ahead as Jo and Jaz conversed in low tones. The Wiccan teen was pointing out something on the side of a bush Dean could barely see ten feet ahead of them. Jaz nodded and the two of them came back to where he waited.

"We found it," Jaz announced. "I'm going to take the lead now. Jo will follow me to help pick up anything I might miss. Dean, you'll come last. Try to keep up. We are going to pick up the pace again as long as the trail is easy to follow. All those demons coming down the hill in one group has torn up the ground pretty well so I think we can easily follow this trail back to the mine's entrance."

"Got it," Dean said with a nod. "Keep up."

Jaz and Jo turned up the hillside and started moving through the brush. Dean stumbled along behind them, doing his best to move silently the way they did and failing at the attempt. He did, however, manage to keep up with the two women. He had thought of Joanna as a Wiccan, a peaceful spell caster. Seeing her in this element alongside Jaz showed him that she was a hunter as well. He wondered how she managed the two sides of her nature and what the rest of the Elk City coven thought of her hunter skills when she arrived at their doorstep, in the future.

The move up the side of the mountain was steep and grueling, and Dean was panting and soaked with sweat despite the cold night air by the time the women called another halt. Jo came back to him where he crouched, gasping for breath. She seemed unfazed by the uphill climb.

"We think we spotted the entrance. Mom is going to check it out and make sure it's clear, then we'll go in," the teen said. She noted his heavy breathing. "Boy, you are really out of shape, Dad. Catch your breath. The exciting stuff happens now."

"Running up a mountain in the dark wasn't in my exercise plan," Dean replied. "And remember, exciting is not always a good thing."

He could make out the broad grin she gave him in reply and realized that she didn't agree with him. Though their ages were not that far apart right now in this time and place, the things Dean had seen over the last year had aged him prematurely. He knew better than to take things for granted or assume that everything would work out the way they planned. The paramedic thought that his hunter counterpart, the teen's eventual mother, would agree with him.

Jaz came back down the hill to where they waited. She looked around and then described what she saw.

"There's an old rusted metal door set in the hillside up there," the hunter said. "I listened at it for a while but didn't detect anything on the other side. The demons definitely came that way and since I don't see them shutting a door after they leave, I have to assume there are other, more intelligent inhabitants inside who closed it after they left. I can see light leaking around the door, so there is light on the other side." Dean liked the sound of having some light for a change.

"What's the plan?" Dean asked.

"We'll go up and you will open the door while Jo and I stand ready to deal with any guards on the other side," Jaz said. "Then we go in, shut and hopefully lock the door behind us to keep anyone from sneaking up on us from behind. If all goes well, we will be able to begin our search. I'm hoping your memory of what you saw in your visions will help us navigate inside.

Dean wasn't sure if he'd be able to do that, but maybe he would remember some landmarks in the passages along the way. He just nodded in response, not wanting to give voice to his concerns.

Jaz must have figured out his lack of confidence, even in the darkness. He remembered she could see his expression clearly because of her amulet.

"Look Dean, you just pay attention to what is going on and tell us when you think something is important. You will remember more than you think you will. I'm going to take the lead and Jo will bring up the rear. We will take care of security, but if things get hairy in there, don't be afraid to use that sword. Its mere presence will keep some of them away from you. Any netherworlder will be able to sense the finality it represents for their otherwise eternal existence."

Dean adjusted his shoulder straps and reached up to touch the hilt of Ashley's sword over his right shoulder. He was as ready as he was going to be. He gave a firm nod in response and Jaz turned to go back up the hill with Dean right behind her.

With Dean's eyes adjusted to the darkness and wide open to any light source, he noticed the outline of the doorway right away. He could see the light leaking around the edges of the door. It had the yellow tinge of fire or lantern light, but he was relieved that he would have some normal light for a change, and any light source would do as far as he was concerned. He reached a flat area in front of the door and Jaz pointed to the door's handle without saying a word. She had drawn her sword and he noticed that Jo was standing just behind him with one hand outstretched and the other resting on the grip of her pistol in its holster.

He gripped the cold metal of the old iron door and looked to his companions. They both nodded to him and he turned the handle and pulled outward. The door swung open with a groan of metal on metal from the rusted hinges. Light spilled out from the entrance and Jaz and Jo both rushed past him in silence. He looked around the door and saw a small room on the other side with a passage leading off from it into the mountain. The two women stood looking down the passage. Jo turned and looked his way with a grin and single thumbs up to tell him it was okay.

Stepping into the room, he pulled the door closed behind him. He looked around the inside for some sort of latching mechanism but didn't see anything. Then he noticed a large iron bar leaning against the wall and the bracket on the door meant to hold it in place. He lifted it up and slotted it into the brackets with one end extending past the door to wedge against the inside of the stone wall. It would hold that door securely for the time being. He was not sure how strong an Oni demon was, but he knew he would not be able to pull that door open from the outside now.

Dean turned to look at his companions. "What now?" he whispered.

Jaz returned a feral grin that was mirrored in their daughter's face. "Now we hunt," the hunter clanswoman said. "It's time for some payback."

24

THE PASSAGE back into the mountain sloped downward a bit, with a dirt and stone floor and the same rough-hewn stone walls with occasional timber supports for the ceiling of the passage. Every twenty or thirty feet or so, the support beams held a kerosene lantern against the wall of the passage from a hook. They created pools of light with long shadowy sections of darkened passage in-between.

Jaz lead the way again, walking in a slight crouch, her sword out in her left hand. Dean figured the gun would make too much noise, alerting others of their presence, plus it might not be effective against their netherworld foes. Dean wondered if he should draw Ashley's sword. He decided that it would just get in the way for now. His hand drifted up again to check it was still there over his right shoulder.

Joanna was behind him, a few steps to the rear. He saw when he checked on her that she turned to look behind them periodically. She was making sure no one caught them by surprise. When she noticed him looking back at her, she gave him a broad grin as if to say she was having the time of her life. He smiled in return and then turned back to pay attention to the passage ahead of him. He tried to remember the view from his visions and tie any detail from there to what he was seeing now. Nothing had clicked for him yet but he hoped that when he saw a defining feature of the passage that he'd recognize it.

There were no side passages for some time and so no decisions about direction needed to be made. They continued on their gentle downward slope for about ten minutes without any changes. While the passage wasn't completely straight, they could see some distance ahead of them with a slight bend in the distance blocking their view. That was why the attack came as a complete surprise.

They had only occasionally looked upwards to check the uneven ceiling. There were the supports that held up the lower sections of the passage but the rest of the ceiling arched upward in dark pockets of shadows that Dean couldn't pierce. There was an upward shaft leading to another level that Jaz missed as she passed under it. A shape dropped down directly in front of Dean between he and Jaz and with the powerful sweep of one arm, knocked him to the ground. He had barely shouted his pain and alarm at the sudden blow before the attack happened.

Jaz didn't have much notice, but Dean saw that it was enough. She twisted in place and grabbed the outstretched clawed hand that reached for her neck, pulling it and using its own momentum to propel the assailant past her into the passage ahead. She was knocked to the ground but had avoided the brunt of the attack. Dean still couldn't make out what it was that attacked. They were between lanterns in the passage so he couldn't make out details, just that it crouched to the ground and was snarling and growling. It landed on the ground just past Jaz and turned to leap back at her where she had been knocked against the wall. Dean was sure that she was going to be unable to defend against it as she struggled to rise.

Jo rocketed past him in a bound. She had her hands outstretched and he could make out her saying something under her breath as she went by. A cobalt blue light glowed from her hands and then he could see a similar glow appear around Jaz. The creature reached the glowing boundary around Jaz and shrieked in pain, drawing back-ward for a moment. That was all the time the hunter needed to recover. She turned, sweeping her sword through the air and the creature's head was rolling off its shoulders, a brief fountain of blood, colored black in the darkness of the passage, appearing in its place. Then the body collapsed to lie next to the head, still rocking in place on the ground. A moment later, the body and detached head disappeared in a red mist.

"What the hell was that?" Dean asked in a whisper. He tried hard to keep his voice under control but he wanted to scream. He hated getting startled like that. It was why he avoided haunted houses.

"Another Oni demon," Jaz replied. "It must have been set there to guard the passage. Well, where there is one, there are likely others. It just adds to the things we have to watch out for. This one was on me. I should have checked the ceilings for hiding places."

Dean was glad she could so easily adjust to the advent of a new threat. His heart was still pounding out of his chest. He needed a minute to collect himself and the women paused to wait for him to get squared away. He could see them exchanging glances, but he didn't care. He was a paramedic. He was not trained to go into dark places and fend off attacks from monsters and demons. Dean took a few deep breaths to calm his nerves and then nodded that he was ready to go on.

A short time later the passage opened up into a small chamber with two other passages branching off from it. The three of them used the small room to take a brief break while deciding to move onward. Jaz checked the passages leading deeper inside the mountain. One sloped upward from the chamber, the other continued down, deeper into the mines. Keeping their voices low, they talked over their options.

"I can see where both branches show signs of recent usage, so I'm not sure which one to take," the hunter said. "Dean, does anything look familiar yet?"

He shook his head. "The general look and feel is right so I think this is where they are holding Ashley, but I haven't picked up on any specific landmarks yet. If anything draws me one way or another, it is to take the downward passage. It feels right."

"I'd go with his feelings on this, Mom," Jo added, ignoring the look Jaz shot her. "He's the one who's come closest to walking this path before."

"Well it's as good a choice as the other," Jaz said rising to her feet. "Let's get going."

Dean got up and joined them as they continued on the descending path. He was frustrated. Every wall, lantern and support looked the same to him. He tried to watch and pay attention to the little differences, but he could detect nothing. Then, when the path had leveled out for a bit, he saw a passage branch off ahead. He whispered for Jaz to stop. Jo came up to join the other two.

"This looks familiar," Dean said. "I think that side passage leads to the cell where Ashley is being held."

Jaz nodded and turned back to look up the length of the passageway. Dean looked around and followed her gaze. Still no sign of anyone else, which was good news. They were on an even tighter guard since the demon had attacked them. Jaz had figured it had been an isolated sentry set there to guard the entrance passage. They moved up to where the passage branched and Dean looked left and recognized the passage he had seen in his first vision. There was a stout door about ten feet down the passage. It stood open, not closed as he had seen it before.

Before she could stop him, Dean rushed past Jaz and ran into the small room where Ashley was held. Correction. Where she had been held. He saw the armchair there where she had been tied up. The ropes that had secured her were coiled and looped over the back of the chair spindles. Jaz and Jo joined him looking at the chair.

"This was where they were holding her," Dean said. The room was tiny and probably served as a secure storeroom when the mine was in operation. It only had the one exit. "Where is she?"

"She didn't escape or get rescued," Jo said.

"Why do you say that?" Dean asked. He wanted to think she had gotten away.

"The ropes," she said, pointing to the chair. "They're coiled. Whoever took her, took the time to leave the ropes in a way that they can be used again. My guess is that she was taken somewhere else in here and they expect to bring her back here later."

"Good thinking, Joanna," Jaz said. "So do we keep looking for her or wait here for them to bring her back?"

"We have to keep looking," Dean said. "Who knows what they are doing to her right now. She's an immortal, but that doesn't mean she can't feel pain."

"I'm not saying you're wrong, Dean," Jaz said. "We can go on searching and return here if we don't find anything or anyone else down here. We know she's been here and will likely be returned here."

"I say we keep going," Jo said, adding her opinion to the mix. "We only suspect they'll come back with her, and every minute we spend waiting is that much sooner that any of the demons might return from the attack on the cabin."

Jaz thought for a moment and nodded. "I'm inclined to agree, Jo. Let's keep going and find her. Dean, can you find the path from here to the room with the portal? My guess is they are trying to use her in some way to hold the breach in the wards between our world and the netherworld open."

"I think I will recognize it," Dean said. "It has to be close to this location. Let's keep going down the main passage and see where it leads."

"Be ready for anything," Jaz said. "If I were the leader of this group of revenants from the netherworld, I'd be at the nexus of the connection."

Dean found his hand drifting upward to the sword again and then pulled his hand back. The sword was still there, and checking on it would only make him look scared. He couldn't let that happen in front of either of his companions. Sure, it was a stupid macho thing, but it also helped him stay focused on them and not his own quivering fear. He never liked enclosed spaces and thinking of how deep they were in the mountain with tons of rock overhead just made his knees weak.

Jaz took the lead again and Jo had moved up closer to Dean rather than hanging further back and checking behind them. All eyes were focused forward. It didn't take too long for the sound of the rhythmic chanting to resonate up the passage to them. The grunting and snarling nature of the voices grated on his eardrums and made Dean's skin crawl. They sounded as inhuman as the beings to whom they must belong.

The three companions stopped at a bend in the passage. There was flickering purple light pulsing from beyond the turn ahead. The chanting was clearer now. It was not a language Dean recognized, if it was a language at all. For all he knew it could be a random collection of phonetic sounds. Dean looked at his colleagues as they paused in the passage and Jo answered the question.

"It's Aramaic, an ancient language used by many netherworlders, as well as their divine counterparts," she whispered. "I don't speak it, but I know enough words to recognize it. I can feel the power emanating from down the passage. They are casting some sort of spell. Whatever they are trying to do down there, it takes a lot of magical energy. The air is crackling with it."

"I think we have found the portal room," Jaz said. She looked at each of them. "When we round that corner we need to have a plan of what we are going to do. Dean, if Ashley is in there, our goal will be to get to her first. Once we get there, while Jo and I keep them busy, you try and free her. Get her out and away if you can. That is our priority. If we have to beat a hasty retreat, we want her to be able to join us."

She turned her attention to the Wiccan teen. "Jo, can you draw on that sun-fire spell again?"

"Yes," Jo nodded. "But only once, or maybe twice. I have some other tricks, though, and the Glock. I can cover my area of responsibility." She patted the gun holstered at her side.

"Okay, then. Based on how you described the portal chamber you saw, Dean, it's a big room." Jaz looked to him for confirmation and Dean nodded. "We will get as close as we can without being seen, and try to see how many we are dealing with in the way of guards and revenants." She paused for a moment and looked at the passage around them. "Okay, I have an idea. Give me a second to rig something here in the passage."

Dean watched as the hunter took off her pack and started pulling a few items from it. He recognized several blocks of C-4 plastic explosive. She took some sort of metal stick and shoved one into each of the blocks. The huntress walked over to the nearest ceiling support where it met the vertical wall support beam and slid the block into a narrow crevice between the rock wall and the wooden crossbar that supported it. When she was finished placing the charges, she came back over to them and handed Dean a small hand-held device.

"That is a detonator, Dean," Jaz said. "If you get Ashley free and you are the last one out, or the only one of us left, you run past here as fast as you can with her and once you are around the bend, flip up the safety and hit the button hard, twice. Two times, close together or it won't work. Got it?"

He nodded, and started to argue the specifics of what she wanted him to do. She shut him down with a hand raised in the air.

"Jo and I are going to be busy in there, at least in the beginning," Jaz said. "In all likelihood, we will be running along with you when you blow the passage. But one way or another, someone needs to seal up this portal for the time being until the magic dissipates and it closes up on its own. You've seen what these demons will do if they get loose. We can't let them run wild in the valley, or get into more populated areas."

Dean thought about all he had seen the demons do and then thought about how the average uninformed human would respond if one showed up where they lived or worked. They couldn't be allowed to get out of this mountain. Dean nodded and slid the detonator into a cargo pocket in his duty pants.

"Alright, that's done then," Jaz said. "Now let's scoot forward, carefully, and see what we can see before we go running in there."

25

THE TRIO CROUCHED and advanced along the corridor until they could start to see into the chamber beyond. Just as Dean had seen in his vision, the room opened up into a huge cavern with the far reaches lost in darkness. Again Dean could hear the sound of running water in the distance. The strange, sickly purple glow filled the room with an eerie light source, casting long shadows on the floor and into the passage where they hid.

Jaz motioned them down and then forward. They all belly-crawled up to the entrance and looked into the room. There was a group of figures clustered in a semi-circle in front of the pulsing portal in the cavern wall. Dean stifled a gasp as he spotted Ashley, held between two humanoid figures in front of another robed figure who wielded a strange curved dagger. The blade was of some sort of black metal or stone and had a serpentine shape. The figure was waving it before the captive Eldara while he and the others surrounding her continued their chanting.

There were seven individuals participating in the ceremony as Dean and the others watched. The one carrying the dagger wore a brown hooded robe and only his forearms and hands showed. The skin showing was pasty and white, like the skin of a dead body drained of blood. He guessed that was the one whose head Dean had seen from when he had his visions assisted by the heavenly blade. The others were dressed in lighter tan robes. The whole group swayed in tandem with the tempo of their chants.

Jaz tapped Dean on the arm and motioned them backward into the passage. The three edged back until they were out of sight of the room's occupants. Then they all leaned close while Jaz outlined their plan.

"Those are all revenants, unless I miss my guess. It is hard to tell for sure from behind." Jaz said.

"So what do we do?" Dean asked. "Can we handle seven of them by ourselves? I'm not so sure we can take on that many on our own."

"Speak for yourself, Dad," Jo said. "Hunters have their own methods to deal with them, and I have my magical resources, too. We can beat them."

"The bullets in our pistols are going to hurt them but not put them down permanently," Jaz told him. "The bullets in our magazines are blessed and infused with silver and arsenic. Those will put them down if we strike clean to the head or the heart. If we miss those vital areas, the slugs will still slow them enough to do what we need to do."

Dean shrugged. He'd have to take their word for it. "So what do I do?"

"You make a beeline for Ashley, Dean," Jaz said. I'm going to take on the three nearest us, then I'll charge the lead revenant. He'll have to pay attention to my sword. It can certainly send him back to hell, whatever protections he might have." Jaz gave him a grim smile. "When he lets go of Ashley, pull her to the side and get her ready to run."

She looked to Joanna and paused a moment. "You are going to have to take on the demons on the other side and then finish off any I miss from the shots I fire at the first three. Are you up to this? I hadn't tackled anything this advanced at your age and you don't have all my training."

"I've got this," Jo said. "You worry about the leader. I'll make sure nothing gets you from behind."

"Okay then." Jaz said. "We can do this. I'll go first, followed by Jo. Dean, you'll follow at the rear. Stay right behind me and grab Ashley as soon as you can."

Dean nodded, checked the sword hilt again to make sure it was there. He didn't know much about how to use it, but it was his only weapon for defending him and Ashley once they got in there. He got in line behind Jo and watched the teen ahead of him bouncing on the balls of her feet in her black boots. She had drawn her pistol, and he saw her rack a bullet into the chamber, flicking the safety to off with her thumb. She shot him a broad grin and turned to look forward again.

Jaz gave one last check behind her to make sure they were all ready and then, with surprising speed, sprinted forward into the room. There was no battle cry or sound at all beyond the scrape of her boots on the rock of the passage floor. Jo was right behind her and Dean was left there, scrambling to catch up. Then the chaos of the battle took over.

Dean entered the chamber to see the closest of the demons in the tan robes go down as its head exploded in a shower of gore. The robe then flattened to the ground, empty as the dispatched demon disappeared in a puff of red mist. One down. The other spun around with multiple bullet impacts and fell to the ground. Dean saw no red mist so he knew that one was still alive. The third took several shots to the torso and then misted as the robe fluttered to the ground. He followed the women in as he ran past the single creature writhing on the ground. He saw the three demons on the far side spin away under a flurry of bullets from Jo's pistol and then a ball of white light erupted from her extended palm, consuming two that were close together. They burst into white-hot flames and soon their charred forms fell to the cavern floor.

He turned his attention to the central figure in the darker brown robes. Jaz was still several yards away, charging in. The hooded face turned and the cadaverous face with sunken red glowing eyes bored into him as it took in the attackers. The lips peeled back in a fierce grin showing dual rows of needle-like teeth in the mouth. As Dean watched in horror from where he charged up behind Jaz, the revenant took his curved dagger and plunged it into Ashley's side, then flung her to the ground in the charging hunter's path. Jaz had to leap to the side and that gave the revenant time to reach into its robes and draw a matching serpentine-bladed scimitar from beneath his them. Dean only had a moment to take all of this in, then the hunter and the demon were battling each other with a mad, flashing flurry of blades.

Dean had no time for that, though. He had to get to Ashley. He rushed over to where she lay on the floor and gently rolled her onto her back. Blood was pouring from the wound in her side and the paramedic flung off his pack, opening the attached IFAK pouch and pulling out a trauma pressure bandage and a pack of quick-clot impregnated gauze to stop the bleeding. He ripped the package open with his teeth and pressed it deep into the gaping wound in the Eldara's side. He followed the gauze with the trauma pressure bandage that had an absorbent pad and the dressing that could be wrapped around her torso and secured by tying on the opposite side. She was an angel on earth, but she could bleed and die. Depending on the nature of that curved blade, her fate might even be worse. He had to keep her alive.

"Dean," Ashley whispered. "I told you not to come."

"Yeah, because you knew I'd listen to you," Dean answered her with a wry laugh. "We'll get you out of here as soon as we finish off the revenant and his goons."

"You found Jaswinder Errington and the Wiccan girl, I take it?" Ashley asked.

"You know about them?" Dean asked. "How?"

"I have been tied to the Erringtons for a long time," she replied. "After some time spent with you, I knew that you would be tied to them, too."

Dean had too many questions to be answered here and now. He needed to do something to stabilize his patient and get her ready to move out of here. Looking up from where he was crouched in front of the portal he saw Jaz still battling with the revenant, their blades moving more quickly than he could see. Jo was circling a pair of wounded demons in the tan robes. He could see scaled skin on their arms and clawed hands that ended in wicked-looking talons. The teen had drawn her Bowie knife in her left hand and held out her hand in a palm out gesture that showed a glowing white light beginning there.

A rustling sound behind him caused him to turn and then scramble backwards as the demon that Jaz had shot, but not killed, crawled toward him. He kicked out at its scaled, flat face with its mouth full of fangs. The creature snapped at him and he kept going backward until he remembered his sword. Reaching back with one hand, he drew the blade and jabbed it forward in the direction of the advancing demon. It shrieked and drew backward, eyeing the blade warily.

He knew they were in a standoff right now. Jaz and the revenant were still battling around the room. One of them was going to make a mistake and lose this battle and Dean was not sure what to do if it was Jaz. Jo had drawn her remaining adversary away from where he was located, but he couldn't get to Ashley and carry her to safety until he took care of the demon nearest him. He got to his feet, and keeping the sword in front of him, walked toward the demon where crawled on the floor. Its legs must be paralyzed by the bullet wounds but who knew how long that would last. He suspected the creatures would regenerate quickly from anything but a fatal wound. He did not have much time.

It swiped at his ankles with a clawed arm and he skipped backward out of the way. He was not a fighter and was not sure he could do this. The alternative, however, was to let Ashley and the others die here in the cavern with more demons coming out of that portal in the future. He moved forward again, and when the demon took a swing at him with its other arm, the paramedic stomped down with his booted foot to crush the clawed hand beneath it. Moving quickly, Dean lunged forward and plunged the heavenly blade into the exposed face of the demon. Black blood fountained out of the wound where it cleaved through the nose and roof of the mouth, then the creature began to shake as if in a seizure and the area around the sword blade began to sizzle. The skin nearest the blade turned black, the charred color spreading outward until the whole head was a blackened, cracked mess.

Dean pulled the blade free and saw the charring of the flesh spread to the exposed arms and clawed hands. Then the beast was still and he was left standing without an adversary. He heard a hissing sound close by and saw the black blood coating the end of the blade smoke, char and flake away, leaving the pristine silvery metal in its place once more.

A flash of white light from behind him caused him to spin around. Jo must have fired off another blast of her sun-fire spell. The demon dodged the ball of solar plasma and took that opportunity to charge at her from the side He shouted a warning. It plowed into her, grabbing her outstretched arm in a clawed hand and biting down across her forearm. The teen screamed in agony and brought her other hand around clutching the broad bladed knife, and jammed it into the creature's neck.

The two of them fell to the ground and rolled over and over several times. Dean watched in horror, holding his sword out but unable to lend a hand, knowing he'd just as likely stab the girl as the demon while they fought on the floor like that. The struggling stopped with the brown-robed figure atop the girl. There was a screeching sound and then the brown robes were empty, as the body disappeared in a puff of red mist. Jo levered herself up on one elbow, still clutching the Bowie knife in her left hand. There were rips in her black body suit where the demon's claws had scraped her and she was clutching her other arm to her side. She got up and came over to him.

"How's Ashley?" Jo asked, her shoulders heaving as she struggled to catch her breath.

Dean looked her over and then moved back to where he had left Ashley on the floor while he battled the demon. "I think she'll be all right if we can get her out of here. I've got her patched up as best as I can for now." He reached out to look at the ragged wound on Jo's forearm where she had been bitten. It was bleeding and the skin was torn in multiple places. He needed to get a dressing on that wound, too. "Come over here and talk with Ashley to keep her awake while I wrap up that arm."

The clash of metal on metal across the cavern drew their attention as Jaz continued to battle the revenant. They were off in the darkness somewhere at this point and Dean couldn't even see them. "Jo, can you make out what is going on?"

"Mom and that revenant are still battling," Jo said. "That thing is good. I need to get over there and help her."

"Stay here and let me bandage that arm," Dean said. "There's got to be a way to distract it or weaken it."

"The sword," Ashley croaked from nearby.

"What?" Dean asked.

"My blade, Dean. It can close the portal," the Eldara said. "That will weaken the revenant. He's too strong for the hunter to beat right now."

"Aunt Ashley, the blade is tied to you, won't that pull you from the earthly plane?" Joanna said.

"It must be done," Ashley said. "We can close this portal forever but we have to do it now, while the revenant is distracted. He doesn't know you have it here. Do it. Now."

Dean looked into the darkness, hearing the clash of swords there. He had to help, but he also had to save Ashley. He looked back at the Eldara lying on the cavern floor. He could still get her some help. A medevac helicopter could get her to the trauma center in time to save her.

"Dean, you saved me," Ashley said. "You already did it by coming here, and by keeping them from using my life force to open the portal permanently. I'm only going to go away for a while. It will only be a few years, ten or twenty at the most, I promise. I'll find a way to come back. I have too much to accomplish here with young Joanna." She looked him in the eyes and reached out to squeeze his hand. "Do it, before it is too late."

Dean felt lost. He had come all this way to rescue her and now he had to let her go again. Everyone who was important in his life was being torn away from him. He looked down at the blade in his hand. The silvery metal gleamed with a light all its own. It was a pure light, unlike the sickly purple light coming from the pulsing portal.

He stood up, letting Ashley's hand slip from his grasp. Walking over to stand directly in front of the portal, he looked back at the Eldara where she lay on the floor nearby. Her eyes met his and she smiled at him. His heart melted under that smile. She nodded to him in encouragement. Dean held up the blade and wondered how he should do this? Did he just throw it into the portal to the netherworld? No, that wouldn't be right. Instead he shifted his grip on the blade, and with two hands gripping it over his head, he stabbed it forward into the center of the swirling mass. He half expected to fall into the pulsing maw of the opening between worlds but the blade struck home and wedged up to the hilt inside the inter-dimensional doorway.

There was a roar of agony in the darkness behind him that was choked off with a shriek. Then the blade disappeared from his hands. One minute it was there and the next it was gone. Gone as well was the purple light illuminating this end of the cavern. It plunged him into total darkness for a moment. He turned and struggled through the inky blackness to get back to where Ashley lay on the cavern floor. As he was making his way back, the golden glow of a pool of light was lit nearby. It was Jo. She pulled her hand down from above her head, but the small ball of soft yellow-golden light remained in the air above her and Ashley. He rushed over, surprised that she was still there.

"Ashley, you're all right, you're here." Dean said as he knelt next to her.

"I wouldn't leave without saying goodbye," she said with a smile. "Besides we don't have much time and you need to tell the hunter something important."

"Okay," Dean said. "I'll tell her whatever you want, just don't go."

"I have to go and I can't hold on too much longer. Listen to me. Tell her that Artur Torrence is behind this. Tell her that the Errington Adversary lured me here. It was all part of an attempt to destroy her family once and for all." Ashley squeezed his hand. "Do you have that? Jo, you too. Remember it. It is important."

Both Dean and Joanna nodded. They had heard her.

"Dean, I have to go now," Ashley said. She looked into his eyes and gave him a smile. "We will see each other again. I promise. In the meantime, you must live your life and fulfill your destiny. You are so much more than the person I thought you were in the beginning. You will figure in many changes coming to this world. Enjoy the time you have and the people around you. Trust in that, and continue to show the good that is within you to the others around you. Promise?"

He nodded, his eyes welling with tears that clouded his vision. He couldn't see her clearly anymore.

"Goodbye, Dean."

He blinked his eyes to clear away his tears, eventually using his hands to wipe them away. When he did so, she was gone.

26

JAZ WATCHED as the revenant's form burst into the familiar red mist in front of her as she pulled her blade from its heart. She had never taken on a greater demon before on her own and she had barely survived this one. She had always had a full attack team backing her up and they had worked together to terminate the target. If this was under other circumstances, she would have swelled with pride and dialed up her father to tell him what she had done. But she could not do that, ever again. She paused, sheathed her sword, and scrubbed at her damned leaking eyes with the heel of her left hand. Her right hand was hanging limp at her side, blood dripping from her fingertips to the floor from a long gash high on her shoulder.

The hunter craned her neck to try to get a look at the wound. The revenant had almost finished her with that attack. She had been forced back under a flurry of cuts and slashes that had ended with that slashing blow to her arm. Only by luck did she duck under the follow-up to the attack that would have sliced her head from her shoulders. She had used it to her advantage, though. She started favoring her right side. It wasn't hard to do. It hurt like hell. It created a pattern the revenant started trying to take advantage of, and when the demon went to complete an attack where that pattern said she should be, Jaz launched her own final, desperate attack. Then just as she was spent, her energy waning, the creature shrieked aloud. It stood up straight and turned to look back across the cavern to the portal. Using the sudden opening in the revenant's guard, she was able to finish it with a single, almost anticlimactic thrust to the heart.

She looked back to the other end of the cavern, hoping against hope that Dean and Jo survived, or at least fought there so that she could lend aid to them in time. She saw that the ugly purple glow of the portal was gone from the far end of the room. There was also the soft yellow glow of witch light hovering over two figures seated on the ground. She saw no others so she hoped that they had been successful in defeating all their foes. Stumbling along, the loss of blood and fatigue starting to take over control of her body, Jaz worked her way back across the broad cavern to the welcoming pool of light at the other end.

As Jaz got closer, she realized that she could not see the Eldara with Dean and Joanna and fear welled up in her. She had undertaken this journey in order to fulfill the clan's duty, and honor their debt to the Eldara Ashley Moore. She had never even met the angelic messenger, but had heard the stories of how she had helped the Errington's on many occasions over the previous two centuries. Had she, Jaswinder Errington, the last of her clan, failed in the quest to save her? She struggled to speed up her pace to get back to where she saw her companions clustered together in the pool of light.

Dean looked up at her as she approached, his eyes red-rimmed with tears. The sword was gone from the scabbard at his back and was nowhere to be seen. Neither was the Eldara. Had she been consumed in the portal? She looked to Joanna. Jaz still couldn't bring herself to think of the witch girl as her daughter.

"Jo, where is Ashley?" the hunter asked.

"She's gone. Her injuries were severe, and Dean and I were not able to save her," Jo answered through her tears. "Her sword might have been used to help her draw on healing energy to save herself, but she had Dean use the blade to seal the portal so that you could defeat the revenant. She said it would kill you otherwise."

"So we failed?" Jaz asked. She looked up and stared at the cavern's jagged ceiling far above them.

"No," Dean's voice cracked as he answered. "We did not fail. Ashley was saved and then she chose to have me save you."

Jaz thought she sensed a hint of anger in his tone. Of course that made sense. She was his girlfriend, even though that relationship was destined to end someday.

"We need to get out of here, then," Jaz said. "I know you are upset about having to leave without Ashley, but we need to go before any surviving Oni demons from the cabin attack return. They will sense the closing of the portal, as well as their master's demise. My guess is they will return here."

"You're hurt," Dean said, looking up at her arm. "Sit down here and let me get a dressing on that wound. While I do that we have a message to give you from Ashley."

Dean had her sit down next to him as he set to work on bandaging her arm. The initial gauze he put on turned warm as soon as it soaked with her blood. She knew the quick-clot formula impregnated in the gauze he used was responsible for the heat she was feeling. When her paramedic companion had finished securing a pressure bandage on her shoulder, he set to creating a sling for her arm to support it while they got moving. His hands were gentle, and she watched him working. He was careful and watched her for signs of pain and avoided moving her arm unnecessarily. When he was done, he pulled out a pre-filled morphine syringe and looked at her with a question in his eyes.

"How's your pain level?" Dean asked. "Do you think you need this?"

She thought about it. They had a long way to walk to get back to the cabin and she was going to need to be clear-headed. On the other hand, her arm throbbed. The pain was a little better now that he had bandaged it, but it hurt like hell.

"Can you just give me enough to take the edge off?" she asked.

"I'll give you half now and if you need more, make sure you tell me, all right?" Dean said.

She nodded in reply and watched as he checked the dose. Then he gave her an injection in her opposite shoulder. He asked Jo to massage the injection site gently for her since she couldn't do it for herself with her arm in a sling. The teen leaned forward to rub her shoulder muscle with her fingertips. Jaz noticed her hands were trembling.

"You did well, Jo," Jaz said. "Is this your first time in a battle like this, other than the fight at the dryad cabin?"

"Is it that obvious?" Jo asked, looking away. The hunter realized she was ashamed.

"Don't look away, Joanna," Jaz said. "I was a complete wreck after my first firefight. I understand what you are feeling, I really do."

"It's different than at the cabin," the teen choked through the tears. "I didn't have a chance to do much thinking before that happened. It was so sudden. Here, I thought I was better prepared, but Ashley's loss and your injury has me realizing how close of a call this was. We almost lost."

"Yes, but we didn't lose," Jaz responded. "Hold on to that. That will help for now. Later, we will have a talk about how to deal with the stress of an event like this. It's the same chat my father had with me, once upon a time. It will help you, I promise."

The hunter looked around the room, seeing little of the aftermath you would ordinarily see in such a desperate battle. That was the way it was with fighting demons and other netherworlders. You destroyed them, sure, but you often had no bodies on the battlefield to mark your success. In those situations there was nothing to show but your own wounds and exhaustion.

"You had a message for me from the Eldara?"

"She told me to tell you that Artur Torrence is behind this attack on you and your family," Dean said, spitting out the words like venom. "I assume that means something to you? It means something to me. Now I have an additional score to settle with Mr. Torrence."

Jaz stiffened at the mention of the hunter clan's hereditary adversary's name. Artur Torrence was the reason behind why the Erringtons had long ago become a clan of hunters. Legend had it that they had been nothing more than peaceful farmers, coming from somewhere in what was now the Middle East. Artur Torrence had come upon their farm and almost succeeded in wiping out their simple farming family before he tired of his sport and moved on. Her surviving ancestors followed, seeking vengeance. Over the intervening years, the family legends say they came close to catching up with him many times. Often they were able to foil his sinister plans, but always missed out on finishing him off.

"Mom," The teen's voice interrupted her thoughts. "Artur has never come after the family before like this, has he?"

"No," Jaz replied. "I don't know if it was because he never had the opportunity, or if it was because we had him on the run so often that he could not spare the time and energy to do it."

"We need to find him and finish him," Jo said.

Jaz turned her head and looked in the girl's eyes. She saw a familiar face as she looked at the Wiccan girl. Her blue eyes reminded Jaz of her own eyes, and her mother's. She still didn't want to accept the revelation that Jo was her daughter, back from the future, but the concept was growing on her. There had never been a witch-trained hunter to her knowledge. It was why she resisted her instincts that the girl's claims were valid. Dean didn't deny it. He had accepted it far easier than she did. Jaz knew that she needed to get over her doubts. They were all that was left of the clan, after all.

"Yes Jo, we do," Jaz said. "We need to finish him, together."

"You aren't alone in this, ladies," Dean said. "I want in on this vendetta, too. Artur's machinations have hurt those I care about twice now. I've met the vampire lord, and I've seen the way he views and treats humans and others he considers lesser beings. I want to be there when he gets brought down."

"It might take a while, Dean," Jaz told him. "We Erringtons have been tracking and chasing him for centuries. If the legends are true, our vendetta dates back to the beginning of recorded history, before the Christian era. We've learned a certain amount of patience in that time frame."

"I can be patient, as long as we are successful," Dean said.

"Then welcome to the family, Dad," Joanna said. "You're an honorary Errington now."

He sort of smiled at that, Jaz saw, as she watched him packing up his EMS supplies and donning his black backpack. Dean Flynn wasn't a bad sort of fellow. She had never had time to get involved with anyone before, and she certainly didn't have the time now, but she admitted he was the kind of guy she had always imagined for herself. Strong and confident, but willing to let her be the hunter she was trained to be.

"Come, on, let's get out of here," Jaz said. "I want to get back to the outside, and I want to make sure we seal up this room before we leave."

"But we closed the portal," Dean said. He pointed to the section of wall where the pulsing purple doorway to the netherworld had been just minutes before.

"That portal is closed, but the tear in the wards between worlds will not heal completely," Jaz said. "Another could come here and try to force the doorway open again if they were able to harness enough power. By sealing off this chamber, we can go a step further and limit easy access to this location. It's not as much as I would like to do, but it will have to be enough."

She watched as they all stood up, each looking more than a little beat up. Time to get this team back to base. The three of them walked out of the cavern, returning up the passage they had used to enter. When they passed the place where she had placed the C-4 plastic explosive charge, she double-checked with her good hand to make sure it was still there above the support beam. She took them further down the passage, turning a bend in the mineshaft before stopping them about two hundred feet away.

"Dean, you can do the honors," Jaz said.

The paramedic took the wireless detonator from his pocket and flipped up the safety cover, revealing the button underneath. He looked at her again and she nodded. She watched as he thumbed the button twice, clicking it quickly in succession. The rumbling blast sent a rolling wave of rock dust down the passageway at them and she heard the continuing fall of rocks tumbling down from the heart of the mountain above them. The portal's location was sealed away for now. It would have to do. Turning to look at her companions, Jaz nodded and led them out of the mines, beginning the long trek back to the cabin in the woods.

27

DEAN WAS EXHAUSTED by the time they returned. It was near dawn as the trio trudged into the clearing surrounding the lakeside cabin. They approached with caution. There were some broken windows visible to show that something had happened here, but no other signs of the battle. As Dean, Jaz, and Joanna walked up to the front porch the door opened and Anya the dryad stood there with Ingrid and Albion on either side of her. She smiled as she saw them.

"Paramedic Dean, it is good to see you and your companions return to us safe and sound," the dryad woman said.

"We are safe, but some of us are not so sound," Dean said. "What happened here, is everyone safe?"

Ingrid gave a broad smile, "My battle sisters and I have not had such fun in years. It was a great way to prepare for the final battle. It will be a story that will make the other battle maidens jealous." She looked at Dean. "I felt Ashley leave for the home planes. Thank you for freeing her."

"But I didn't save her, Ingrid," Dean said. The guilt that told him he had failed wracked him. "I couldn't bring her back with me."

"You succeeded in keeping the revenant from using her to create a breach between the worlds," the Valkyrie said. "She is not destroyed, and she will return to this plane to help people again. It will not be long. You saved her very existence, Dean, take heart in that."

"How did the battle here go?" Joanna asked.

"It was glorious," Ingrid said. "My sisters and I pinned the demons against the cabin when we attacked them from behind. We destroyed five of the eighteen before they even realized we were here. When they turned to face us, the shifters exploded from the cabin's entrance and pushed them into our blades. We destroyed twelve of them with our heavenly blades, and the shifters sent the others back to their masters in hell. None escaped."

"That's good," Dean said. "It was better than I hoped would happen. Were there any major injuries on our side?"

Albion shook his head. "A few of the shifters suffered some bites, cuts and bruises, but they have all regenerated. Ingrid told us that she sensed your success in rescuing her sister, so the others all returned to their homes. Anya and I waited for your return to see if there was any further assistance we could provide. We owe you a debt for ridding our valley of this threat."

"We banished the revenant for now and sealed the portal. We also blocked off the mine shaft with explosives," Jaz said. "There should be no further trouble here."

"There is one thing, Ingrid," Dean said. "Artur was behind all of this again. I don't know how, but he rebounded from the last failed attempt to disrupt lives in Elk City and instituted this whole series of attacks to provide the revenants a foothold in this world."

Ingrid's eyes burned with a feral gleam. She looked at Jaz and said, "Your adversary returns, Ms. Errington. I, too, have long had a score to settle with this one. I have looked for him over many years, in between my other travels. I know that your clan has been hunting him as well."

Dean watched Jaz for a response, but it was limited to a hardening of her eyes and pressing her lips together until they disappeared. She had found out back at the cave that the vampire lord

Artur Torrence had destroyed the rest of her family. Now he discovered that Ingrid and Artur had history, too. It was something else that connected the two of them.

Ingrid continued, "Jaswinder Errington, I pledge my services to you and yours now and in the future in the hunt for this creature. We have been working separately, but now let us work together to track and defeat this evil."

Jaz looked the Valkyrie in the eyes and nodded, extending her good arm to clasp hands in agreement.

"Good, that is settled," Ingrid said. "I will watch for signs on my travels and send word of anything I find. Dean knows how to invoke me if you need my assistance, since the two of you are tied together in this, as well. Until then, I must return to my work gathering souls of warriors in preparation for the last battle." She turned to Jo and pulled her in for a quick hug. "Hang in there, kiddo. Your parents are good people. Give them the time they need to get used to having you in their lives."

"I will, Aunt Ingrid," Jo said.

Ingrid took a step back away from the cabin in the clearing, manifested her great white wings again, and launched herself skyward with a few broad strokes. Then the Valkyrie was gone, blinking out of sight as she sped away skyward.

Anya took the opportunity the break in the conversation offered and came forward to Jaz, pointing to her injured arm. "And your injuries? We must do something for you. Come inside and let Zora and I make you something to eat and treat your wounds. Come." The dryad woman gestured to the open cabin door and Jaz led the way inside to enter and rest.

Dean watched her go inside and turned to Albion. The werelion had been a strong ally in this fight for the valley's residents and against the demon incursion into this world. Dean hoped he could keep that friendship alive. He stepped forward and extended his hand to shake the other man's hand. Albion took it and merely nodded, then he turned and started off into the forest. Dean watched him leave and then turned to go inside. Jo had already gone in following Anya and Jaz.

Once inside, they sat while Dean looked at Jaz's injured left arm again. She needed stitches to properly close that gash in her shoulder, as well as an antibiotic and a tetanus shot. They could stay here for a few hours, but he needed to get her to a hospital for the needed treatment. Anya and her daughter set to work providing a breakfast for all of them. It was good to sit and relax in relative safety for a change. Dean looked around the room at the assembled group. Anya walked around with a smile serving the breakfast meal and doting over Jaz, worrying over her injuries. Jo and Zora were in the corner chatting together, bonding as only teens in the presences of adults, or in this case, parents, could. They were close in age and he was glad that Jo had relaxed enough to find a friend here.

He felt like someone was watching him and when he looked around the room again, he caught Jaz staring at him. She smiled a little when their eyes met. A lot had happened to them in the last few days. He was concerned about her. She had yet to deal with the loss of her family in the explosion back in Elk City. Dean knew that it was probable that she was the last of her hunter clan. A series of giggles from the two teens on the other side of the room distracted him and he remembered that, no, she wasn't the last of them. Somehow Joanna was the continuation of the Errington line, and while he had trouble believing in the beginning when it was revealed to them, he could see what might attract him to Jaz. It was not impossible at all that, in some way, the two of them would end up together.

Dean shook his head. Ashley was only a few hours gone. What was he thinking? He felt guilty that he was considering another relationship so soon. But, this was different, wasn't it? The two of them had not hit it off in the beginning, but the last few days of events had brought all three of them closer together than he would have thought in the beginning of this quest.

The paramedic's thoughts drifted back over the previous year. He thought about his time in the fire academy to become a paramedic, his initiation into the Unusual world at Station U, his realization that, despite the true nature of his patients, they were people in need of care just like anyone else. Now he had fought his way through a series of battles that had truly been about good versus evil. It was so different than what he had become used to. Getting back to Station U and the ambulance calls serving his Unusual patients would be a welcome return to normal. It would be good to get back home.

EPILOGUE

INGRID HAD ONLY FLOWN a short distance away, using her innate ability to mask her presence in the mortal world to disappear from view of those on the ground. The Valkyrie stopped and hovered in the air over the cabin. The other shining form before her exuded a blinding light that dazzled even her divinely created eyes. Vaguely humanoid in shape, it hovered before her in the air where she flapped her great wings to maintain position.

"Does he know his true nature yet?" the light pulsed as the form spoke to her, more like words echoing directly in her mind than spoken in the air.

"No, my lord," Ingrid said, inclining her head in respect. "He did not question how he could handle the heavenly blade without harm, nor his position in this conflict. I followed your instructions to keep it from him if I could, though you know I cannot lie in response to a direct question."

"It is well that he remains in the dark for the time being," the form pulsed. "It is not yet time to reveal his relationship to all of this."

"My lord, Dean Flynn is not an ignorant or foolish man," Ingrid said. "He will begin to question what happened here in this valley and the things he was able to do."

"When the time comes I will reveal myself to him and explain his place in the world," said the voice in her mind. "For the time being, I must attend to your sister. She was sorely injured by the revenant scum. I will assist her recovery so that she may regenerate faster and return to earth to continue her work there."

"Thank you, my lord," Ingrid said, bowing slightly again. "I know my sister will appreciate that."

"In the intervening time, Ingrid, you must undertake the task of watching over him, assisting him to fulfill his destiny. My son must come of age in his own time but time is short and he must be ready for the battle when it comes. Everything depends on it."

"It will do as you say, my lord," Ingrid said, bowing in the air again as the form faded from sight. She glanced back down at the cabin below before soaring higher into the blue morning sky, setting off to Valhalla, awaiting the time when she was needed again on the earthly plane. Needed again to help Dean Flynn realize his destiny.

Read on for a preview of Book 5 - *The Paramedic's Witch*

ALSO BY JAMIE DAVIS

Get a free book and updates for new books.
visit JamieDavisBooks.com/send-free-book/

Extreme Medical Services Series

Book 1 - *Extreme Medical Services*

Book 2 - *The Paramedic's Angel*

Book 3 - *The Paramedic's Choice*

Book 4 - *The Paramedic's Hunter*

Book 5 - *The Paramedic's Witch*

Book 6 - *The Paramedic's Nemesis*

—

Eldara Sister Series

The Nightingale's Angel

Blue and Gray Angel

—

The Broken Throne Series

(Released beginning July 2017)

The Charm Runner

Prophecy's Daughter

The Queen of Avalon

Stolen Destiny

The Mended Throne

—

The Accidental Traveler Series

(a LitRPG series to be released beginning August 2017)

The Accidental Thief

The Accidental Warrior

The Accidental Mage

The Accidental Emperor

Follow on Facebook for updates, news, and upcoming book excerpts

Facebook.com/jamiedavisbooks

THE PARAMEDIC'S WITCH PREVIEW - CHAPTER 1

THE BABY WEREWOLF TRIED to bite him while he worked on his assessment. "How long has she been like this?" Paramedic Dean Flynn asked the concerned parents standing in the doorway of the baby's bedroom.

"We heard the growls coming from her room about 15 minutes ago," the mother said. "When we saw her we called 911 right away."

Dean was glad to be back on the job at Station U after the events of the past few weeks. He had rescued his kidnapped girlfriend Ashley, an actual angel from heaven, only to have her slip away as a result of her injuries during the ordeal. She wasn't dead, but it would be years before she could manifest again in person on earth. Along the way to rescuing Ashley, he had teamed up with a female demon hunter named Jaz Errington and a witch or Wiccan named Joanna. The surprises and complications continued when he and Jaz found out that Jo was their daughter, returned from the future to assist in their quest to rescue the angel.

So managing the snarling werewolf baby in the crib in front of him was a welcome change of pace back to his normal life of treating his special type of emergency patients. Those patients were the creatures of myth and legend, called Unusuals, who lived alongside their unknowing human neighbors. Dean, his partner Barry, and the other paramedics of Elk City's Station U were tasked with helping these underserved members of the city's community.

"I thought that Lycans didn't start changing until they reached adolescence?" Barry asked, trying to hold the baby without getting bitten by the were-child. "What do you think is going on, Dean?"

"My guess is that the baby is having a seizure of some kind that is causing it to shift and change sooner than expected," Dean surmised. He turned to look at the concerned parents standing nearby. "Has she been sick lately, had a cold or flu bug, or anything?"

The mother answered. "She has not been sleeping well and had a fever last night when I put her to bed. I didn't think anything of it. Did I let this happen? Is it my fault? I've never heard of one of us shifting form so young before. Is she going to be alright?"

"I think she is going to be fine," Dean reassured her. He wasn't sure, but he thought the baby was having a febrile seizure. It was a common enough occurrence in some infants when they spiked a high fever suddenly. It kind of caused the brain to reset. That might be what happened here. The seizure must have triggered the change to werewolf.

"You're thinking febrile seizure?" Barry asked.

Dean nodded. "So what do we do?" The paramedic asked his probationary partner, testing him.

"Actively seizing infant, we give Midazolam IM or IN," Barry replied. He meant give the drug commonly known as Versed by injection or aerosolized spray up the nose. It was a sedative that would break the seizure and hopefully, the baby would return to human form. Hopefully.

Dean nodded in the affirmative and took over securing the snarling infant, avoiding the snapping teeth. Barry crouched down to draw up the medication in a syringe while his partner secured the patient. The new guy was coming along alright, Dean thought. He wasn't a new paramedic, which helped. He was just new to the knowledge that some of his patients were creatures like werewolves, even werewolf babies.

Barry stood back up with his syringe and supplies and Dean turned the baby on her side so Barry could give the injection. Barry used an alcohol prep to swab the little hairy butt and then gave the intramuscular injection. It would take a few moments to begin to work so Barry took over holding the struggling and snarling infant from his partner after putting the needle and syringe in the sharps box in the side of their med bag.

"Now we just need to wait and see if the drug we just gave her does the trick," Dean told the concerned parents. "In the meantime, while a febrile seizure is usually an isolated incident, given the startling change that occurred, we should probably take her in to the hospital to get checked out. Okay?"

"Are you sure she'll be alright?" the mother asked.

"Look," Barry said. He had let go of the child. The snarling had stopped and as Dean and parents leaned over the crib to look at the baby, they saw the tiny werewolf shift back into a normal baby girl. Her clothes were a little shredded from the previous struggles, but she was sleeping comfortably and looked none-the-worse for the experience.

"See," Dean said. "She seems to be just fine. Like I said, it's probably an isolated incident but I'd like to have you come with us while we take her into the hospital and get checked out. It may never happen again. Still, it's better to be safe."

"We can go to the hospital if that's what you recommend," the father said. "Thank you so much for helping us. I come from a long line of Lycans and I have never heard of that happening before."

"It's new to me, too," Dean said. "Still, this job is all about new and exciting experiences." He chuckled and started helping Barry pack up the gear. He would head out to the ambulance and get the car seat for the baby set up in the back of the ambulance while Barry got the baby ready to transport and brought her and the parents out to the ambulance behind him.

When they got there, mom climbed in the back with Barry and the baby while Dean pointed to the front passenger seat for the father. Dean got in behind the wheel and waited while the dad buckled his seat belt. He checked the rearview mirror to see the thumbs-up from Barry in the back that signaled him it was time to go and he pulled the ambulance out from the residential driveway, onto the street. Then they were on the way to Elk City Medical Center.

——————

BY THE TIME they got back to their station after dropping the baby off at the ECMC ER with the nurses and doctors there, Dean was ready for the end of a long night's work. It was nearly dawn, and he and Barry worked together back at the station to get the ambulance restocked and make sure everything was done for the end-of-shift checks. The next crew of paramedics came in at six in the morning to relieve them, and another emergency call could come in at any time so the ambulance and gear needed to be ready.

The restocking didn't take long and the two paramedic partners walked into the squad room to the smell of a delicious breakfast in the air. A gravelly voice across the room in the small kitchenette area of the station called to them.

"I've got steak and eggs with home fries for you guys to round out your shift," the shambling chef said. That was Freddy, their live-in chef. He was a zombie who had been a premier chef on the national restaurant scene until his voodoo priestess girlfriend had caught him cheating with one of his waitresses. One spell later and he was one of the undead, forcing him to leave the profession he loved. Dean and the other paramedics had adopted him after his house trailer was burned out in a hate crime. Now he lived in the station and made the paramedic teams five-star, restaurant quality meals in gratitude. The food was great as long as Freddy checked to make sure he hadn't lost any body parts during the cooking process.

"Man, I'm starved," Barry said. "Keep it warm for me, Freddy. I have to finish up my paperwork from the last call. It'll only take a few minutes."

"Will do," Freddy croaked.

"Well, I'm not waiting," Dean said. He took the plate offered by the zombie chef and grabbed himself a bottle of water from the fridge before sitting down to eat in the Station U squad room. The room served as an office between ambulance calls, as well as a lounge during their downtime. There were two recliner lounge chairs and a sofa, as well as a large flat screen TV mounted on one wall.

The best part of the station, in Dean's estimation, was the extensive library on myths and legends in a bookshelf on the wall. The volumes were annotated with notes from various Station U paramedics over the years to help teach later crews the lessons learned about their special patients. Dean made a note in his smartphone to remind himself to make an annotation on one of the werewolf stories about his encounter with the werewolf baby, the first he had ever heard of.

Once he set up the reminder for later, he dug into the plate of delicious food. Savoring every bite, Dean took his time with his breakfast. That was unusual in itself. He knew that most paramedics ate their meals as fast as possible to make sure they finished before another ambulance call came in. Dean used to be that way, too. He had changed in the last few months, though. There had been a lot going on. Racist hate crime attacks on his Unusual patients, a takeover attempt of the whole city by a rogue vampire lord, and the kidnapping of his girlfriend by demons had all left him with a new perspective on life. He was determined to enjoy and savor these quiet, peaceful moments whenever he could. He knew all too well how quickly they could shift into chaos and loss.

His phone buzzed on the table next to his plate and he checked to see that a text message had come in. It was from Joanna, his recently revealed fifteen-year-old daughter. He was still getting used to that fact himself. He was too young at twenty-three to have daughter that age under normal circumstances, but she had traveled back in time via a powerful spell to come here and help rescue Ashley. She was from twenty years in his future and only knew him as her dad. He was still struggling with thinking of her as his daughter, let alone that he was somehow responsible for her while she was here in this time and place.

He checked the text message and saw that she was up early and wanted a ride over to her mother's apartment. Jo was staying with him because he had a spare room in his place, though he knew nothing of raising a teenaged girl. Now she wanted to go over to her mother's place. She probably wanted to help her mother continue the job of sorting through the few remaining items left after her own parents and much of the rest of the extended family had been killed in a suspicious gas explosion and fire just a few weeks before. Dean sighed. He supposed he could take her across town to Jaz's apartment after he got off work. This was his final night shift in the rotation and he had a few days off, so he had plenty of time to give her a ride over before he got some sleep after working all night. He could use his tiredness as an excuse not to stick around too long.

Dean didn't relish running into his parenting counterpart. She had been as surprised as he was by the revelation they had a child together at some time in the future. It was doubly awkward because the two of them had not hit it off well when they first encountered each other. Jaz was a strong-willed individual and took umbrage whenever anyone tried to tell her what to do, or worse - didn't immediately listen to her commands when she was in charge. Dean was willing to stand up for himself when he or someone he knew was being wronged. This dichotomy led to the two of them arguing over who had the right to reprimand Dean's probationary paramedic Barry when he was late to a class Jaz had been teaching.

It had not gotten much better when Dean and Jaz had evaded a demon attack aimed at him and had to leave town, picking up a stray witch on the roadside who turned out to be their future daughter. The daughter who wasn't to become a hunter like her mother, but was already committed by her father to becoming a member of a Wiccan coven. Dean saw nothing wrong with joining the coven at its most basic level. He had made a difficult decision that affected not only him, but two other people as well. He had been the one who made the deal with the coven for his firstborn daughter to someday join them in exchange for a spell they cast on his behalf. 'Someday' had seemed so far away at the time.

This was the root of the awkwardness that lay between he and Jaz Errington. Then there was the problem that existed because of their opposing careers. She was a member of a hunter clan, committed to hunting down demons as well as those Unusuals she perceived as evil. She drew that line at anyone taking advantage of humans or perpetrating crimes against humans with evil intentions. He, on the other hand, was a healer and a paramedic committed to saving many of those same individuals when they needed medical care. They said opposites attracted, but he thought this was not what the proverbial "they" meant when it was said.

Dean picked up his phone and texted his daughter. He told Jo that he was fine running her over to her mother's place. He told her to be ready when he showed up after work. She texted back a thumbs-up emoji. He finished his excellent breakfast and prepared to welcome the next shift. Bill and Lynne, the next shift's paramedics, both showed up soon after he was finished eating. Grabbing his gear as six o'clock rolled around, Dean said goodbye to Bill, Lynne, and Barry, and headed out to his pickup truck to drive home and pick up Joanna.

CHAPTER 2

DEAN DROVE the few miles back to his apartment, located over a detached garage in a residential neighborhood on the outskirts of Elk City. When he pulled up out front, Joanna was there waiting for him in the driveway. She was dressed in shorts and a tank top, carrying her purse on one shoulder. They had gone shopping for some new clothes when they returned from their rescue mission in the mountains to the west. Jo had been transported back in time pretty much with just the clothes on her back. Her outfit at the time was not what a normal teen in this day and age would wear. Apparently, twenty years from now, the fashions revisited what he would have called nineteen-sixties' "hippie" style. Now, at least, she looked like any other teen he saw walking down the street.

"Hi, Dad," she said as he climbed in the pickup with Dean. "I appreciate this. Mom will, too, I think. She's having a problem adjusting to being the last living member of the Errington clan. She's overwhelmed with all the responsibilities to run the security company, plus having to manage getting her parents' estates in order."

"Did she invite you or are you inviting yourself to go help?"

"She would never ask for help. You know that, Dad."

Dean was still getting used to this whole family man thing. A week ago, he had been a normal single guy. Okay, maybe not normal, but certainly not the father of anyone - especially not a fifteen-year-old girl. Now he not only had a teenaged daughter, he also had a future - what would you call her? Wife? Girlfriend? Baby-momma? He still had trouble seeing him and Jaz Errington getting together, even with the apparent proof that they did sitting in the truck next to him.

"Have you given any more thought to how and when you're going back to when you came from?" Dean asked.

"I can't do it on my own. I have an idea of how it's done, but the spell has to be cast on me by another Wiccan. It took a group casting to send me back here. It might take more than one of us to send me back."

"We should contact the local coven then. They sent you back here in the first place, at least their future selves did." Dean was getting a headache trying to wrap his brain around the whole time-travel thing.

"I want to stay a little longer and help Mom out. She is all alone now. She doesn't even have you to lean on yet. She needs someone else to help her through this."

That comment brought them to an awkward silence. They were mostly quiet the rest of the ride downtown. Jaz had taken an apartment about a block away from the location of her family's bombed-out building. The fire marshal and the feds at the ATF had determined that it was not a mere gas explosion as had originally been reported in the news. Since they were federal security contractors, it was being treated as a potential terrorist incident, given the company's federal security ties, especially since Jaz and her team had just returned from an unnamed mission in Syria. Dean knew from the news how dangerous that middle-eastern country was. It was a testament to how tough Jaz was, and to her skills as a demon hunter that she had been sent there and survived to come home again.

Dean found a spot on the street, thumbed a few quarters into the parking meter, and followed Joanna into the building. They caught the elevator up to the sixth floor where Jaz was staying and knocked on the apartment door.

Jaswinder Errington opened the door. She could have been Jo's older sister, they looked so much alike. Dean saw right away she had been crying. He knew that she would be embarrassed by his noticing it, so he shot her a big grin when she looked his way and pointed to Jo.

"Look, I brought you a teenager to lend you her snarky comments while you work."

"Oh, joy," Jaz said stepping back and gesturing to them. "Come on in. I told you I didn't need your help, Joanna. It's busy work for the most part. It's stuff that I just have to slog through and get it done."

"No one should have to do this stuff alone, Mom. Besides, Dad is off for the next two days so he can stay and help, too. Together we can get it done faster than you could do it alone."

"I told you, Joanna. Stop trying to force Dean and me together. I don't doubt that we are your parents anymore. That is something I accept now. I do doubt that we are going to become more than friends just because you keep coming up with ways for us to stay in close proximity to each other."

"Jaz is right, Jo." Dean jumped in to help Jaz out. "If we end up as more than friends in the future, it will have to happen in its own time and can't be forced. I mean, you didn't want us to just start jumping on each other as soon as you snapped your fingers, did you?"

"Ew, Dad, don't be gross. That is not an image any daughter wants to think about."

"Well, then, leave us alone," Jaz said. "Let things happen naturally. You aren't even born for almost five years, right? Dean and I have plenty of time yet to get to know each other."

Dean saw the teen's shoulders sag a little. If he thought about it from her point of view, he could understand how she felt. She wanted to see the parents she had left behind in the future. They were a happily married couple, not the barely-friends she saw when they were together here in her past. He had very little memory of his own parents together before his father left him and his mother on their own. He had been three when his father left them. After that, his mother had avoided talking about him, at least in front of Dean. He knew almost nothing about the man who had fathered him.

Dean changed the subject. "On the bright side, we are here together now. Let's see what we can do to get some work done. What do you think, Jaz? Do you have any work for the kid and me to help you with?"

"The fire marshal dropped off some boxes of personal items recovered from the fire. I have not wanted to, but maybe since you both are here with me, we can sort through them. I've got nothing else to do until a conference call coming up at noon with some of our satellite office managers. I need to make sure that all the Errington private and federal security contracts are being served."

Jaz's family had been one of the world's great hunter clans, serving as the guardians of humans against demons and those Unusuals who saw fit to take advantage of them. Once they moved to the United States before the Civil War, the family set up a security and private detective firm to serve as a basis for them to investigate demon and Unusual attacks on humans. Since then, the Errington Security Firm had become one of the preeminent private security and personal bodyguard companies in the nation. They provided protection to people like movie stars and corporate leaders around the country. They also took special jobs from a clandestine federal agency related to their core mission, hunting demons who broke through to the human world from the netherworld. It had been one such group of demons the three of them had battled to rescue the angel, Ashley Moore, just a week before.

"So where are these boxes?" Dean asked looking around the room. He saw a stack of six large cardboard boxes on the far side of the room along with some charred, hard plastic Pelican cases in various sizes.

Jaz pointed to the boxes and Dean and Jo walked over to them.

"Where do you want us to start, Mom? Do you want us to just pick a box or case and dig in?"

"Yeah, sure. Pick one. I don't care."

Jo picked up one of the cardboard boxes and moved over to the dinner table with it. She unfolded the flaps and looked inside. Dean noticed the smoky odor coming from the contents of the box. Jaz came over and the three of them started to pull some picture frames and other odds and ends from the box.

———

IT TOOK them about two hours to go through all the boxes, and it wasn't until they got to the last box that Dean found something strange.

"Jaz, what's this?" Dean asked. He pulled a small jade figurine from the bottom of the box. It had been hidden under a piece of charred linen.

Jo hissed in alarm and Jaz drew in a sharp breath.

"Dean, where did you get that?"

"What? It was in the box. Here," he said trying to hand it to her.

"Don't hand it to me. Just set it down on the table, quickly. You shouldn't touch it at all." Jaz looked at Jo. "Do you have any protection magic that will counter that?"

"Just a normal ward against evil. It might work."

"Cast it. Now."

Dean was confused but set the figurine down. Jo closed her eyes and started chanting under her breath. He looked at the jade figurine. It was about the size of his fist and portrayed a short, squat man-shaped figure holding a sword. It appeared to be smiling, but as he looked closer he saw there were double rows of sharp teeth in the figure's mouth that made the smile more of a grimace.

The hair stood up on the back of Dean's neck as Jo's chanting got louder. He didn't understand the language, but knew that many spells were spoken in Latin, Greek, or even other, more ancient languages. She finished and opened her eyes. Looking at Dean and the figurine, she nodded.

"That should do it, Mom."

Jaz stood up and looked in the box Dean had been unpacking. He looked inside, too. It was empty except for a few scraps of paper.

"Crap, where are the other two?"

Jo looked alarmed. Dean looked from one to the other, still not understanding.

"There were three?" He asked.

"Yes, a matched set of three that were kept in a specially warded box. The wooden box must have burned in the fire, but the jade would have survived, as we've seen."

"Will someone please explain to me what is going on?" Dean asked, careful to stand very still. He had been afraid to move and touch anything.

"It's a summoner, Dean, and Jo's spell should serve to contain it for now. They are meant to be used to summon the presence of a demon lord to earth. They work when all three are set at three of five points of a pentagram scribed in a warding circle."

"They can also cause really bad luck to those who hold them, Dad. Like evil sorts of bad luck! I think I cleansed the effects from you with my spell. You only held it for an instant."

"Why would your family have a way to summon demons, Jaz? You're demon hunters after all."

"Dean, we didn't use them, we kept them safe from others using them. My clan captured them centuries ago when we wiped out a ring of demon worshipers back in the old country, if I remember the family lore correctly."

"Wow, Mom. I know you can't see it but the aura radiating off that thing is disgusting and really powerful. If I look at it for too long it makes me queasy. I can't imagine what it would be like with all three of them in one place. We need to see if we can find the other two. If someone else picked them up in the rubble of the fire and ran off with them, we could have a big problem on our hands."

"So it causes bad luck. So what?" Dean asked.

"So what, you say? The problem, Dean, is that this is evil associated directly with bad luck," Jaz said. "Like Jo said, it won't just be stubbing-your-toe, or tripping-over-a-fallen-branch-on-the-sidewalk kind of bad luck. This will be run-out-of-gas-in-the-middle-of-a-railroad-crossing-while-a-train-is-coming bad luck. This is the kind of bad luck that brings down fully loaded passenger airliner while you're on board."

"And it will get worse unless it can be contained. There could be other effects on an unprotected person, as well," Jo said.

"Well, let's head over to what's left of the building," Dean suggested. "There's a construction crew there. Maybe they have seen something or someone. If not, we'll see if we can find the other figurines in the rubble. Jo, you can see the glow of the figurine's aura, so if we get there and the other figurines are there, you should be able to find them, right?"

"In theory, Dad, yes."

"Good. Then let's go before some homeless guy decorates his cardboard box with a new knickknack and brings down an asteroid on the city."

————

"Look honey," Sam said. "Today was my lucky day. I found these cool bookends on my demolition job. I thought we could use them on our bookshelf."

The matching figurines he held were set on the shelf and turned so they looked out over the construction worker's small apartment. Sam didn't see the eyes flare with an internal light for an instant, glowing and pulsing a sickly green before they faded.

CHAPTER 3

DEAN, Jaz and Jo left the apartment building and started the short, two-block walk to the burned out remains of the former Errington Security headquarters. They had just gotten to the intersection across the street from the site when a delivery truck swerved out of passing traffic. It hopped the curb heading straight for Dean. He wasn't paying attention. He was going through some emails on his phone and looked up, startled by the noise and shouts, to see the truck barreling towards him. He couldn't move. He just froze in place.

He tried to move out of the way, but felt like he was mired in glue. Then he felt an iron grip clamp onto the collar of his uniform jacket and yank him backwards out of the path of the out of control vehicle. He fell backward as he lost his balance, and landed on top of whoever had rescued him. He realized after a moment of struggle that it was Jaz.

"You can get off me now," she said.

"Oh, sorry." Dean rolled off of her onto the sidewalk and got back to his feet. He extended his hand to help her up, and after looking up from the ground for a moment, she took it and he helped her back to her feet. "Thanks for that. I couldn't move. It was all going in slow motion, kind of like one of those dreams where you can't get away, no matter how hard you try."

"Dean you need to be more careful. I mean seriously, Jo and I told you that you've touched a demonic idol that will bring you bad luck. You would think that you'd be more aware of your surroundings when you know your luck is compromised."

"I thought Jo's spell solved that problem." Dean looked at his daughter. "What was all that mumbo jumbo back in the apartment about if it wasn't to protect me?"

"It was a protection spell, Dad, and it worked. Mom grabbed you and saved your life. You were lucky. That truck could have splattered you all over the sidewalk."

Dean turned to look at where the truck had come to a stop just before crashing into one of the shops that lined the street. The store owner had come out and was shouting at the driver. Dean looked around to make sure no one else was injured. There didn't appear to be any other casualties, just his own pride.

"Come on, Dean, we need to get over there and find the other two figurines before it's too late," Jaz said.

Dean joined the two women and together, after carefully checking that all oncoming traffic was stopped by the light, crossed the street to the newly erected construction fence that surrounded the remains of the Errington Security building. The three of them had to walk halfway down the block to get to the construction entrance where trucks and workers were coming and going from the site.

"Let me talk to the construction foreman when we get inside. They are pretty careful about anyone but their demolition workers coming on the site," Jaz said once they got inside. She walked up to an office trailer nearby and went inside.

While she was inside, Dean and Joanna looked around as the workers went about their work knocking down the remaining brick walls. A front end loader was scooping up rubble and filling a dump truck nearby.

"Do you see anything, Jo? Any sign of the other figurines?"

"No. They could be covered by the rubble and wouldn't show as easily, but I think I would still see the aura emanating from where they were."

Jaz came out of the trailer, followed by a tall man in work khakis and a blue button-down shirt. He was wearing a white hard hat and carried two others. Jaz was putting a similar hard hat on, adjusting it for her ponytail.

"Guys, this is Joe Anderson, the construction foreman."

Dean shook his hand and took the offered helmet, putting it on. Jo did the same.

"Yeah, we need to be careful," the foreman said. "I've had three guys injured in the last three days by fluke accidents and the insurance inspectors are due here any minute. Everyone on the site has to wear their helmets and I have to ask you three to stay back from the work. I know you are looking for some personal effects and I've had my guys keeping an eye out. We've been putting whatever we find over in that storage trailer over there. If you'll follow me."

The three of them filled in behind him as he walked over to storage container trailer nearby. Dean brought up the rear and leaned forward so that his companions could hear him over the machinery. "Fluke accidents sounds like we have a confirmation that the other idols were here, right?"

"I was thinking the same thing, Dean. Jo, keep your eyes open."

"I am, Mom. Nothing pops out to me so far."

Joe unlocked a padlock and opened the other trailer. There were a few boxes and dusty items set on tables inside. There was no light in the trailer, just what streamed in the door.

"I'll be outside if you need anything. I've got to keep an eye out for that inspector," Joe said. He stepped outside the trailer and left the three of them to look through the piles of stuff.

Jaz went in first. To Dean, it seemed as if her steps were tentative, as if she didn't want to be there. He knew this must be tough for her. Jo followed her and stayed close to her mom.

Dean kept back a few steps to give the two of them some space. This was all that was left of her family. To Jaz and Jo this was something like visiting a grave site. Jo had grown up hearing about this in the future.

After a bit of searching, Jo let out a squeal of delight and rushed forward past her mother to one of the tables. Dean thought they had found what they were looking for. He craned his neck to look past Jaz in the dim light streaming through the open trailer door. He saw Jo pick up something and turn around holding it out in triumph.

"Look, Mom. It's Grandma's sword. My sword. You gave this to me when I turned thirteen."

Jaz stepped forward and took the katana in its scabbard from her daughter. She held it in front of her, brushing her fingers across the pattern on the lacquered wood of the scabbard. Then she reached out and pulled Jo into an embrace. Dean could see Jaz's shoulders shaking from the sobs and saw tears streaming down Jo's face over her mother's shoulder.

He turned around and gave them some room while he looked at the scattered items on the table next to him. Most of it appeared to be junk, or the items were ruined enough in the fire and building collapse that they would not be usable anymore. Dean looked through all the items on the table in front of him and looked over at the other two tables in the trailer. A thought occurred to him.

"Jaz, what happened to all the guns? I know your family had to have a lot of guns and ammunition in the building."

Jaz pulled away from her embrace with Jo and wiped at her eyes. "We did. Most of them were in the building's armory which largely survived the explosion and fire. It was built with additional structural and security support. There is a large gun dealer we know outside of the city that has taken possession of them until I can get some place secure to store them again."

Dean knew that the Erringtons' national security business had an arrangement with the FBI and U.S. Marshal's office that gave the qualified team members nationwide carry permits. Jaz had once mentioned that the close relationship with the Marshals carried back to just after the U.S. Civil War.

"I still have all the gear from my personal SUV, so I have my full load out. I don't need the rest right now. The other weapons will have to wait for me to go over them. I can't do that until we get local offices set up again. Right now the remaining staff is stretched pretty thin covering all of our existing contracts."

"I know your parents and two cousins died in the blast," Dean said. "Were there many staff members lost in the fire as well?"

"No. Luckily, it happened after regular business hours and all the staff had left. Now I have some new offices rented in a building on the outskirts of town. I have stopped in but haven't set up an office there for myself yet."

"I'm sure it's hard, Mom. You have to take over for everything that both your mom and dad did. Maybe Dad and I can help in some way."

Dean cringed. He didn't know anything about security work and was still uncomfortable with many of the ways that the hunter clan looked at some Unusuals. He realized that Jaz noticed his reaction.

"Sorry, Jaz, I just think that me working there part-time would not be a good fit. I feel like it would be a conflict of interest."

"Actually, Dean, I could use your expertise if you'll give it. We were in the process of refitting our medic bags and gear. Now all of those supplies were destroyed inside the building. None of it is salvageable and I have no idea what my Dad was doing with the project. I could use your help fitting out an updated tactical EMS bag equipment list."

"Oh, I could help with that certainly."

"What about me, Mom? It is a family business after all."

"I didn't have anything planned for you, Jo. I thought that Dean and I were going to find a way to send you back to your own time. You need to go back to the future time frame. I'm concerned that you being here in the past too long could mess up something in the future."

"Nah, the Coven told me before they sent me back it was unlikely that I could do anything to change the timeline as long as I returned before I was actually born. It seems that if I interact with myself at all, even as a baby, I could change something in myself which could really mess up both me and the timeline. They had a huge discussion about it before they sent me back. Some of the members didn't agree because of the risk if I couldn't come back."

"So there is some risk to the timeline?" Dean asked. He was thinking about how Marty McFly started to disappear in "Back to the Future" when he screwed up his parents getting together in the past. "I think we need to focus on getting you back sooner rather than later. It's better to be safe than sorry."

"But I want to stay here. I like you guys as your younger selves. You're not all parenty and stuff."

Dean and Jaz shared a look. Jaz stepped in.

"Dean's right, Jo. We don't know how many things might get shifted in time, even just a little bit, just by you staying any longer than is necessary. Dean will contact the coven right away, and see when they can send you back."

"But, don't you need my help to find the other idols? Who is going to cast your protection spells?"

"There are other Wiccans around, Jo," Dean said. He hated to be more 'parenty' as she put it, but this was important. "No more argument. You have to go back."

Jaz looked around at the tables one more time. "We know the idols are not here and there's nothing else of value beside my mother's sword. Let's go and head back to the apartment. I need to show up at the office today and I have that conference call coming up. They need to see my face and know that everything will be alright." She saw Jo's pouting face. "Jo, you can carry the sword if you want. I promise that when the time comes in the future, it will be yours."

That seemed to perk the teen up a bit, but Dean could see she was still disappointed and her shoulders had sagged a bit as they left the storage trailer. Dean collected the helmets when they got to the gate and took them over to the foreman. Joe waved to Jaz as he took them back, and then returned to his work directing the demolition of the building.

The three of them headed out to the street and started walking back to Jaz's apartment. Dean wondered aloud where the other two idols could be.

"Someone must have picked them up," Jaz replied. "Either it was one of the firefighters, investigators, or one of the construction workers. It should be a small list. I'll have one of the staff at the new office put together a list. Once we have that, we can take some time to track each of them down. These things are powerful enough that we should see some signs of their presence if we end up with the right person."

Dean hoped so, he worried about how some poor, unsuspecting person might react to supernatural bad luck in their life.

CHAPTER 4

SAM CONTINUED his search for the perfect, creepy magic words to use in the weekly Dungeon Masters game with his friends. They had been participating in this role-playing game campaign with him as the Dungeon Leader for the last five years. He, his wife, and a few of his old high-school buds had been playing off and on for years, but this was the longest running game any of them had been involved with.

They had each invested a lot into their characters, and Sam worked hard to make each week's adventure special in some way. This week, he had them invading the lair of a Lich, a supernatural being of the undead variety. This particular Lich he had designed was a real bastard and he was going to enjoy playing his part in the upcoming gaming encounter.

The Google search had turned up several options for old incantations and it was hard to choose from them. He wanted something that was not English and would lend a dark tone to the pretend spell-casting he had planned. In the end, he let random choice make the decision for him, closing his eyes and stabbing at the screen with a finger to pick one of the search engine's choices.

Sam opened his eyes and saw a link to ancient transformation curses. Perfect, he thought. Sam clicked the link and hit the print icon on his computer screen to print out the strange and alien words that came up. He got up to start setting up the dinner table for the game in the small apartment he and his wife leased. A black table cloth went on the table first, followed by the three electric candles from the bookshelf. On a whim, Sam brought the two jade idols over, too. They would add a nice supernatural touch to the Lich's lair.

His friends would be arriving soon, and he went back into the bedroom to see what was keeping his wife from coming out to help set up for so long. He didn't see the faint glow in the eyes of the two green figurines on the dinner table, or the shifting text on the printed paper nearby.

————

A GROAN WENT up from around the table as Eddie exhibited another of his horrible rolls on the pair of twenty-sided dice. The low result on both dice meant the team would fail to find any traps as they entered the passage that led to the Lich's lair. Sam just smiled and gave a mock laugh "mwa-ha-ha-ha." He was enjoying this night's game a lot. Every one of the four players had shown horrible luck when rolling their dice for the game and several characters had come close to dying. Everyone was tense and the mood in the room was both excited and a little annoyed at the string of bad luck.

Sam asked them what they wanted to do next. He knew that there was no real choice. They had come here to play the game and the game led them down into the underground lair of the undead creature waiting for them. The trap had been laid.

"Man, Sam, you've outdone yourself this time," Sandra said. "The whole scenario tonight is super-creepy. The hair on the back of my neck is standing up."

"Thanks, Sandra. Jill and I like it when you guys come over and play. I thought we could go the extra mile for tonight's session. So what do you all want to do next? Eddie detected no traps ahead."

The players all looked at each other around the table. Eddie and Steve had both gone to high school with Sam and even though they had gone off to college, they both had kept in touch with their old friend, rejoining his weekly games when they graduated and returned to Elk City to settle into their adult lives. Sandra was a work friend of Sam's wife, Jill. She was a divorcee and the newest member of their group. He suspected she was using this as a way to get out of her house once a week now that her ex-husband had moved out. She added a lot to the group, though, and she was easy on the eyes, too.

"We will go down the passage to the door at the far end," Steve announced. "It's what we're here for. Let's kill this Lich and steal his treasure."

There were nods of approval and Sam smiled. Now it was time for the fun to begin. Eddie had failed his attempt to find traps and the party of adventurers was about to walk right into the Lich's first defensive trap, laid out just for invaders like them.

"You step forward and hear a 'click' from down the hallway," Sam announced.

"Run away!" Sandra shouted

"I duck to the floor," Eddie proclaimed.

"I draw my sword," Steve said standing up.

"Me, too," Jill added.

"Too late," Sam said. "You are all transported by magic to a large room. There is a pentagram drawn on the floor and you find yourselves within it. None of you can move so much as a muscle. You hear a weird deep voice begin to speak nearby and you can't understand what the words are saying. It is in a language you have never heard before."

Sam picked up the sheet of paper and began to read the words printed there. He was really in the groove and was surprised that he didn't stumble over the unfamiliar word structure he encountered. There was a strange, green glow from the center of the table as he read and he heard the players gasp as he continued reading. He wondered where the glow was coming from, but found he could not stop reading the words once he had started. It was like someone else was reading them through him. He did not hear the spell's final words. He felt his consciousness fade to the background as the being now speaking from inside his mind took over, finishing the dual spells of summoning and transformation. In the small apartment, there was a flash of bright green light and then the darkness came.

———

"GREAT GAME, SAM," Steve said as he stood up to leave.

Eddie joined in. "Yeah, that was the best one yet. Keep it up."

"Eddie, can I get you to walk me out to my car?" Sandra asked

"Sure, we can all go down together."

Jill closed the door behind them and looked up at him. "You outdid yourself this time, honey. Come to bed. We can clean up this mess in the morning." She walked back to the bedroom in the tiny apartment without looking backward.

Graadu smiled to himself. None of them suspected that Sam was no longer in control of this body. He was still there, but not in control. The demon lord could hear the pitiful screams and protests in the back of Sam's mind. Once the spell had been cast, the four players had been put into stasis while Graadu took some time to acclimate to his new surroundings. He spent two hours deciding what he would do to the band of adventurers in the apartment. In the end he decided to transform each of them in a different way. Each would begin to cause havoc in this small earth city, and each would be unaware of how they had become the monsters of their own nightmares.

The demon turned his attention to the two figurines on the table. Together, the pair had just enough power to help the human fool, Sam, to bring him here in this limited form. He recognized that the idols were actually part of a trio of summoning stones. If he could locate the third summoning idol of the set, it would allow him to fully manifest himself on earth, rather than merely possess this flimsy human body. This fleshy shell was so fragile and delicate. He would have to find the other stone figurine if he were to complete the summoning and enter this world for real. It had been more than six hundred years since he had come to earth. He longed to come back, take revenge on humankind for banishing him away in the first place, and see what this newer, modern world offered in the way of entertainments.

He had been amused by the way the humans of this time and place "played" at the tasks that would have been all too real for individuals just a few hundred years earlier. Had they all forgotten that things really did go bump in the night? Maybe this time, he would be able to remain on earth and create a hold over an entire region. If the humans were all so unsuspecting and unprepared for a true manifestation of evil, this was going to be easy.

Graadu looked at the statues again and asked Sam, cowering in the back of his mind, where they had come from. When he discovered they had been found at a nearby construction site, buried in the rubble after a fire, he became excited. All he would have to do is search the site. He would turn up either the third idol or maybe find the previous owners. They would likely know where the other stone idol was located. It would be child's play to take the last one away from its owner if all the humans of the present time were such fools.

"Sam, come to bed. You've got work in the morning," Jill called from the bedroom.

"Be right there," Graadu said. He could start the search in the morning. Tonight he had other plans. It had been far too long since he had enjoyed the pleasures of the flesh. He had left Jill unchanged so he could savor her fear and terror when she realized her husband was not the man she thought he was. He was not a man at all.

CHAPTER 5

TWO DAYS LATER, Dean got up and made breakfast. It was his day off and ordinarily he would be getting ready to do some chores around the house and yard for his landlords, the Baxters. They were a nice elderly couple that Dean liked a lot. They offered him a break on the rent if he mowed the lawn for them and did other odds chores around the outside of their house and property as they needed.

That would have been his normal routine for a day off, but this wasn't a normal day off. This was the day they sent Jo back to the future. The local Wiccan coven had to wait until the "stars and heavens were aligned" or some such nonsense. He didn't know how magic worked, though he had benefited from it several times before since he started working at Station U. It did work, though, and if all went well, Joanna would be going back home today. He had mixed feelings about the spell and sending her back.

He and Joanna had become close over the last few weeks. He had come to grips with the fact that he had a daughter, and that she was the future teenaged version of that child. She was a good kid and had turned out alright. He had always wondered what kind of parent he would become when the time came. He had grown up with a single mother and a missing father. It turned out that, for all that he could see in Jo, he was a pretty good dad despite not having a good role model of his own growing up.

He was thinking about this over a cup of coffee and a bowl of cereal when Jo came padding out of the spare bedroom. She was still tired and had a serious case of bed-head hair going on.

"Hey, Jo," Dean said. "There's some more coffee on if you want a cup. Are you ready for today?"

"I guess so, Dad. I'm not sure I'm ready to go back. You and Mom need me to help you out with things. How are you going to find those other two figurines without my help?"

"We'll just have to make do, I guess," Dean laughed. "Seriously, Jo, how did you think we got along and got things done before you got here?"

"I don't know and the two of you didn't get along before I got here. It took me to make you stop fighting and start working together." She had a big grin on her face. She wasn't exactly wrong.

Dean didn't have the heart to tell her that she was not the cause of the friendship between him and Jaz. He considered himself easy-going and he made friends easily. He would have found a way to get along with Jaz even if Jo had not come back and forced the issue while they searched for Ashley.

"Well, you can't keep staying here, Jo. People would talk. I told the Baxters that you're my niece and that you're only here for a short time. No one will believe you're my daughter and it will make me look like some sort of creepy guy with a teenaged girl living with him."

"Eww, Dad. Way to make it weird."

"See, that's just what I mean."

Jo came over and made her breakfast while Dean cleaned up his. The two of them chatted about other things while she finished her food, and he admitted to himself that he would miss her when she was gone. She was a good kid. The two of them cleaned up the break-fast dishes together one last time and then they headed out to drive to the Wiccan coven in Elk City where they would cast the spell to send her back.

———

ANYA, the leader of the Wiccan clan met Dean at the door of their large home located in one of the more prestigious neighborhoods of the city.

"Welcome, Dean, and welcome Joanna," Anya said, gesturing for them to enter. "It is wonderful to finally meet you after all that Dean has said about you."

Jo rushed forward to give Anya a hug that startled the older woman for a moment, then she enfolded the teen in her arms and returned the hug. She smiled at Dean over his daughter's shoulder.

"Jo, your father sent us the details you shared about the spell that sent you here and we believe we have the necessary power and items needed to cast the reverse of it to send you back. We must be careful, though, in that we do not wish to have you cross over and alter the timeline in any way. This could be disastrous for all of our futures."

"We are confident that you can do this, Anya," Dean said.

"Don't be so sure, Dean Flynn. The Coven has not always had great success when it comes to casting spells on your behalf."

Dean remembered the magical explosion when they had tried to do a scrying spell to uncover who was at the heart of an anti-Unusual terrorist plot just a few months before. That had been the spell that had required the promise of his firstborn daughter to the coven in the first place. Jo would not have ended up in the hands of the Wiccan coven were it not for the price paid for that spell. It made him think. Nothing came for free.

"Anya," Dean asked. "What is the price for this spell? I know there is always a price."

The older woman laughed as she led them into the communal casting room with its circle of chairs and the waiting women of the coven arrayed around it.

"Payment is for outsiders, Dean. Joanna is one of us, promised to us by you in your past. This spell is for one of our own. We will assume the price for the magic cast here today."

"Well, I certainly hope that this one goes better than the last spell you cast for our family. I do not wish there to be any problems or injuries from such a powerful spell."

"Dad, this is not a spell like the scrying spell where the Coven had to pierce the defenses of another magical being. That was what caused the danger before in that instance. This is more of a magical price to be paid in drained power and fatigue. They can only cast this type of thing once in a while."

"She is right Dean," Anya added. "We will not be up against those types of countering forces today, although, the power of the spell required to pierce the veil of time is significant. We would not try this were it not for the fact that young Jo here is proof that it can be done. The sun, moon, and planets are in a good position to assist our efforts as well. We will have ample power to do this today."

Dean heard a knock at the door behind them in the hallway and turned to see Jaz being led into the room. He heard a sharp intake of breath from several of the assembled Wiccan sisters. They could see that she was a hunter, one who, in another time and place, might have been chasing Wiccan casters down. Anya shushed them with a sharp glance.

"Welcome, Jaswinder Errington," the elder Wiccan leader said. "Your presence here is an important part of the casting and we wish you well while you are within these walls."

Jo walked over to her mother and gave Jaz a hug. Dean was pleased to see the two of them continue to bond, although this would be the last chance for a while.

"Thanks for coming, Mom."

"I was told that my presence was necessary for the spell to work out. Plus it is my last chance to see you before you go." Jaz smiled at her daughter. "Of course I would be here."

"It is time," a voice intoned from the circle behind the family. "Will the spell's focus please enter the circle."

Dean and Jaz turned to watch as Jo walked to her place in the center of the large casting circle. Anya had assumed her place at the apex opposite from where Dean and Jaz stood. Dean could feel something, he wasn't sure what it was, as the low chanting began. He watched as Jo closed her eyes and tilted her head up toward the high domed ceiling, painted with a motif of heavenly bodies and zodiac symbols.

The chanting grew in intensity and Dean looked around as the light streaming in the windows from the sunlight outside seemed to dim. The room grew dark and the chants reached a crescendo, stopping with a sudden shout and then Dean turned to see Jo collapsing in the center of the circle. He started to rush forward, but Jaz's steel grip on his arm stopped him. Dean knew she was right. His entry into the casting circle would only serve to break up or even alter the spell.

The chants began again and the whole process repeated itself as Dean and Jaz watched. This time, there seemed to be an edge to the tone, something that had not been there before. The darkness returned again and this time Dean kept his focus on the casting circle. He watched as the thirteen women leaned in from their seats around Jo as if forcing their wills to push her back to when she belonged. Then there was a collective gasp and the light returned to normal.

Dean heard a whimper and saw Jo struggling to rise from the center of the circle. She was unsteady getting up from where she lay on the floor. This time he could not stop. He broke free of Jaz's grasp and rushed into the circle to Joanna. As he got closer, he could see her crying.

"Are you alright, Joanna?"

"Daddy, it didn't work. I tried to release myself to the spell. I did everything right, I promise."

He embraced the teen and looked around at the circle of watching women. Anya came forward from her chair as the high priestess of the coven. She looked pale and drained of energy. Jaz came and joined him at the center of the circle, too. She rested her hand on her daughter's head where it lay on Dean's shoulder. The girl was sobbing now.

"Anya, what happened?" Dean asked.

"There is something holding her here," the Wiccan leader said. "Some great evil has entered the region and young Joanna is tied to it magically somehow." She looked down at Jo. "Child, have you cast any spells recently? I told you that you must be free of any magical ties to this timeline in order to be sent back."

Jo looked up at the three adults clustered around her at the center of the casting circle. Her brow was furrowed as she considered the question.

Jaz answered for her. "The protection spell."

"What?" Dean asked.

"The protection spell. Jo cast it on you, and the figurine, when you pulled the summoning idol from the box back in my apartment."

"What is this summoning idol you speak of, huntress?" Anya asked.

"It was one of three placed in my family's care for safe-keeping. When my family was attacked and the building burned down, the protection spell and the box for the three summoning idols were both destroyed. We only found one of the idols in the items salvaged from the fire. The other two belonging to the set are still out there. We thought they were at the demolished building site but a search there proved fruitless."

"And young Jo here cast a protection spell over the one idol to keep its effects from harming her father, yes?" Anya asked.

The three of them nodded.

"Well, there is bad news and worse news, then," Anya announced. "The bad news is that Jo cannot be sent back until the other idols are recovered. The worse news is that our spell's failure revealed that the other two must have been used by someone to do evil. That evil is now tied to her. If she does not break that tie before the next time we might cast this spell, the autumnal equinox in three months, she will never be able to return to her correct time."

Jaz spoke up. "I think you're missing the bigger picture, Mistress Anya."

They all turned to look at her.

"Those stone idols are powerful. If they've been used, even partially, to summon a demon here to Elk City, then the whole city is in danger. The demon lord tied to those figurines is one of the most powerful I've ever heard of. My family's lore masters were clear in their records. His presence here will spell doom for Elk City unless we can find a way to send him back to Hell."

***

Read on! Get Book 5 - *The Paramedic's Witch*

HELP THE AUTHOR

I Need Your Help ...

Without reviews indie books like this one are almost impossible to market.

Leaving a review will only take a minute — it doesn't have to be long or involved, just a sentence or two that tells people what you liked about the book, to help other readers know why they might like it, too. It also helps me write more of what you love.

The truth is, VERY few readers leave reviews. Please help me out by being the exception.

Thank you in advance!

Jamie Davis

ABOUT THE AUTHOR

Jamie Davis, RN, NRP, B.A., A.S., host of the <u>Nursing Show</u> (<u>NursingShow.com</u>) is a nationally recognized medical educator who began educating new emergency responders as a training officer for his local EMS program. As a media producer, he has been recognized for the <u>MedicCast Podcast</u> (<u>MedicCast.com/blog</u>), a weekly program for emergency medical providers like EMTs and paramedics, and the Nursing Show, a similar program for nurses and nursing students. His programs and resources have been downloaded over 6 million times by listeners and viewers.

Jamie lives and writes at his home in Maryland. He lives in the woods with his wife, three children, and a dog.

Follow Jamie Online

www.jamiedavisbooks.com

Made in the USA
Monee, IL
02 May 2022

95734469R00142